BELLADONNA

Other books by the author include:

A Wing And A Prayer (Book One)

Once Upon A Time (Book Three)

A Long Way To Die (Book Four)

Past And Future Sins (Book Five)

BELLADONNA

THE SECOND BOOK OF GABRIEL

ERNEST OGLESBY

iUniverse LLC
Bloomington

Belladonna
The Second Book of Gabriel

iUniverse books may be ordered through booksellers or by contacting:

iUniverse LLC
1663 Liberty Drive
Bloomington, IN 47403
www.iuniverse.com
1-800-Authors (1-800-288-4677)

ISBN: 978-1-4759-3597-4 (sc)
ISBN: 978-1-4759-3598-1 (hc)
ISBN: 978-1-4759-3599-8 (ebk)

Library of Congress Control Number: 2012912185

Printed in the United States of America

iUniverse rev. date: 07/18/2013

Prologue

The mark's name was Beppo Lombardi, a high-level enforcer for one of the Mafia Dons. Beppo had made two serious mistakes in his life. His first mistake was becoming too high-profile amongst the drug trade in Rome, and his second mistake was in coming to the attention of The Sword of Solomon. The drug trade had been quiet these last few years, and no one wanted to see it escalate again.

Normally, Belle would use a more delicate approach, when carrying out a hit such as this, but the Cardinals wanted publicity on this one, to serve as an example amongst the other pushers and lowlifes.

Lombardi jogged in the public park, most mornings, and his usual route entered from Flaminio, routing east past Villa Borghese, and coming out on the Corso D'Italia, where one of his other bodyguards would wait for him with his limousine. He ran with only one bodyguard, a heavyset, but younger, man. He was the one to watch out for. Luis Giordano. He looked fit, and probably a handful in a fight. She would need to take him out before attending to Lombardi.

Belle had also run in the park these last few days, letting her face become part of the scenery. There was no timetable on the hit, and she liked to survey the ground, and become part of the background. Wait till they were used to her presence, and they would pay her less attention.

The lump at the back of Giordano's tracksuit meant he was armed during their run. She had checked both men out carefully in their brief contacts over the past week. The two men had checked her out, in turn. Belle's form-fitting running clothes were designed to attract attention, and to lower their guards. In this instance, her high visibility was perceived as less of a threat. The weapons she carried were not visible, yet no less deadly than the gun the bodyguard carried on his person.

Her long, normally black, hair was tied up at the back using a small wooden dumb-bell shaped clasp. This week it was died a bright shade of red. One more piece of eye-candy, and misdirection. The clasp came loose in less than a second, and once in her hand, the edges of the dumb-bell protruded from either side of her fist. Atemi-waza was a sub-discipline of karate, one of many martial arts in which Belle had received training. It targeted pressure points on the human body.

The early morning mist was just clearing as Belle entered the park, but pockets of greyness clung near the trees. The warmth from the sun could barely be felt at this time of the morning. Belle ran in a smooth rhythm, her muscles already toned, and she barely felt the cold through her thin, blue and white striped leotard. It clung in all the right places, and was the eye-catcher she intended.

As she approached the two men, Belle had already worked up a sweat, and she appeared to be breathing hard, as she used one hand to sweep back her hair. The clasp came loose, and was in her fist as she struck out sideways at the bodyguard, aiming for his temple. He cried out, managing to duck and divert the blow slightly, but it was enough to drop him to his knees, and she followed up quickly with a blow to the top of his skull. This time it put him down for the count. He would live. Lombardi wouldn't.

Lombardi caught on instantly. He wasn't dumb, but there was nothing he could do about what was about to happen. Cries for help were useless, with no one to hear. He looked around hopelessly. No one else in sight at this hour, and his only bodyguard was down. The woman pulled the knife from the sleeve of her tunic. He could tell she knew how to use it from the way she held it.

"Please . . . I'll pay you double whatever you're being paid. Triple . . . ." he offered, bargaining for his life.

"Nowhere to run, this time, Beppo . . ." Belle's face was impassive. The fat man backed up against the tree. Please, no begging . . . she pleaded, mentally, and lunged forward to end it.

Lombardi's mouth opened, and a gust of stale air was expelled into Belle's face, as she thrust the knife through his ribcage. He grasped at the knife-hand, but it did no good. Belle withdrew the knife, as easily as she had thrust it home. A clean kill. Straight to the heart.

In the few seconds it took for his brain to register he had been killed, his eyes looked from Belle's face, to his bloodied chest, then his knees sagged, and Belle stepped back, trying to avoid getting any of his blood on her running clothes.

Quickly, scanning about, she bent and wiped the blade on the grass, and replaced it in the forearm sheath she preferred. Then she turned, and ran off along her usual route, towards Flaminio. It would be another ten minutes or so till the bodyguard recovered, or the other man in the limousine realized something was wrong. A job well executed.

Chapter One

The morning sun shone down, reflecting brightly off the disturbed waters of the private swimming pool in the walled estate. As yet, the water was still cool, but would warm up throughout the day, heated by the sun's rays. The whitewashed walls of the villa were hard to look at on sunny days like this, for the sun and heat reflected off them. The shimmering curtain of heat formed a modicum of privacy from a distance.

It was a fine, if typical morning just outside Buenos Aires. The sweet smell of flowers was on the light breeze, and the noisy cicadas were heard across the lawn separating the pool from the lush garden and trees.

Laura Donovan swam gracefully, and energetically, cutting through the water with ease, as she completed her twentieth length of the pool. The water was still cool in the hot Argentine sun, and she paused at the end of the pool, turning and hooking her elbows onto the paved edge, her naked breasts glistening wetly and invitingly as Gabriel paused from reading his newspaper and turned to look at her.

She smiled wistfully, enjoying his appreciative stare. The scars of her recent bullet wound were barely noticeable, and would disappear entirely, Gabriel assured her. She found it hard to credit the speed of her recovery. As a recipient of the Blood of Christ many years ago, she had experienced an accelerated metabolism, but nothing like what she had experienced after drinking Gabriel's unadulterated life's blood.

Gabriel stood up from his late breakfast, and, untying his robe, he draped it on his chair. Naked, he dove into the pool to join her, surfacing alongside her as her arms reached out for him, thrilling in the sensation of his naked body pressing up against her.

Skinny-dipping was a pastime she was getting used to, secreted away here in Gabriel's villa. His manservant Manuel discreetly stayed away from the pool area when either Gabriel, or herself, was using it. A simple buzzer by the table sufficed to call upon him when needed.

Gabriel kissed her, softly, tenderly. Her lips opened to take his tongue. Laura loved him with all her heart and she knew the feelings were reciprocated. She could feel him hardening down there, despite the coolness of the water. Chuckling, she reached her hand down to grasp him, Gabriel gasping.

Her head dipped down below the water, and Gabriel gasped once more at the sudden heat he felt, but for a moment, and then she surfaced, laughing, as she swept her long blonde hair out of her eyes. "Mine, all mine," she chuckled, then, shrieking with laughter, she pulled away, and began swimming away from him. Gabriel surged after her, eager for the chase, his powerful strokes overtaking her halfway down the pool, and caught her leg, pulling her back into his arms, and she surrendered willingly this time.

* * *

Up in the computer room, Manuel was dutifully checking feedback from the search program instituted by his master, and downloading e-mail responses from many of Gabriel's varied associates across the world. He had enlisted worldwide aid in tracking down a woman known only as Mirabelle. Contacts old and new were requested to find out anything they could about a woman Gabriel could only give the vaguest details about.

Certain questions had to be phrased so as not to reveal anything about her longevity, therefore old contacts were only asked about possible sightings of such a woman in the distant past, and not seemingly possible sightings of her in present day circumstance, though some of these contacts, the ones Gabriel maintained more frequent contact with, had their obvious suspicions about his continued youthful appearance.

There was still a chance that Mirabelle was no longer among the living. Only seemingly immortal and very hard to kill, it could still be done, indeed it had been done in the past. Gabriel thought himself the last survivor of his species. Or had, until learning about his daughter.

They had no description of her, only a name. Not much for his friends around the world to go on, and he focused most of his hopes on his maintained Mafia contacts in Rome. Even after Grimaldi's death, his family had continued their support in whatever activities he required. It had been a sad, and private funeral in a small cemetery in the foothills overlooking the sprawling city.

It was always risky to venture into Italy, even via Sicily where the Mafia was so strong. The Holy Catholic Church was always there in the background, hovering like a vulture, and awaiting the opportunity to strike. Still, he had wanted to go. A senseless death. One of many, in the Mafia's internal feuds over the years. The Grimaldi clan remained his staunchest allies amongst the Mafia even unto present day, and it was there he hoped to have most success in the possibly fruitless search.

Manuel gathered up today's printed matter, sifting through it, preparing for Gabriel to peruse later in the day. Sightings of women, some blonde, some dark, some modern, some dim remembrances of years past. Gabriel looked for similarities of either description or personalities.

If she had been brought up within the Church, then obviously as a child she would have been fostered somewhere, and as an adult, she would have maintained close relations with the Church, possibly as a nun? There were so many possibilities.

Manuel had been diligently sifting this information for the last few weeks, descriptions came and went, but a name kept cropping up from time to time, both from past and recent remembrances, possibly a code name. Belladonna.

Was the name coincidental? Was it indeed the same woman? Manuel took it upon himself to initiate further searches using various points of reference unearthed by Gabriel's large network of contacts, thus possibly saving his master time in his research.

Belladonna was indeed a code name it seemed, and used within the Sword of Solomon organisation. The codename had been in use for the last 40 years, but no further information was available to him. Perhaps

Gabriel himself knew of a way of hacking into the Vatican's private computer systems?

*   *   *

Later that afternoon, after lunching with Laura, Gabriel was presented with the latest search updates by his manservant, and he sat down in his study to go through them, occasionally initiating further internet searches via his computer link at his desk.

His own hacking skills were formidable, better even than that young English boy, Luke. Still, the Vatican's system was locked out from external interference, as there was no physical link between external phone lines and its own private internal communications set-up. What firewalls existed were extremely sophisticated. If he could find a way to access them, it would be no problem to find out everything he wanted to know, but there was presently no way in; not even a mobile phone allowed in the place.

Was the code name handed down from one operative to another? Or was it indeed used exclusively by one person? Was that one person his daughter? He needed a description, and descriptions seemed to vary judging by the few people who had actually caught sight of her. This Belladonna seemed to be a very shrewd operator. Not many people ever got a good look at her and lived to tell the tale. As deadly as her nom de plume, to be sure.

It was time to ask Laura of her time spent with the organisation. Perhaps her memories might give them a clue. Laura was out in the gardens, enjoying herself with a pair of pruning shears among the shrubbery when he called to her, and joined her there in the shade of an overhanging tree. She turned to greet him, kissing him lightly as he embraced her. Gardening was a long-forgotten pleasure, in which she now indulged herself in this home of Gabriel's, and in which she was beginning to feel at home herself.

"We need to talk," he spoke softly, using a finger to lightly brush her pouted lips. "Let's go into my study and I'll show you what we've found out to date." Arm in arm, he walked her back inside the house.

Scattered across his desk were reports and printouts, and he scooped up a few of them as he sat down with Laura on the soft upholstered sofa. "Cast your mind back to the time you spent with Ryan in Italy.

All the reports I'm getting back are pointing to a female operative within the Vatican's Sword of Solomon organisation who uses the name Belladonna. Does the name ring any bells?" he asked.

Momentarily, a shadow fell across Laura's eyes, as she sought to drift back in time, searching her memories. "I seem to recall hearing the name, but I don't think I've ever come across her," she replied. "The Sword of Solomon was a big organisation, and the people that worked for it, the actual 'operatives' very rarely came into contact with each other," she explained. "Only the Cardinals dealt frequently with their network of agents."

"Then we need a better description of who we're looking for, if indeed this Belladonna is our errant daughter." Gabriel smiled ruefully. "I think you'd better get changed. We're going to take a little ride up into the mountains," he explained.

*   *   *

An hour later, as Gabriel's 4x4 negotiated the well-worn mountain track, Laura's curiosity could stand it no more. "Just where is it you're taking me?" she asked. Gabriel turned around from the wheel, and smiled mysteriously, as he peered over the top of his mirrored sunglasses.

"I recall your surprise when you realised the truth about me, and my origins. Well, let's just say you still have a lot to learn about this world in which you live, Laura," he smiled wistfully. "In my many years I have seen countless strange and unexplained things. Things which you and most of the modern world write off as fiction and fairy-tales to frighten children, and adults alike. Some of them aren't," he added, warningly. "Some of these *myths* still walk this earth." Laura looked puzzled by Gabriel's words, and he relented, and continued. "We're going to see an old woman, who lives up in the mountains. Her name is Juliana," he said, simply. "She is a witch."

Chapter Two

A further two hours went by, and the roads began getting narrower and progressively worse, till it seemed they were non-existent. Laura was starting to think Gabriel had lost his way, when she noticed a wisp of smoke rising above the tree-line in the distance.

Within a small clearing, a tiny log-cabin nestled against the rising slopes of the mountains. A small stream ran past, mere yards from the old-looking structure. Gabriel finally halted the vehicle about fifty yards from the place, raising a small cloud of dust. He switched off the engine, and beckoned to Laura to alight.

Together, they began to approach the cabin, which showed no outward signs of life other than the plume of smoke from the chimney. "Perhaps she's not home?" suggested Laura.

Gabriel gave her an amused glance as he took off his sunglasses and put them in his top pocket. Then he reached for the door to turn the handle, opening it to reveal a dark and gloomy interior. The strange smell hit Laura, as he beckoned for her to precede him into the cabin. "Hello? Anyone home?" she called out softly, slightly wary.

"Do you think I'd leave the door unlocked if I wasn't home, child?" an amused, aged voice replied from the murky interior, "in such troubled times?" Laura stepped back, momentarily startled, backing into Gabriel as he followed her inside.

"It's okay, she won't bite. Lost her teeth years ago, didn't you Juliana?" Gabriel joked, and then quickly ducked as the old woman's stick swung through the air, his lightning-fast reflexes enabling him to grab hold of the offending weapon. "No way to treat your guests, Juliana," he scolded her, wagging a finger.

"Arrogant as ever. Come here and give an old woman a hug," she smiled. Gabriel let go of the stick and moved forward, arms widening to embrace the wizened old figure, when the stick swung back and caught him high on the forearm before he could block the blow a second time.

"Owwwww . . ." he cursed. "Juliana, that wasn't funny," he warned. Laura stifled a chuckle, as she sensed the intimate rapport between the two of them.

"You're late," the old woman snapped. "I was expecting you an hour ago. The soup's almost ruined," she announced, turning away into the interior of the cabin, which Laura noticed, as her eyes grew more accustomed to the dim light, went deeper into the actual mountainside.

The strange smell, she recognised now for what it was, a pot of soup, boiling away on an old cast-iron wood-burning range. "I had it brought up here years ago," Gabriel explained. "No utilities out here, and Juliana likes to live well off the beaten track."

Gabriel and Laura took their seats on plain wooden chairs around a small kitchen table. There were only three seats, though plainly enough room for four around the table. Seeing Laura's look of slight puzzlement, the old woman offered an explanation.

"The missing chair broke. It went into the stove." Juliana chuckled as she ladled the thick aromatic soap into bowls. "I don't get many guests here, so it wasn't missed." She handed out the bowls, then offered a basket of fresh home-baked bread around.

The three of them settled down to enjoy their soup, as Gabriel explained to Laura his relationship with the old woman. "I came to Argentina in 1964 . . . . " he began. Laura's eyes flashed a warning, interrupting his narrative momentarily. "It's okay, she knows about me," he reassured her, then continued. "Lucifer and I had been stalked halfway across Europe by former friends of yours, and we needed to put a lot of distance between ourselves and the Vatican at the time." He paused, dipping the fresh bread into the soup, then wolfed it down hungrily. "The military junta was causing havoc with the populace back then, so it took a lot of money to ingratiate ourselves and buy the villa. Friends of friends put me in touch with Juliana's husband, who was a member of the opposition party at the time. He helped open a few doors for me back then. Then came the dawn raids as the junta clamped down, and Juliana and her husband were arrested." The old woman concentrated on her soup as Gabriel recited his memories of unpleasant times. "Marco was put before a firing squad within hours of his arrest. Fortunately, we managed to get to Juliana and remove her from the prison before she was due to be executed as well."

"You went into the prison to get her out? I've passed that place. It's a fortress." Laura's eyes widened.

"Not me, personally. Lucifer was the one who went inside. I just took care of a few 'distractions', to take their minds off things."

"He only blew up half of Buenos Aires," the old woman cackled. "Never heard fireworks as good, before or since," she managed a pained smile.

"Since then, Juliana has lived up here in the wilds. Her choice, even though things have improved with the military over the years."

"Is peaceful here. Where else should I live?" Juliana shrugged her shoulders, breaking off more bread for her soup.

"You could live anywhere now Maldano's dead," Gabriel complained mildly.

"Who's Maldano?" asked Laura.

"Generalissimo Maldano was the bastard who trumped up the charges to have members of our party arrested," the old woman explained. "He survived the fireworks, but he did not survive me," she smiled cruelly, an expression which did not seem to fit on her face.

"You killed him" Laura asked in disbelief, for the slight figure of the woman in front of her, even as she must have looked thirty years ago, did not seem capable of such an act.

"Not personally." The old woman chuckled, as Laura looked puzzled. "A little of this, a little of that," she shrugged her shoulders, obviously not prepared to go into details.

"I told you," Gabriel butted in, "she's a witch." Juliana started to laugh, and then coughed and spluttered as some soup caught in her throat, and it was Gabriel's turn to laugh. Laura too, as the old woman turned to hit him with the spoon.

"That night, I crossed a line, over which there can be no return," Juliana reminisced. "I had power then, but I had never used it for my own benefit, and never in such a manner. His death was not easy. It gave me immense pleasure." She returned to her soup, her explanations over for now.

The three of them continued with their meal, only small-talk interrupting. Laura felt the old woman's eyes were on her throughout the meal, and she caught the glance Juliana shared with Gabriel, who nodded quickly in affirmation of whatever it was that passed between them.

Gabriel had told her about the instinctive almost telepathic bond that he had shared with Lucifer before the chemical torture he had undergone beneath the catacombs of Rome. Apparently it was quite common among Gabriel's kind, another benefit of the strange blood which now also flowed through her veins. She had noticed a similar 'bonding' between the two of them lately, more instinct than true telepathy, but hadn't had chance to raise the subject with Gabriel yet. As if sensing her interest, Juliana looked across the table towards her, and nodded slightly herself, her dark eyes catching Laura's own.

After the meal was concluded, Gabriel explained the reason for their visit, which again, the old woman claimed to already know, and Laura wondered whether indeed Juliana was joking at her expense. She watched as the old woman washed out the large black pot which had contained the soup, and then went out of the shack to refill it with water from the tiny mountain stream. She came back in momentarily, and began adding to the pot a mixture of herbs and strange looking things she kept in jars of preservative on a shelf in a dark alcove in the corner of the kitchen. She then placed the pot back on the range to boil.

"A strange story," Juliana commented, as they waited for the pot to boil. "A daughter that neither of you knew existed, and now seek to find." She shook her head, long greying hair hiding her face for a moment, till she swept it back. "Mirabelle is a nice name. If she still lives, I can help you. My magic, helped by yours . . ." she added pointedly, "will reveal her to you."

As the small pot gradually bubbled and boiled, Laura enjoyed listening to the interplay between Gabriel and Juliana. It was obvious she knew of Lucifer's death, and Laura assumed that Gabriel must have visited her at some time since his return to Buenos Aires, for he was always flitting here and there, leaving her to convalesce on his estate.

Eventually, the steam rose from the boiling pot, and Juliana used a rag to lift it off the range, and brought it onto the table around which they all sat. "Roll up your sleeves," the old woman instructed. Gabriel nodded at Laura to do the same, as he rolled his sleeve up, baring his forearm.

Juliana went away into the darkened alcove once more, and came back brandishing a small wickedly curved knife, the edge of which looked strangely black with age. Gabriel knew what was expected, and held out his arm over the still bubbling pot.

The old woman turned his arm, exposing the vein, which she sliced through quite deftly, and red blood flowed, dripping into the boiling liquid. Laura was taken aback momentarily, then, seeing it was expected, offered her own arm, wincing as she felt the hot slice of the knife, and her own blood mixed with Gabriel's in the boiling concoction as the old woman began her strange mutterings, half-whispered, strange monosyllabic sounds, guttural and basic, like no tongue she had ever heard before.

The wounds on their wrists began to noticeably close, healing themselves as the blood-flow diminished, and then stopped altogether. Still, Juliana kept up her chanting. As Laura looked on, the swirling steam coming up out of the pot seemed to contain shapes, as if containing something 'else' within.

A face, for it was surely a face, was taking shape within the steam. Gabriel and Laura looked on avidly as the face took shape before their eyes, solidifying, growing clearer by the second. A young woman's face, looking in her early twenties. Black hair, skin that strange golden sheen of Gabriel's. Laura's own eyes stared back out of the steam at her.

It was a beautiful face, which suddenly made Laura gasp involuntarily, and also caused a cold shudder to run down Gabriel's back.

"Your daughter," announced Juliana.

Chapter Three

The drive down from the mountain was made mostly in silence after having bid goodbye to Juliana. Both Gabriel and Laura lost in their own thoughts. They had seen the face of their daughter, and from Juliana's comments, this meant the girl was still alive.

Unbeknownst to the other, both of them had recognised the face in the steam, the recognition hitting each like a knife between the ribs. As Gabriel drove, they both tried desperately to deal with the dilemma each of them now found themselves in. At length, Laura broke the silence. "What now?" she asked, not able to bring herself to look him in the face.

"Now we have a face to go on, I'll make some sketches and circulate them," he explained. "My contacts might be able to come up with a photograph. Once we know where she is, I'll go to her."

"She's my daughter, too," she said. "I should be the one to go to her," she argued.

"Out of the question." Gabriel was quite resolute. "You may have been an agent for the Church, but no longer. All your contacts are gone, and it won't be long before the rest of that organisation knows you've joined up with me. It's far too dangerous. She might even kill you herself. She's one of their agents, remember?" he reminded her.

"I was a pretty good agent too," Laura protested.

"You're not in the same league," Gabriel blurted out, almost too quickly, without meaning to. "I'm sorry, Laura. I didn't mean that the way it sounded," he managed to disguise his words glibly. "It's just that from what we know, her track record takes some beating, and your work for the organisation was hardly in the same line," he explained. "If she is indeed this Belladonna, then she's a killer. Our daughter is an assassin, and one of their best."

Laura bit her lip sullenly, hiding her face by pretending to stare out of the window. She knew Gabriel talked sense, but there was no way she could afford to let Gabriel find the girl first. The past had a terrible way of catching up with the future, and it could destroy everything.

For his own part, dark thoughts filled Gabriel's mind as he drove, dark remembrances of an even darker night, high on the cliffs above Marseilles, and of a pretty face that he had thought would haunt him forever. The girl he had known only as 'Belle'. How could he tell Laura what he had done?

That night, Gabriel slept uneasily. Not wanting to wake Laura, he crept quietly from their bed, unaware that she was laying there awake herself, staring at the wall on the far side of the moonlit room, watching the shadows from the lightly billowing curtains. She too was finding it hard to sleep.

Gabriel went into one of the other bedrooms, to sit and brood on the edge of the bed, his mind awash with the recent events which had led them here, and were now causing him much remorse. The Church had pursued his kind for centuries, ever more organised after the Roman martyrdom had allowed them more religious freedom. He could only guess at how the Church had discovered his kind, and what their blood contained for mortal men.

But learn they did, and he had crossed swords with them on more than one occasion. The last one had changed his life forever, he thought, and then almost laughed. Forever was a long time to an immortal. Lucifer had been the bait. It was a bait he could not refuse to take. His best friend for over 2000 years. He blamed himself for the way it had gone wrong, all his careful plans awry at the last moment. The unexpected was always there, just waiting to catch you out.

Startled, the figures on the rock crowded together. "Look at the big bird . . . ." cried the boy, pointing up. Gabriel circled above them as they watched. Slowly, he swooped lower, approaching the flat rock from the valley side, flaring his artificial wings to slow his descent as they stepped back from the edge, allowing him plenty of room to land.

Their mouths gaped at the sight of this angel come to earth, eyes staring wide with wonder, Lucifer's with the first glimmer of recognition as he had hoped. The woman. There was something about the woman. She looked so familiar.

And then alarm bells went off inside his head, gasping as though an invisible hand had reached into his chest and solidified around his heart. It couldn't be . . . . it just couldn't! Now it was Gabriel's turn to gape in sudden recognition, sudden realisation, frozen with shock, as the woman finally regained her senses, clawing open her handbag and fumbling for the gun, the gun she quickly pressed to Lucifer's temple as she grabbed him from behind, taking him by surprise.

"Mary, what . . . . what are you doing?" he exclaimed in sudden shock. His mind whirled, fog lifting in slow swirls. Gabriel . . . . his friend Gabriel. Mary, with a gun . . . .

"Stay still! Still, I say, or I'll shoot you . . . ." Mary commanded. Her lip trembled as she tried to remain in control of herself and the situation. Luke backed away, horrified at what was happening.

Slowly, Gabriel was mentally piecing together the unknown events of the last 58 years. There was only one explanation, and it inwardly sickened him. For one brief second his heart had soared higher than his makeshift wings could carry him, and then the crushing revelation had brought with it only blackness and despair.

"I take it this is no chance reunion?" he said, sullenly, baleful eyes glowering out from beneath his dark rain-soaked brow.

Mary looked wildly at him, her eyes barely focused as her mind flashed back oh so many painful years . . . . Back to the day she had recovered from the anaesthetic, and Father Ryan telling her that her second child had been delivered stillborn, dead because of the mental stress she had been under at the time, caused by Gabriel. "Take off that ridiculous suit," she ordered. "Father Ryan will be here soon, and he will see you delivered to the Church, to pay for your crimes." She spoke hurriedly, the gun wavering back and forth from Gabriel to Lucifer.

"So he lives, too?" Gabriel shook his head. "I wonder how, with all those bullets I put into him?" he asked, rhetorically.

"Mary . . . . Mary, put the gun down, please. I think he's a friend of mine,' said Lucifer, memory beginning to flood back, in bright sudden flashes, which made his legs weak, and he wavered unsteadily.

Gabriel locked eyes with the woman. Burning coals glowered out from under the dark wet fringe which clung dripping from his forehead. "Is that what she told you her name was, Lucifer?" he said simply, then to her he spoke again. "I always said I would introduce you, didn't I?" He choked on the words. Overhead, a tremendous thunderclap exploded, as if one cue, and sheet lightning lit the face-off in an eerie sheen. "Lucifer, meet Laura Donovan . . . ."

The initial shock reunion with a woman he had long since thought dead had thrown Gabriel's strategy off-kilter, and then the appearance of Michael, one of the long-since believed lost Aerie, a vengeful, angry Michael, blew his plans all to hell . . .

He had time only to react, and fight for his life in the rain-swept skies above the north of England. The fight he had thought he had won, but which had allowed Ryan and his men to capture him, and then the shock and numbing horror, as a still burning Michael rose up behind him, wings aflame, spear raised on high, like an apparition out of Hell.

"No . . . . He dies . . . He dies . . . ." he roared, hurling the spear with all his waning might at Gabriel's chest. Frozen into immobility as much as Gabriel himself, the Irishmen could only watch, and it was only the recovered Lucifer who was galvanised into action.

"Michael. No . . . Nahhhhhhhh . . . ." he flung himself in front of Gabriel in a split second, trying to force his friend out of the way of the deadly spear. Too slow by far, the force of the blow taking the spear almost a foot out the other side of his body. Lucifer, his long-suffering friend of centuries, would suffer no more.

He took what seemed like a long time to fall to the ground, lifeless. And the Irishmen looked on, shocked, but not as shocked as Michael himself, who had wanted so badly to kill Gabriel, and who had now killed instead his former lover. Indeed, even through the centuries, he had never stopped loving Lucifer, never stopped cursing Gabriel for his role in their parting. He looked on for three, four seconds, ignoring the pain of his still smoldering wings, his mind finally snapping, and he roared in anguish and frustration,

*rounding on the Irishmen. "Your fault . . . . Your fault . . . . yours . . . .
not mine . . . yours . . ." he accused, starting towards them painfully, then
ignoring his pain and running at them, bellowing his hate.*

*Connor and Patrick began blasting away at him with their handguns,
terrified as most of the shots missed. Some didn't, but for all the blood and
flesh they blew away from his mighty body Michael kept on coming, his
huge arms sending Connor smashing into the nearby rock face, and leaving
a messy trail of blood on the rock as the limp body slid to the ground.*

*As mighty hands reached for him, in desperation, Ryan triggered the
transmitter in his pocket, and the explosive charge implanted in the angel's
brain did it's work. Michael's skull exploded, showering them all with blood
and brains. On the ground, Gabriel could do nothing, except sob helplessly.
Lucifer was dead. Michael was dead. They had him at last!*

In many ways, Gabriel would have given his own life to save Lucifer,
for their bond went beyond mere friendship. They had been separated
over the many centuries, but had always managed to find each other.
One loss had been exchanged for a lover he had thought dead. A bitter
balance of Fate.

On the other side of the wall, Laura lay now on her back, resenting
Gabriel's absence from their bed. She needed his warmth and comfort
now as she lay there, tormented by her own demons. What if he found
out?

She had asked herself this question a thousand times since this
afternoon. Would he hate me for it forever? There was no way of
telling. If he found their daughter first, and she told him, Gabriel might
never forgive her, and then it would all have been for nought. Why, oh
why? She gripped the sheets tighter about her as she tossed and turned
restlessly. She found herself wishing she had had more bullets in that
gun, when she finally had Ryan helpless at her feet.

*Laura stood, wide-eyed, gun in hand, as she checked on Gabriel's
condition. "Ryan ran off through the cornfield, using the car as cover. He's
wounded, but he's still got the gun." Gabriel could see the look in her eyes.
"Let him go, he's dangerous." He tried to sit up, fighting the affects of the
paralysing drug still coursing through his system, but could not. Blood still
flowed from the fresh wound.*

"So am I!" she said resolutely, 'You've no idea just how dangerous!' her eyes flared wide, and she turned quickly away from him, keeping low as she ran over to the overturned car. She checked inside to see Sean slumped over the wheel. His neck was obviously broken.

"Laura!" he called out to her, "Laura!" but she didn't hear him. Her mind was set, and nothing would change it. Looking quickly around, she saw where Ryan had entered the cornfield, and she quickly followed his tracks, feet squelching into the mud. "Fuck it!" Gabriel swore, as he forced himself to his feet. The flow of blood was easing. As long as he could stop the bleeding, his wound would heal all the faster. Yet he had no time. Laura was chasing that mad priest across the countryside. He gathered Laura had been given training whilst under Ryan's care, but what sort of training, and how good was she?

He limped over to the overturned car, to find a weapon. As he did so, Luke finally got out of the car, having looked in his rearview mirror to see headlights approaching, through the rain. He stepped out into the middle of the road, to wave the driver down to get help. The car slowed as the headlights picked out the boy. Patrick smiled as he recognised the boy. He was already drawing his revolver as the boy rushed up to the car.

Laura ran after Ryan as fast as she could, feet slipping in the mud, till she kicked off her shoes and went barefoot. It proved to be quieter anyway. There was no way she was letting him go. As she approached the copse, she heard him cry out, and looked up to see bushes moving over to her right. Crouching now, she slowed her pace. Ryan was wounded but still mobile. He had taught her a lot over the years, taught her too much.

Controlling her breathing, she kept low, traversing the edge of the woods, looking for movement, dark patches that shouldn't be there. Growing up on a farm, she was well versed in woodcraft. She had been born in the countryside, and knew all about hunting game, stalking prey. The rain both helped and hindered her. Ryan's tracks were easy to follow, but moving was noisy unless she took it slow, and Ryan was moving, trying to put as much distance as he could between them.

She heard him cry out once more, heard the sound of breaking twigs, and she rushed forward using the sounds to mask her own movements. Ryan had slipped and slid down a muddy bank. She saw him across from her, trying to climb up the other side, which was just as muddy, just as slippery. His right arm hung limply at his side, the sleeve of his jacket dark red with the blood he'd lost. His collar bone was damaged, she guessed, from the way he was holding himself. In a lot of pain. Good.

Ryan used his left hand to put the luger in his pocket, needing leverage to help himself up the slippery slope. Laura rose up behind him as he did so. "End of the road, Father," she said coldly, as Ryan froze at the sound of her voice. He turned around slowly, face contorted in a half-smile, against the pain.

"Laura, me child. So you've come on your own then?" he asked, scanning the woods behind her for sight of Gabriel.

"I think this little talk is best kept between just the two of us, Father. Don't you agree?" she asked, face set like a mask.

"Maybe you're right. Gabriel knows very little about the last 50 odd years, does he?" Ryan asked. "I understand, there are certain things you'd rather he remained ignorant about." His breathing was still laboured, as he tried to catch his breath from his exertions. "You always were good with that gun, weren't you, Laura?" he smiled again.

Laura felt in control of the situation now, and she hefted the gun comfortably in her hand. "Fifty eight years ago, Father, I was pregnant with Gabriel's child. You told me it was stillborn, you lying bastard!" she accused.

"Ahhh . . . so that's what all this is about?" he managed a chuckle. "I wondered how he managed to turn you against me so quickly."

"You knew I'd already lost one child." her voice was pained, the memories still haunting her. "How could you put me through that agony again?"

"It seemed the most plausible excuse at the time," he started to explain, then looked up quickly, over Laura's shoulder. "I thought you said you came alone?" he queried. Laura automatically half-turned, and instantly cursed her own stupidity as she heard Ryan's gasp and he fumbled the luger out of his pocket with his left hand.

Dropping onto one knee, Laura whirled, her gun-hand reaching out, pointing . . . firing all in one smooth movement, and Ryan screamed as the bullet shattered his forearm just below the elbow, falling backwards into the mud, the luger dropped from nerveless fingers. Carefully, as Ryan gasped at the fresh pain, and lay there panting, she made her way down the slippery bank. "Now we'll have our little talk, Father. I'm going to enjoy it, and you're not!" she said, aiming the barrel of the gun at Ryan's left kneecap. "Forgive me Father, for I am about to sin."

Four bullets she had used, aimed cruelly, for maximum pain, yet not anywhere that would let him bleed to death too quickly. Ryan had talked, and Laura had learned of how he had deceived her, how they had all deceived her. The drugs, the lies, and fifty odd years of loneliness, and misery, as she tried to justify herself amidst an organisation that had offered her a home, a family, a refuge. In reality, it was responsible for her despair, and her unjust hatred of the man called Gabriel.

She had learnt her lessons well in that organisation, and had become one of their better agents. Ryan told it all, the Cannucci's, the girl's own misdemeanours, her own training in the Sword of Solomon, before Borgia himself had taken her under his wing. Satisfied finally, the last bullet had put the old man out of his misery, and she felt no remorse at all, as she stood looking down at the frail broken corpse, leaking blood onto the already damp woodland floor.

She didn't know why the tears finally came, for it was not for Ryan she cried. He could rot in hell for what he had done to her, to Gabriel, to their daughter. The rain washed them away, as she walked slowly out of the wood.

And now she lay here, pondering the future. The face in the smoke she had recognised only too well, for their paths had already crossed. It was a wonder she hadn't thought of it before, when Ryan had first revealed Mirabelle was also one of their agents. She had found happiness again after nearly sixty years of self-torment. Was it all to be taken away from her once more?

Chapter Four

*R*ome, 1942

The Cannucci's were a simple farmer and his wife, who tended a small farm about twenty miles out from Rome. The couple had been married seven years, and remained childless, despite their efforts to conceive a child. They were known to the Catholic Church, and seemed ideally suited as foster parents, and so Father Ryan approached them one evening, timing his visit to coincide with the farmer's return from the fields. He was welcomed by the couple, and invited to partake of their evening meal.

Over the meal, Ryan laid the groundwork of deception that was intended to persuade the couple to take and care for the child as their own. A fictitious brother and sister-in-law had supposedly been touring Europe, on their way to visit him, when they had been 'killed' in an automobile accident, leaving the girl-child as Ryan's only surviving relative, which of course, he was in no position to raise himself. Ryan suggested that, as he thought the two of them ideally suited to care for the child, and with their own childless situation, it would be a mutually beneficial arrangement for them to raise the child on his behalf, with a suitable monetary recompense arranged through the Church for her care and upkeep.

So it was that the child was given into their care, and christened by them in a small ceremony as Mirabelle Cannucci, after his wife's mother. The baby girl was doted on by both parents, and by relatives alike, who believed the child to be the product of a secret pregnancy. Not unusual as the Cannucci's rarely made the journey into the city.

Mirabelle was a healthy child, and soon grew into a fit and strong young girl, who delighted in the country life, and the chores she helped in around the farm. The farm was seven miles away from the nearest other habitation, and so Mirabelle had no other children to play with, but she didn't mind. Her mother had been a former schoolteacher, prior to her marriage, and so managed to educate the girl to a basic level. The girl seemed to have a gift for learning, obviously very bright, and her mother, even though she was not her real mother, was very proud of her daughter.

The arguments with her husband occurred regularly though, as had the beatings. Mirabelle had grown up to accept them as normal, for her 'mother' never once complained about her treatment, merely accepting the bruises and harsh treatment, fearful of angering her husband further.

Mirabelle was never witness to any of the actual assaults, merely hearing the sounds, or seeing the aftermath, the bruises. Her father had a quick temper, and her mother always shooed her out of the way when she recognised his mood swings. Giuseppe Cannucci was not a well-educated man, coming from a long line of farmers, he had not needed to be. His marriage to Maria Bartone had seemed a strange mismatch at the time, but who knows what to expect from true love?

He saw the girl's fluency with numbers and language, although useful in helping with the accounts, as a pointed reminder of his own shortcomings. As though his wife had set out to do this to personally embarrass him, though this was not the case. He was a very insular man, suspicious of anyone and everyone. So it was that he began to alienate himself from his wife and daughter.

On the day of the accident, Giuseppe had been drunk. Maria had been behind the wheels of the tractor trying to help push it clear of the mud, when he had accidentally put the tractor into reverse. It had left Maria crippled, unable to walk without the aid of a crutch, her leg refused to set properly because she could not keep up with the farm's chores and remain in her sickbed. From that day on, Mirabelle found herself doing more and more of her mother's work around the farm.

In her tenth year, the first changes of puberty were making themselves apparent in her body. The aching swellings on her chest, the growth of hair between her legs. Not knowing what they were, she was unconcerned about the slight changes in her body.

Time passed, and one hot summer's day, sweating from her exertions in the fields, the twelve year old girl paused from her toil to remove her clothes and bathe in the cool waters of a stream that ran through one of the fields. It was while she was bathing, that her 'father' happened upon her on his way back from the upper pasture.

Giuseppe stopped in his tracks at the sight of the naked girl splashing happily in the water. She was very obviously growing into a young woman, a very pretty young woman, he admitted to himself as he felt his cock harden as he watched her bathe from a distance.

He hadn't had sex with his wife since her accident. She had blamed him, and always complained that her leg gave her too much pain. He found himself walking towards the stream uncontrollably, drawn by the naked young girl's naïve frolicking in the water.

The girl's sudden shock as she saw her father approaching, quickly turned to screams as he pulled her kicking and loudly screaming from the water, and he forced her down onto the grassy bank, cuffing her as she resisted. Her screams frightened a flock of nesting birds into flight, as her lust-crazed 'father' pulled open his trousers, and forcibly penetrated her, the actual penetration almost as painful for him as for the girl, but it didn't stop him, so great was his lust.

When the act was done, Mirabelle ran home in tears, pausing only to pull on her clothes once she was far enough away from the old man, and ran tearfully up to her room, locking her bedroom door behind her and refusing to acknowledge the worried calls of her invalid mother.

When Giuseppe finally came home, the guilty look on his face was plain to see, and Maria launched herself into a tirade of abuse, which the old man batted aside as easily as he did herself. Knocking her to the ground and kicking her repeatedly as she cried out. "I am the master of this household! Me!" he bellowed as he kicked her. "It's not as if she were my *real* daughter," he excused his actions. "I keep her, I clothe her, I feed her. It's about time she paid me back!" He left his wife there on the floor, semi-conscious. He felt like a man again, and he felt no shame in his actions. He was the man of the house, and the women were his chattels, to do with as he wished.

From then on, Maria dared offer no argument to her husband. Her only token show of resistance was to protect her daughter by keeping her away from the old man, but she couldn't do it forever. The second rape occurred two weeks later, almost to the day, as her 'father' caught her behind the cowsheds. "Come here, girl!" he grinned as he grabbed for her, the milk bucket spilling onto the ground as he forced himself upon her. Mirabelle's life turned into one of fear, fear at the treatment her own father was now giving her.

The old man felt rejuvenated at the availability of such succulent young female flesh, and the attacks grew more frequent. Soon, even her own bedroom was no longer safe. Her mother was too frail to protect her from the old man's lusts. As time went by, Mirabelle found herself resisting less and less, accepting the inevitable to save her bruises. She learnt to please the old man in various ways, anything to lessen the brutality of the act.

Her mother could no longer look her own daughter in the eye, and Mirabelle thought herself abandoned to a life of sexual slavery. How could two such formerly loving parents treat her like this?

Giuseppe thought he had broken the girl's will, but he was wrong! Not daring to openly defy the overbearing monster that she called her Father, because of her size and lack of strength, Belle waited and waited, till the opportunity for revenge finally presented itself.

Chapter Five

*T*wo years went by before the girl's situation came to the attention of the Holy Church. The Cannucci's were found dead in their own home, poisoned with rat-poison, the old man mutilated, and the girl missing. The police forces initiated a search which found her hiding out in the hills, and Father Ryan was recalled from his overseas posting to Southern Ireland.

His first sight of the wild-eyed girl in the police holding-cell shocked him. As she heard the inspection visor open, she flew into the corner of the room, huddling with her knees drawn up beneath her on the bare bunk, obviously terrified, for as he understood it, apart from her foster-parents, Mirabelle had had little other contact with the outside world.

He understood from the police, that the girl had fought like a wildcat when they had finally cornered her after a long chase. Two of the police officers were still recovering from wounds received at her hands from the knife she had carried with her. The same knife which had later been proved to have been used in the old man's castration. It had taken fully four grown men to subdue her. Her strength and speed were far superior to those of a normal girl of her age. Ryan was to attempt to salvage the situation with the girl, whilst other forces behind him smoothed the way to resolve the legalities of the double-murder.

Mirabelle glared defiantly as the cell door swung open. Caged animal that she felt herself to be, she had already made two attempts to force her way out of the cell on previous occasions. Unsuccessful, despite her efforts. The police had overpowered her with sheer numbers, and used batons on her, though strangely the bruising soon vanished. This time she remained there in the corner, as Ryan entered the cell alone, seating himself on the single stool across from her.

"Hello, Mirabelle. My name is Father Patrick Ryan," he said, speaking Italian with a noted soft Irish lilt to his accent.

"Why should I care what your name is?" she answered sullenly.

"Perhaps because I can help you, help you leave this place, help you start over," he said simply, careful not to reveal too much of his knowledge of her situation. "Terrible things were done to you, and no one really blames you for what you did," he went on. "But the authorities are now faced with a problem, to which we, the Church, can offer a solution that will please them, and help you at the same time."

"How can you help me? Can you get me out of this shit-hole?" she asked, half derisively.

"Child, I can make you disappear off the face of this earth, as if you never existed," he stated simply, yet with a hint of menace. "I can take you out of here, offer you employment, something to suit your obvious skills," he smiled. "You would want for nothing ever again, and no one would mistreat you," he promised.

"How can one man do all that?" she asked.

"I am not just one man, child. I speak for the Holy Church, which stretches across the whole wide world."

"I don't want to be a nun," she replied, curtly, dismissing the offer.

"You may serve the Church in many ways, child. A nun is only one such example. I myself serve the Church in a similar capacity to which we hope to employ you." Her eyes seemed to burn into him, across the room. So like her mother's that Ryan was taken aback for a moment. "There are many branches of the Holy Church, child," he eventually continued. "I work for one special branch, which requires certain skills not normally associated with the cloth. If you agree to this, I will take you from here to a monastery near Como in the north-west. My organisation uses this place as a sort of specialised training camp."

"What about the police?" Mirabelle asked.

"If you agree to leave here with me, the police will not bother you. Arrangements are already being made," he promised. Mirabelle seemed to be assessing his words, and the man himself, as if she could sense the truth or lies in his words. After a few moments, the girl seemed to make her mind up.

"I need some clothes." She stood up, displaying the thin and grubby prison-shift they had given her to wear.

Ryan stood up, turning towards the door. He knocked and the cell-door was opened warily. Ryan turned again to the girl. "A nun will visit you shortly, with appropriate clothing. We leave for Como this afternoon," he promised, and with a smile, left the cell. The door clanged shut behind him, and all that Mirabelle could do was to wait.

Just over two hours later, the nun arrived at Mirabelle's cell, with clothing finer than she had ever seen before. Used to coarse homemade fabrics on the farm, she was amazed by the silks and the cotton garments the nun presented her with, and she left the cell while Mirabelle dressed herself, marvelling at the feel of such luxurious garments against her skin.

Once she was ready, the nun returned, and this time the cell door remained open as the nun beckoned to her to leave her cell. "Come, child. We go now to meet with the Holy Father, who is waiting outside in a car to take us to Como." The nun stood to one side, as did the policeman, who had had cause to respect the girl's physical prowess the last time she had tried to escape. His ribs still ached.

Mirabelle walked hesitantly out of the cell, as though expecting it to be all a sick joke, and she stood there just outside the steel door for a moment, till it finally sunk in that it was all really happening. They were letting her go. "Come," called the nun, politely, as she led the way. Mirabelle enjoyed the feel of the hot sun on her face again as they left the entrance to the police station, and she followed the nun down the steps to where a long black limousine waited. She could see the priest sat in the back of the car, and he now reached across and opened the rear door for her to enter.

It was then that Mirabelle chose her moment, looking up and down the street, seeing the many alleyways where she could easily lose herself in this strange and wonderful city, and whirled to run off to find her own freedom. Despite lightning reflexes, before she could take a second step, she cried out as her wrist was grabbed, twisted savagely up behind her back, and her face slammed down hard against the rear bodywork of the car. Mirabelle cried out with the sudden pain. Despite her superior strength, the woman held her easily with this strange grip.

Behind her, the 'nun' offered little in the way of scant consolation. "Not unexpected, girlie. I was warned how good you are. But I think you'll find I'm pretty good myself. Now get in the fucking car!" she ordered, twisting the arm further as she pushed Mirabelle's head down and through the open car-door.

More shocked than actually hurt, Mirabelle allowed herself to be bundled into the back of the car, where she seated herself alongside Father Ryan. The 'nun' got in the rear of the car as well, and Mirabelle glared at the smirking face, as the car door was closed, and the limousine began to pull away from the kerb. "I see you and Sister Angelica are getting on famously." Ryan chuckled.

Chapter Six

Belle was pleasantly surprised by the Monastery. High amid the foothills of the Alps, it started the day in shadow, the sun taking its time to appear over some of the small surrounding hills. Looking up to the higher peaks to the north, she could see the ever-present caps of snow on some of the peaks. Lake Como was less than a few hours away by car, and available for weekend visits, under supervision, the Father advised her.

The air outside was cooler this far north, noticeable in the three day journey. She found Ryan's company and conversation amiable, and quite pleasantly reassuring. Once they had transferred onto the train, she had decided against her earlier reservations, to go with the flow, and see what the old man's offer of a new life was like.

Angelica sat across from her in the carriage, keeping her distance, yet close enough to be a veiled threat should she show any signs of offering violence to the good father. She smirked occasionally at Belle, and Belle definitely did not like the woman. She glowered back at her, which just seemed to amuse the silent nun.

Ryan noted the friction between the two, but refused to comment on it. Truth be told, Belle was a bit in awe of the older woman. She had realised her own strength and speed in the fight with the police, and was then surprised that the woman had been able to subdue her so easily. If Ryan wanted to train her, then she was willing to be trained. At least until she could meet the woman again, on her own terms.

The nun, if nun she was (and Belle doubted it), had already made her assessment of Belle. Raw but gifted. A possible useful asset to the organisation. But she had no doubt that Belle's value would be second to her own, for she had enjoyed the last three years as Ryan's personal agent, and though the Father looked to be getting on in years, he was still a useful field-agent himself, having learned his trade in Southern Ireland fighting the British. So sprightly was he for his apparent age, that she thought he must be 'chosen'. Angelica herself had not yet been offered the Blood of Christ, and it was her aim in life to achieve the same status as Ryan within the organization.

The Abbot met them at the station, and then took them by car to the monastery. It looked like any other, set high amid the foothills. High walls which were not overlooked except by keen mountaineers, hid the inside from view. Only the aged terracotta roofs and the tall chapel belfry were visible from outside.

Two monks opened the large solid gates, and as the car drove through, Belle quickly saw that this was no ordinary monastery, for within the large grounds she could plainly see an obstacle course, what looked like a barracks, and other strange looking structures and buildings. Apart from the Abbot himself and the two monks at the gate, everyone else she could see wandering around inside the walls was wearing ordinary everyday clothing.

After introductions were over, Belle was shown to her quarters, a small barracks which she shared with nine other women. Angelica, one of the instructors, had private quarters of her own. All the other women were obviously wary around her as she showed Belle around, and indicated which bunk she should take.

The monastery was run more on military than religious regime, with harsh courses in physical training intermingled with scripture and religious classes. Prayers, Mass and Confession seemed strange bedfellows to unarmed combat, knife-fighting and handgun practise.

Once the other women realised the friction between her and Angelica, they warmed to Belle more. One woman in particular, who had the adjacent bunk, named Jessica, became a close confidante. Friendships with the men were more difficult, for the two sexes were kept apart when not training together. The religious overseers, Belle wasn't sure whether they were really part of the clergy or just conscripts like herself, frowned on fraternisation between the sexes, just like a real Monastery or Priory.

She found the training hard but interesting, and soon began to excel. The more physical sides of the training she mastered easily, endurance, obstacle course, running, climbing. Her gun skills were improving. Her knife-work was excellent. Blades just seemed like an extension of her arm once in her hand. Her unarmed combat was left to Angelica to administer, who she found was one of the combat instructors.

Although teaching Belle, instructing on technique, method and application, she seemed to take a delight in applying harsh lessons when Belle seemed slow to pick up on what she had been taught. More than once she taught Belle painful and embarrassing lessons on the practise mat, in front of the other women.

Judo, Karate and a number of other skills were taught. None were dedicated. It seemed like the best moves from a number of different martial arts were taught. It was deemed best to be able to switch fighting styles as required, in case they ever came up against an opponent who could counter some of their moves. Some came more readily to Belle, though Angelica was obviously a master of them all, and was keen to vigorously demonstrate the fact to any of the women who dared meet her on the practise mat.

Belle nursed her latest round of bruises one evening, after a refreshing shower. They still had ten minutes or so before they were scheduled for evening prayers and supper. Jessica sat down on the bunk next to her, and put an arm around her friend. "She beat the shit out of you again, didn't she?" she shook her head, hugging Belle close. "Why the hell do you always volunteer ? You know she loves kicking your ass." Jessica just couldn't understand her friend. Belle managed a smile, through a cracked lip, which immediately started to bleed once more.

"But every time, it takes her a little bit longer to do it, and she knows it!" Belle grinned, her tongue flicking out to catch the blood on her lip.

"I hope I'm there to see it, the day Angelica finally gets her comeuppance," Jessica smiled back, and then she leaned forward and gently kissed Belle's broken lip, which seemed perfectly natural under the circumstances. Belle thought nothing of it, even though she had heard some of the giggling and low moans from some of the other bunks during the nights. The two women giggled, as Jessica came away from the embrace with blood on her own lips, too. Belle leaned forward and licked Jessica's lips, taking the blood away. The two women looked into each other's eyes, both of them seeing something similar reflected therein, and then the moment was broken as the muster bell sounded for evening prayer.

Later that evening, it was no surprise when Jessica slipped into Belle's bunk. "Move over," she whispered, and then she giggled as she slid under the blankets, pressing herself against Belle. She giggled too, as she cuddled against the 15 year-old, enjoying the body warmth.

"Are you in love with me?" Belle asked, gasping as she felt Jessica's hot mouth on her neck, and her hands move over her body. She needed to be loved so badly, after the shambles of a life she had lived so far.

"Does it matter?" chuckled Jessica. "We're not likely to get hold of any of the men while we're here. The instructors enforce that curfew," she moaned as she held Belle's breast in her hand, feeling the nipple all hard against her palm. "I can make you happy," she promised.

"I loved my father, once," Belle started to say, and then paused as Jessica's fingers slid down inside her panties. "Then I learnt to hate him. Ohhhh . . ." she gasped.

"Hush now, little one," Jessica soothed and stroked. "Don't hate me, just love me back," she moaned, and buried her hot mouth on Belle's own, kissing her hungrily.

In the months that followed, the two women grew ever closer, and the relationship was easily spotted by Angelica, who smiled at the realisation. Ryan wanted Mirabelle nurtured and trained to be the best, and had given strict instructions that all care was to be taken with her training.

Taking an instant dislike to the now 15 year-old, which she knew was mutual, she enjoyed humiliating and beating the younger girl, though taking care not to cause any permanent damage. She found herself more and more of a mind to arrange a training 'accident', for which she could not be blamed. One which would leave Belle either dead or permanently injured. Now she had a new 'weapon' to use against Belle. Her lesbian relationship with Jessica.

*   *   *

In the weeks that followed, Angelica often ignored Belle's raised hand when wanting to demonstrate the latest lesson in unarmed combat. Instead she chose Jessica to join her on the mat. The lesson taught was hard, and needlessly cruel, as was Angelica's intent. She smiled deliberately at Belle, as she went to help her friend up at the end of the brutal lesson.

By the time this had happened twice more, the older woman's motives were plain for all to see. Jessica's face was black and blue, and badly swollen after the third beating. Even Belle's lips hurt, where they touched the bruised flesh. "She's going to kill me." Jessica sobbed into her lover's shoulder, as Belle held her reassuringly.

"No," whispered Belle, as she kissed Jessica's hair. "No, she's not," she promised.

*   *   *

When next Angelica was the instructor at the practise mat, Belle was the first to put up her hand. More hands went up than usual today, for a number of the other girls had also noticed how Angelica seemed to be picking on Jessica, who was a popular girl in the barracks, and they would each save her from a beating if they could. But Angelica ignored the show of hands and went along the ranks of the kneeling girls, stopping in front of Jessica once more.

Belle shot to her feet, finding it hard to control her temper. "Fight me!" she demanded. "Or are you afraid to?" Everyone stared as Angelica turned slowly toward the younger woman, smiling in disdain.

"Never fight in anger, child," she admonished, "and where possible, always choose the time and the place, seeking the maximum advantage over your foe," she smiled thinly. "I choose to fight Jessica, here. Stand up girl," she ordered.

"You're not getting a choice. I choose *here* and *now*, you *fucking* cow!" bellowed Belle, as she launched herself at her tormentor in a high kick that Angelica almost didn't avoid, Belle's foot dislodging the bun in Angelica's red hair, and it flew wild and free around her shoulders, as she backed away onto the training mat. The rest of the girls roared their approval, and crowded around the mat, sensing blood.

A confident grin appeared on Angelica's face as she and Belle circled warily around each other. Belle had finally taken the bait.

All the girls were cheering Belle on. The noise was deafening and distracting. "Come on, 'little girl', let's see just how much you've really learned," Angelica taunted, as Belle launched another flying Savate kick, which she parried easily with her forearm, and then launched into an attack of her own. Angelica came at Belle in a flurry of blows, some previously taught, but most of which the girl had never seen before, and the younger girl had only her instinct and reactions to protect her against Angelica's age and greater skill.

Both hands flashed out almost faster than the eye could follow, lightning aikido strikes to the throat and solar plexus, Belle grunting as she parried the first two, crying out as the third hit home, and she threw herself back, rolling away from the older woman, who followed her quickly.

Turning retreat into attack, the reverse roll was suddenly halted, and Belle's leg flew forward, tripping Angelica as she lunged forward. Belle sprang up and down onto her tormentor, slamming an elbow down into her midriff as Angelica tried to block, and Belle snarled with keen satisfaction at the grunt of pain from the older woman.

The rest of the girls scented blood. They roared their encouragement as Angelica forced the younger girl back, longer arms and legs being used to their fullest advantage, till she caught her breath back.

The noise was bringing more people to watch the fight. Some of the men and the other instructors were now gathering around as the two women went at each other. Belle's face was cut by the long nails of Angelica, but she felt no pain in her rage.

A high kick from Angelica caught Belle on the side of the head, and she fell backwards, the screams from the other girls warning her that Angelica was rushing in for the kill. Turning her forward roll into a sprung handstand, she lashed back with a high kick, catching Angelica full in the crotch, and the older woman screamed in pain, clutching herself and falling back away from Belle who whirled round quickly to take advantage.

She flew at Angelica in a rage that few could have survived. More high-kicks followed, interspersed with chops and jabs, alternating her styles as Angelica herself had taught her. A good old fashioned straight right, something she hadn't been taught but which came naturally, smashed into Angelica's nose, fist breaking cartilage as the watching girls screamed for more. The sight of free-flowing blood from their tutor's nose was pleasant indeed.

More enraged than badly hurt, Angelica redoubled her own attack, more respectful of Belle's skills this time. The girl was a natural fighter, tenacious and fast to make up for her lack of skills, and this combat was proving more difficult than she had thought. More blows were exchanged, Angelica using her longer reach to advantage, her blood-smeared face contorted with hate. She aimed a two-knuckled blow at Belle's throat, and some of the watching girls gasped as they recognised it. It was a killer! Angelica was no longer looking just to teach the girl a lesson.

Belle was too caught up in the fight to realise the rules had just been changed, automatically using a block, and then twist, to try and throw the woman, all instinct now. Angelica rolled with the throw, as Belle tried to follow up quickly, and Angelica came up fast off the floor, launching herself at the younger girl before Belle could back off, closing her down quickly and slamming a knee into her solar plexus.

Winded, and gasping for air, Belle broke free and rolled away, but not quickly enough, as a vicious Savate kick slammed into her side with all the venom Angelica could muster, making Belle scream as she felt a couple of ribs go. Angelica was on her before she had time to recover, straight-fingered jabs slammed into her pained ribs as she tried frantically to block, and then Angelica towered above her, as she lay momentarily dazed, arm pulling back as she grinned in triumph. "Not good enough, little girl!" she taunted, and her right hand knifed down at Belle's bared throat.

The killing blow never landed, for two of the male combat instructors had recognised what was happening just in time, and rushed forward to break up the fight. Angelica screamed in frustration as she was hauled off the semi-conscious young girl. Mirabelle was quickly attended to by the rest of the girls, as the Abbot himself made an appearance.

The two women were escorted to the infirmary, where they were treated in separate rooms and well-supervised. Mirabelle was detained, whilst Angelica was discharged after treatment, her presence being requested by the Abbot who had been questioning some of the witnesses to the fight.

* * *

When Mirabelle was released from the infirmary after a few days, Angelica had already left the Monastery, her presence now deemed a de-stabilising influence. Her pained ribs still hurt, though her recovery was amazing the camp-physicians. She tried to curb her laughter at the description of the Angelica's taped-up nose and two black eyes, as Jessica and the other girls came to congratulate her for getting rid of the 'wicked witch'.

The two women enjoyed life much better after that incident. Both of them enjoyed and excelled in their training under the tutelage of skilled instructors, who treated them fairly if harshly, depending on the circumstances.

Mirabelle was looked on as a rising star by the Abbot, who was kept well-informed of her progress, passing the information on to Father Ryan.

*   *   *

The next year kept Belle busy at the monastery, as she was trained in martial arts, covert surveillance, intelligence, and assassination techniques.

Encouraged to develop her own skills, Mirabelle found herself favouring the knife more and more. Always reliable, where a gun might jam. Shorter range, but not necessarily so in the right hands, and Mirabelle could throw a knife accurately over twenty feet or more. One of the male mechanics in the workshop helped her develop a pair of weighted throwing knives, light enough for her to handle and throw easily, heavy and sharp enough to penetrate powerfully whatever she was aiming at.

By the time she was 16, Mirabelle was allowed out of the monastery for brief sojourns with actual field-teams, learning her craft on the job, albeit in a supervised role. She would be gone for 2 to 3 weeks at a time.

This happened with some of the other girls as well, and they all treated it as a big adventure, until the day one of the girls didn't come back. This brought home the reality of their roles. They were being trained for a purpose, and once word got out of the girl's fate, the rest of them knuckled down all the harder into absorbing their training.

This didn't prevent mishaps in the field, but certainly reduced them. Barring a few injuries, there was only one other fatality that occurred on these field-trips, and that was Jessica.

When her friend and lover didn't return as expected, a fearful Mirabelle asked to see the Abbot. By the time she left his office, she was shaking uncontrollably, and rushed back to the barracks to sob into her pillow. Jessica had reportedly been a casualty in an altercation with a group of Mafia thugs, and had been stabbed to death after a surveillance mission had gone wrong.

The rest of the girls did their best to console Mirabelle, and the mood in the camp darkened as more and more of them realised the time for playing games was over. They either made the grade, or they would not survive. It stiffened resolve among all of them to excel at their training, and Mirabelle forced herself back into a physical regime, to try and get over Jessica's death.

A week later, a small parcel arrived at the monastery, addressed to Mirabelle Cannucci. Mail was indeed rare, but not unknown at the Monastery, for the Church often forwarded mail from people's families to keep them in touch and thus allay any suspicions as to their whereabouts. Mirabelle had never previously received any mail, even from Father Ryan, and so was surprised to receive the small parcel, addressed in a neat script. She opened it with curious fingers. It was small, light. What could it be?

Her mouth dropped as she opened the package, and saw what was inside. A pair of tiny, bloodstained earrings were pinned to a small piece of card. She had bought the earrings herself for Jessica as a birthday present last year. The card was written in the same flowing script as the front of the package, only this time it was written in blood.

"I took my time killing the little bitch!" was all it said, and beneath it was a cupid's bow imprint of lipstick. A shade Mirabelle remembered well. Angelica!

Chapter Seven

The Cardinals amused themselves with the weekly ritual of bringing the young novitiate nuns to witness their very own Miracle. They were brought into the subterranean chamber which housed Michael, the last known winged angel on Earth.

Michael's sexual needs were easily catered for, and they were voracious. The young nuns were in awe at the sight of him, so magnificent in his regal silks and his huge broad ever-moving wings, so tall, so handsome, so manly. His matted chest was oiled and perfumed, his beard manicured and curled into ringlets

He could scent them before they were brought before him, scent them even while they were still in the outer chamber. His nostrils flared as he inhaled their feminine musk, sniffing their virginity like a heady perfume.

He beamed down at them, from a suitably raised and regal plinth, where he reclined on a marble throne, all festooned with gold silks. He truly looked like something out of legend, straight out of the scriptures. The room was done out in whites and pastels, silks and cottons. Careful not to create too ostentatious a setting, the Cardinals did indeed wish to convey a heavenly background to the young impressionables, who would doubtless go from this place with their faith both renewed and strengthened.

During the audiences, the nuns were allowed to converse with Michael, some allowed to touch him, and all the while he deported himself with decorum, in a manner fitting the role he was required to play, feeding the Church's fantasies, supporting their doctrine of life after death, and glory ever-after. He had long since learned the role the Church would have him play.

If not his freedom, it got him his women. Michael could not imagine life without women. Some of them were overcome in his actual presence, fainting away, so that the other attendants had to take them out of the room to recover.

Michael made his choices by a casual stroke of the back of his hand across the brow of one or two of the young nuns, and it was later that the Cardinals approached the young women, broaching the delicate subject, and justifying what they were asking the women to do by remembering the angel who came down to Mary to begat Jesus (even the Cardinals did not know of Michael's actual involvement there). It was a holy duty to perform this service to an angel.

Michael was thus never short of naughty nuns to cater for his sexual needs. Some of the Cardinals even watched secretly, amused by his antics, and lustful of the young women themselves.

*   *   *

This opulence was a far cry from his last period of confinement, in the Tibetan Monastery high on the Himalayan borders, where today's modern day Catholic Church had 'rescued' him. In reality, it was merely swapping one type of confinement for another. At least this one had women, as well as catamites.

Michael had had sexual relationships with both men and women in his long life, though by far his greatest love had been his fellow 'angel' Lucifer. Did he still live, Michael wondered? Wingless, and confined to the earth, as a result of his friendship with Gabriel, his lover had remained behind, as Michael had lead the Aerie north, fleeing the advance of the Roman legions and the civilisation they brought with them.

All their lives had seemed one long migration, as he looked back on 2000 plus years. As man had become more worldly, and spread like a rash on the face of the globe, Michael and his kind, whom had once been looked upon with awe, quickly became denigrated to the ranks of oddities and freaks, to be hunted and persecuted when they came into contact with the wingless humans.

Mankind had spread too rapidly for Michael's brethren to stand their ground, and they had perpetually sought the vast wilderness, and the high ground, only coming into closer contact where they needed water, food or other things in the ways of supplies. They made the mountains their homes, in the highest reaches where man could not come. Not in those days anyway.

His earliest memories were clouded with time, though the warm climes of the east had seemed their home, he remained unaware of his origins. There was no childhood he could remember, no parents, and no females.

Human females had thus attracted their curiosity and their lusts, though most were not averse to relationships with each other, having no females of their own race. Such liaisons had caused problems in the past, in Judaea and other kingdoms, as the might and influence of Rome spread.

By the time the Aerie reached Britain, Michael's own longstanding relationship with Lucifer had been threatened by the latter's friendship with Gabriel. A friendship which later ended in tragedy, with both Gabriel and his lover being shorn of their wings by the Druid Priests. Although Michael had led the Aerie on a rescue and revenge mission, saving their lives, they were then earthbound, and no longer able to fly with the Aerie, and eventually abandoned to live a life amongst the humans who had crippled them.

Leaving Lucifer and Gabriel behind, the migration had continued westward, longer ago than he could almost remember, till the legions of Rome had pushed them as far as the great Western Sea, which they tried unsuccessfully to cross. Left with no alternative, as civilisation marched on, they were forced northwards, till halted by the frozen waters and then eventually they gradually retraced their steps to the north and east, across Scandinavia and Russia, being hunted all the way by the savage humans, then being forced south again by a savage winter, till at last they reached the Himalayas. The Roof of the World.

The Aerie's numbers had been savaged over the years, during their long flight, for the humans' numbers had greatly increased in the last few hundred years, and they met armed resistance with every turn. Some of the nations had learnt the use of the bow, and hunted Michael and his kind as they would the hawk and the eagle. Only a handful were left. The rest had fallen to the humans' warlike ways and ever increasing intelligence.

Sorely wounded himself as they reached the high mountains, Michael had no longer the strength to fly at the altitude it required to cross them, for the thinner air required greater effort to fly, and as Matthias, Nathaniel, and the rest of his friends pressed on, he sought a passage through the lower peaks. The storm erupted in all it's fury around him, as his mighty wings beat against the ferocious winds, which ripped open wounds to bleed and matt his feathers where the wind froze them.

He was finding it harder and harder to fly, and could hardly see through the blinding snow. Finally, his strength failing, he swooped down to seek shelter, in the leeward side of one of the tall peaks, but as his sandaled feet sank into the snow, it began to move. His weight had been enough to trigger an avalanche.

Michael's world erupted around him in a mighty roar as the snowfield under his feet slipped. Caught up in the moving mass, he had no chance to seek the skies. Before he could beat his wings even once, he was engulfed, turning end over end, buffeted as even the mightiest of storms had never buffeted him before. His mouth filled with snow as he attempted to cry out, and then he lost consciousness.

*   *   *

It was many hours later, after the storm had abated, that the weary traveller was making his way through the mountain passes, heading for the Monastery on the higher slopes. Noting the excess of snow, he was moving slowly and cautiously, and unable to take the most direct route.

Ordinarily, a frozen wing sticking up out of the snow would not have been enough to attract his attention, except for the sheer size of it, and the man's curiosity got the better of him. Picking his way carefully to where the huge bloodstained wing stuck up from the fresh snowfall, the man began to dig, curious as to what sort of bird this was, that had perished in the fierce mountain storms.

His fingers dug down through the soft snow, scooping away. He paused momentarily at the darker shape his digging revealed, and then his fingers found the arm, cold, yet not yet stiff, and he screamed in shock, instantly murmuring a prayer of appeasement to Buddha.

Turning, the man pulled his robes more closely around him, and hurried on up the pass with renewed vigour. The brothers must be told. They would know what to do.

*   *   *

So it was, that Michael, mightiest of the Aerie, was brought low. Rescued by the monks from the monastery, they took him on a litter up to their remote mountain retreat, and nursed him as he slowly recovered from his ordeal. These tiny men cared for him, fussing over him, though at first he could not understand any of their strange language.

His wings had suffered severe frostbite, which took many years to heal fully, and then when finally Michael felt well enough to fly, he found the air too thin to support his mighty frame, the effort requiring more air for his lungs and lift for his wings, for the Monastery was in the remote high peaks of the mountain range.

Trapped on the Roof of the World, Michael's only choices were to set out on foot, into an unknown landscape, and try to reach lower slopes where he might fly once more, or remain with his new found friends in the Monastery. These monks were the only humans whom had ever offered Michael friendship, and so Michael decided to remain.

*   *   *

The years went by, turning into centuries, and eventually a traveller of a different faith called upon the monastery. Father Angelo was travelling through the Far East, engaged in research for a doctorate on the many diverse religions of the modern world. Travelling through China, he had chosen a route back through Tibet, and had heard of the monastery here so high above the snowline, where the priests deliberately cut themselves off from the outside world, restricting contact to the barest minimum. Villagers from the lower slopes of the mountains supplied the brothers with food and tools when needed. In return, the monastery's workshops provided prayer-wheels and other craftwork, which were sold in the villages, to repay their kindness.

Father Angelo was well-received by the monks, though he spoke little of their language. The Abbott gave him an audience, where an interpreter from the village helped explain the reason for his visit. He was then shown to a cell which was not in use, and bade welcome to stay here while he continued his research. A similar cell was found for the interpreter, who had agreed to stay on and help the good Father for a week or two, until he learned enough of the language to communicate his scant needs, and talk to the various monks about their beliefs.

He was in the monastery for three days before he got his first sight of Michael. The shock almost killed him, for he suffered from a mild heart condition. His medication was in short supply, but was sufficient to control the chest-pains the sight of a winged angel had brought on.

The tall muscled figure of Michael stood head and shoulders above the shorter monks. Broad wings flexed constantly, and it was an unnerving sight to see such appendages affixed to an otherwise human body. The angel spoke their tongue easily, and was obviously a popular figure with the monks, taking part in the many chores, especially revelling in those which required the sort of great physical effort that the slighter-framed monks found difficult.

Talking to the monks through his interpreter, Father Angelo found that the angel had been here longer than the monks had been alive. On rare occasions, they would see him fly, though not very high and not for very long in these extreme temperatures and thin air. The air was thin enough to make physical effort very strenuous. You had to take things very casually at these altitudes.

Father Angelo continued his research with the monks, but also wrote down other information concerning Michael, and his many sketches included layouts of the monastery itself. All this information he intended to pass on to other members of the Church.

He left on good terms with the brothers, but once he left his guide in the village below, he was eager to find civilisation and a phone. "Zola. I need to speak to Cardinal Zola . . . ." Father Angelo explained once a connection to the Vatican had finally been established.

* * *

The attack on the monastery took the monks completely by surprise, as agents of the Sword of Solomon scaled the walls one night, and, like white ghosts in their camouflage snow-suits, ran through the dormitories and halls, spraying death from silenced handguns. No one would remain alive to bear witness to this night.

Michael and his latest paramour dozed lazily in his chamber. Out of deference to his greater size and physical needs, subsequent Abbots had made structural changes to allow four of the normal-sized cells to be made into one, in which Michael made his home. Michael had outlived many such Abbots in the years since he had found refuge here.

He did not know what had awoken him, and looked down at the sleeping head on the pillow next to him. Affectionately, he ran a hand over the youth's shiny black hair, wondering if he had stirred in his sleep.

He heard a noise from the corridor, and eventually a scream went out, causing Michael to become fully awake, and more screams followed, as the monks realised their fate. It was against their beliefs to raise arms, or offer violence, and the older brothers merely bowed their head when accepting the inevitable. Only the younger novices fought, or tried to resist. Unarmed, it was useless. The twelve man Solomon hit-squad were professionals.

Michael entered the main hall as the sounds of death and the dying had awoken him from his private chambers. Mighty wings flaring, he waded into the attackers with nothing but his fists, mighty though they were. Two men died with their skulls crushed from his mighty blows, before the guns were turned on him, and drugged darts turned him into a pincushion.

Screaming his fury, Michael pulled at the annoying darts, as his senses swam, eyes losing focus, his legs growing weak. He fell to the stone floor, rolling over onto his back, losing consciousness. He caught the words "Get the sleds ready. Radio ahead to prepare the truck. This one has a long journey ahead of him."

*   *   *

On the day Mirabelle was to be brought before Michael, it was three months to the day, since she had received the bloody earrings in the mail. Belle was not in a good mood. Though continuing to excel at the more physical side of her training, her tutors thought she would benefit with some spiritual tutelage, and one or two of them had suggested she be allowed to see the Angel, to help restore her faith, which had been badly damaged by the death of her friend.

Belle had heard the rumours, but could scarcely believe that were really such things as Angels. Surely Angels were just a kind of metaphysical concept? Beliefs and faith were all very well, but to actually find proof of that belief? Such a thing was unheard of, and certainly more than she expected.

She was approached by Cardinal Zola, who informed her that she had been chosen to accompany a party of novitiates to a 'special place' deep under the Vatican City. A place where spiritual beliefs would be reinforced. Belle had heard enough rumours to have guessed the rest of it, what she was being taken to see. But did it really exist? Was it a fake? Were her beliefs really up to such divine scrutiny? Would she be found worthy, or lacking?

She had her faith from her mother's teachings on the farm, a deeply religious woman, whose prayers hadn't been enough to keep the old man's hands off her. Faith had to be strong to work, that she knew. Faith without strength was nothing. Belle had faith, but more faith in herself, than the Almighty. Life on the farm had proved that you could only rely on yourself.

A car took her from the monastery in the foothills, down into the nearby town, where a small train station awaited her. The old engine had been cleaned, but the smell of it's fumes, and the hiss of it's steam was still enough to make her choke. Once inside the carriage though, Belle recovered her composure, and found that opening the window allowed fresher air inside once the train was underway, chugchugchugging along the old tracks.

Another, more modern, train awaited her once she hit the main line, where she would transfer to a more direct route to Rome and the Vatican City. She would arrive tomorrow morning, spending the night aboard the train, whereupon she would be met at the station, and escorted into the Holy See.

She was dressed informally for the journey, her habit and surplice were in her accompanying luggage. To the other passengers on board the train, she was just another pretty girl off to Rome, where a lot of young girls sought their fortune. Some succeeded in finding it. Others didn't. It never seemed to put off the rest of them from trying their luck.

The old train wasn't crowded, and there was only one other occupant to the carriage Belle chose. The man busied himself in a book, and Belle took out some magazines she had brought with her. Enforced periods of motionless were something she did not enjoy, for she was not a good passenger. She would have to get herself either a car or a motorbike, she thought to herself. She liked to retain control over her own life.

Belle was met at the Roma Termini station and taken to a hostel, run by the Church, on the Via Delle Sette Sale, near the park, to freshen up, and change. After a few hours, she was collected again, and joined a small bus-party of similar novitiates as they drove into the Vatican City, which proved to be every bit as grand as her expectations had lead her to believe. Swiss Guards stood to attention, in their colourful purple and gold dress uniforms, as the bus drove through the gates,

She was soon shown the entrances to the underground complexes, and was in awe as she realized the extent of the underground excavations which had greatly increased the original catacombs. The Cardinal who was escorting them on the final leg of their tour explained that everything above the ground was just for show and pomp. The real business of the Holy Church was conducted here, below ground.

*   *   *

In his reception chamber, Michael sat, impatient to see the day's fresh meat. He dined on cooked fish, washed down with an acceptable wine, and attendants waited on his pleasure, hurriedly cleaning up his plates and cutlery before the day's visitors arrived.

Michael seemed strangely uneasy, as if sensing something was different about the day, and he straightened up, sniffing the air. He had a very acute sense of smell, and he strove to understand why the hairs on the backs of his arms and legs were standing on end.

Further away, the giggling band of novitiates were enjoying their tour into the inner workings of their Church, honoured to be found trustworthy of new knowledge. They came closer and closer to Michael's chambers as their tour progressed.

The watching Cardinals noted Michael's very obvious apprehensiveness, which was unusual, for he normally looked forward to the nuns' arrival. Michael was pacing about the chamber, his wings flexing impatiently, and his attendants had a hard time avoiding them as they hurried to placate him. His mighty head thrown back, long hair flicking back, nostrils flaring wide as he sniffed the air repeatedly. Some faint trace, faintest of smells, was setting his senses on fire. What was it? He knew it, and yet he didn't know it. What in Hell's Name was it?

"What is it?" he cried. "*What?*" roaring now in angry frustration. Closer and closer, room by room, came the party of nuns. Michael could smell them by now, smell them and something else, something he hadn't smelt in centuries, and at last he knew what it was. "GABRIEL!!!!!!!!!!" he screamed, whirling around, his mighty wings flexing wildly, and scattering his attendants as they tried to quiet him down. "He's here! GABRIEL!!!!!!! Come to me Gabriel. Come to ME!!!!!!" he screamed, a mighty fist smashing one of his attendants in the face as he sought to restrain the angel.

The room exploded as attendants tried to force Micahel back from the door, and Michael attacked the two men, throwing one the full length of the room. His mighty wings beat as he tried to fly, screaming his frustration as he could not. The ceiling was too low. Mighty fists beat on the outer doors which were normally kept locked until the novitiates arrived.

"Give him to me!!!! Do you hear, you sycophants? Give him to me!!!!! I know he's here. I know! I can smell him! GABRIEL!!!!!! Your death awaits!!!!!! Come to me, you coward!" His tirade continued.

The watching Cardinals panicked, one of them rushing to find the control device, which they normally did not need whilst Michael was indoors, but Michael had never before erupted with such uncontrolled anger. The party of nuns could hear the noise fully three chambers away, and the escorting Cardinal wisely decided to cut short their tour, guiding them back the way they had come, whilst the noise and screams died down.

As the button was pushed, white fire lanced right through Michael's skull, and he screamed anew "Damn you Gabriel!! Damn you!!!!!" he screamed and screamed, till at last, the pain was too much, and he fell unconscious to the floor. The two Cardinals looked at each other, then back into the bloodstained chamber, neither of them understanding just what had transpired.

*　　*　　*

Belle was disappointed the visit had been cut short before they had actually seen what she had come all this way to see. To make amends, the Cardinal arranged for them to be escorted through the Vatican City, showing them all the splendours of the above ground world, from the Plaza of San Pietro, through to the Sistine Chapel itself. All the girls in the party were suitably impressed by the grandeur of the architecture.

A couple of days were allowed for the girls to explore Rome itself, and do the usual shopping that teenage girls do in the big cities. The Church gave each girl an allowance, which they held onto and released on such days as this, where they went out beyond the cloistered walls and into the wider world. Belle enjoyed the adventure, amazed by the big shops and boutiques. Skirts were getting shorter, she noticed, in the streets around her, and momentarily dared herself to go and buy one, but then thought better of it. The Church was not that forgiving.

Finally, arrangements were made for Belle to return to the monastery. She left Rome with a little bit of her faith restored, though no amount of it would make her forget her loss, or forgive the person responsible for it. Sooner or later there would be a reckoning.

Her Catholic Faith was strong, but her Italian blood was stronger. A vendetta was sworn, which would one day end in blood!

Chapter Eight

1966 France

Quid pro quo. Gabriel could hardly refuse when he had a call from his old friend Grimaldi. Although he had respect for the Mafia, for its size and organisation worldwide these days, it seemed to have grown beyond its initial purpose. Its dealings were ever darker these days.

Although at times it had proven itself a useful ally, and he still called the man, Grimaldi, his friend, he was ever wary of maintaining close ties with what was these days becoming more and more a purely criminal organisation. Grimaldi, he knew, was deeply enmeshed in its workings, and yet he still strived to regain some of it's earlier glories. Crime was still crime, but there were degrees, depths to which the old man would not stoop, and he always fought to keep his own dealings within his own personal code of ethics, ruthless though it could be, in its own way.

Luigi Grimaldi had risen through the ranks to be the personal capo of Don Morricone, an old man who wasn't long for the world, and would likely nominate Luigi as his successor, rather than his weak nephew.

Gabriel had received the call two weeks ago in Portugal, and listened to his old friend explain the problem with which he needed Gabriel's assistance. The Don's nephew Fabio Casiraghi had been kidnapped in Marseilles, whilst there on 'business'. Some of the French showed the Mafia little respect these days. Grimaldi rankled at the idea of paying a ransom for the irksome little bastard, and he had never trusted the French since his wartime adventures. Collaborators, all of them, in his eyes.

Grimaldi's own assets had learned that Casiraghi was being held in a little fishing village near Marseilles, and rightly assumed that any attempt at rescue by his own forces would probably result in the young man's death by his kidnappers. A specialist extraction was called for. Grimaldi knew he could trust Gabriel to carry out such an extraction. Duty to the Don led him to call Gabriel to attempt a rescue. If it was up to him alone, he would let the ungrateful whelp rot in whatever hellhole his kidnappers were keeping him.

Lucifer had suggested they used the excuse to try out their new yacht, The Sea-Angel, which was moored in one of the ports on the western Portuguese coast. It would give them a good chance to see what the boat could do.

*   *   *

The sun was barely rising over the horizon as the two of them put into the fishing port of Cassis, early one morning, before most people were up and about, but late enough so that the early morning boats had already put out to sea to try their luck with their nets. The flock of seagulls could still be heard in the distance as they followed behind the fishing fleet.

The harbourmaster took one look at their boat, and had them pegged as rich playboys within an instant, and this was the impression they wished to give. Questions would always be asked of strangers in such a small community, so why not give them something to talk about? From here, Marseilles was only a few miles away, and their absences would not be so readily questioned if folk thought they sought the playgrounds of the richer port.

The harbourmaster found them a berth, and they tied up their boat. Lodgings were sought in one of the local hotels, and a few phone-calls arranged for a hire car to be delivered. Once the car arrived, the two of them revved it up, and rode off in the direction of Marseilles, though turning back once out of sight of the main village, and driving off up into the hills, where Lucifer pulled out a small pair of binoculars to use for scouting out the locale. They would need to familiarise themselves with the area, and the local inhabitant, until they found out where Casiraghi was being held.

Night found the two of them wandering around the local bars in the village. There were only three of them, and not much of a walk between them, such was the size of the little port. Gabriel and Lucifer played their part, appearing friendly and affable to the locals, not shying away from buying people drinks to loosen their tongues, and gradually steering the conversation around to any other strangers that might have been seen around recently.

The clientele was run of the mill in two of the bars, and they soon found the rougher elements of society, the people they really wanted to talk to, frequented Le Mistral, the third bar, which seemed to feature an evening cabaret. Both of them were busy 'socialising' with some of the local men and quite obvious whores, plying them with drinks to loosen their tongues, when the cabaret started.

A lone piano player started up to one side of the small stage as a man and woman came out from behind the purple brocade curtain, introduced simply as Belle and Max. A classic Apache twosome. Both Gabriel and Lucifer had seen this type of act before, and were of no mind to pay it any particular attention, when they caught sight of the beautiful woman whom the spotlight now revealed.

Long black hair hung down past her shoulders, curling slightly at the bottom, and seemed to shine in the harsh artificial light. A Bettie Page lookalike, but much more beautiful than that famous model. A red rose was pinned behind her ear, beneath the black beret she wore slightly askew on her head.

Her skin seemed to have a lustre of it's own, visible even under the spotlight, and those lips glistened in invitation. The low-cut top allowed a hint of cleavage. Lucifer started, as he realised every man's eyes were all staring in the same direction as his own. There was something very striking about her. Even the women were looking at her, and not at her male partner, as the spotlight singled her out.

Gabriel admired the black silk skirt, slit high to the waist on her left side. A red silk garter embraced her thigh on top of the dark fishnet tights she wore. Her legs were incredibly long, and shapely. She stood stock still in the spotlight, enjoying being the centre of attention. Gradually, the spotlight widened out to encompass her male partner, a big six-footer with a chest like a barrel. Clean shaven of chin, yet with a large dark handlebar moustache, which had been recently waxed. He too wore a beret.

The costumes were simple, stark but effective. The mixture of black and white striped sweaters, contrasted with the plain black of skirt and trousers. As the music picked up tempo, the apache dance commenced, with the two partners dancing discordantly under the spotlight.

The whore on Lucifer's left, put her hand on his thigh, rubbing to get his attention, but Lucifer's eyes were transfixed on the small stage. As if noticing his avid view, the female dancer made to leave her male dancer, and approach him, her eyes seductively meeting his own. This was an accepted part of the act, the excuse for the rough treatment of the woman by the man to begin, and it did so as expected. She cried out as the larger male pulled her roughly back towards him, wrenching on her arm.

The music tempo altered slightly, becoming more loud and discordant to reflect the drama being enacted on the stage. A slap cracked loudly on the woman's face, as she recoiled from the blow, and fell down onto the stage. Her hair was pulled by her partner, forcing her back onto her feet as he crushed her in his embrace.

Back and forth they danced/struggled across the stage, the woman seeking to break away, the man seeking to keep her at his side. It went on for only just over a minute, though seemed longer, as Gabriel enjoyed the nuances of the dance.

Nails clawed out, raking down the side of the man's face, and drawing blood. Max cursed as the audience gasped, not expecting such realism. The piano halted, for brief moments, to accentuate the drama being performed up there on the stage. The pianist was very good, thought Gabriel, enjoying the spectacle. So were the performers.

The woman's teeth showed, as she enjoyed the sight of the bloody tracts down the man's face, and she cried out as he cuffed her to the floor. Belle rolled with the attempted kick that followed-up, and then they were enjoined in the grotesque dance of death once more. Both of them played their parts quite to perfection, in time-honoured manner.

The coup de gras finally came as the man pulled out a flick-knife from his pocket, the blade snapping open in dramatic fashion, bright in the spotlight, and the pianist hit all the wrong discordant keys on purpose, heightening the drama to its climax.

The watching spectators cried out in horror, though some had doubtless seen the act before, as the tall male pulled the woman suddenly towards him, onto the waiting knife-blade. Lucifer was momentarily fooled by the sudden spilling of blood, though Gabriel had noticed the slight lump of the plastic bag of blood the woman had concealed under her sweater, against her side, and she cried out once as she fell to the stage.

The man stood over her, head bowed, and finally doing a masterful job of feigning remorse, as the lights dimmed and the audience applauded. After a suitable period of clapping and a few whistles, the lights grew to reveal the man and woman both standing in the centre of the stage, bowing gracefully to accept the applause which they were indeed due. It had been a very well presented, and believable act. Lucifer was quite smitten with the woman.

As the two of them came down from the stage, Belle made her way towards the bar, while her partner delayed to speak to the pianist, seemingly complaining about the accompaniment. The dark eyes flashed at Lucifer, and then at the whore who had latched onto him. The fingers clutching his arm suddenly loosened, as the whore quickly took her leave, leaving an empty seat, which Belle slipped into quite readily. "Buy me a drink, m'sieur?" she smiled seductively, and Lucifer found himself beckoning for the barman before he had time to reply.

"That was a great number. You must have practised it a lot," he complimented her. She smiled knowingly.

"Max and I often have such disagreements," she chuckled.

"Forgive me, my name is Lucifer, and this is my friend Gabriel," he introduced himself.

"Mais ouis? How devilish?" she laughed, and accepted a martini from the barman, who was obviously familiar with her choice of alcohol. She took it to her red lips, and took a deep draught, then smacked her lips, now moist as well as invitingly red.

"Are you and Max . . . .?" he started to ask, but Belle interrupted him.

"Max and I are just friends, though he may wish we were closer," she replied amusedly, and then swivelled on her seat to flash a smile across the room to where Max now sat with a male acquaintance of his. Then she examined her sweater, which was still soaked with blood. "I must change. The blood needs to be washed out or it will stain," she explained. "You will excuse me, non?" she got up off the barstool. "I will take a quick shower. Will you stay?"

"Of course. We're not planning on leaving. Are we?" he turned to ask Gabriel, who shook his head briefly, though annoyed slightly that Lucifer was allowing himself to be distracted from the real purpose of their visit here.

The woman left, vanishing back behind the stage curtain to where the dressing rooms obviously where. "She's nice," Gabriel commented.

"Nice? She's gorgeous," Lucifer exclaimed.

"Well, maybe I'll leave you two lovebirds to it," he suggested. "I'll do some more talking around and see if I can find out any more about any other strangers in town. They must be holed up in some remote farmhouse, from what we've seen of the countryside around here." Gabriel finished his drink and got up to leave. Max glowered at him as he made his way through the crowded tables. Gabriel merely smiled in return. He wanted no trouble, and hoped Lucifer knew what he was doing.

Lucifer, for his part, ordered another round of drinks, and waited for the raven-haired beauty to reappear. When she did, minutes later, she seemed disappointed to note that his friend had left.

"Your friend does not like this club?" she asked.

"He was tired. We've had a busy day. He went back to the hotel," Lucifer explained. Belle joined him at the bar, and took her second glass of the evening, and he then went into his cover-story about coming over here to look at vineyards, a subject he fortunately knew a lot about. Now dressed in more formal evening wear, a dark green low-cut silk gown, which hugged her in all the right places, she looked even more beautiful, if slightly less formidable, than she did earlier.

Her English was good, and Lucifer's French was good too, but he thought it best to feign ignorance. Over the years he had learnt to be wary of revealing too much about himself to people he didn't know. Belle for her part told him of her struggle to make a living, being an orphan, and how Max had taken her in and introduced her to cabaret life, and how they went from town to town, always on the road looking for the next club to perform at. Good as their act was, it was only good for a few weeks until patrons got bored and looked for something different. Lucifer sympathised. He ordered more drinks.

*   *   *

Outside in the cool night air, Gabriel walked back along the darkened quayside. Deserted, the only sounds were the lapping of the waves, and the occasional squawk of a gull out to sea. The fishing boats were tied up, awaiting the morning's tide, and mooring lights twinkled as they rocked back and forth with the waves.

The man following him was good, and if it hadn't been for Gabriel's acute hearing, he would not have known he was there, for he remained invisible, for as long as Gabriel wanted to maintain the charade. If he turned quickly enough, he would probably catch sight of him. But he couldn't very well do this in a casual manner. The watcher would know he was onto him in a second.

He took a slow walk through the town, mulling things over. A pickpocket wouldn't be so discreet, or stay so far away. Someone was interested in him. Possibly someone connected with the local organisation that had kidnapped Casiraghi. They would be stupid not to think the Mafia might send someone over here.

How should he play this? Confrontation before they knew the lie of the land might be hasty. True, he might get the man to talk, but then he might have to kill him. He didn't know how skillful the man was. If he were good, Gabriel might be left with no alternative. You don't give an opponent any opportunity if it could be avoided. He decided to let the man make his move, at whatever time suited him.

Heading back towards the hotel, Gabriel took his time. Their car was still parked outside, and he noticed no obvious signs of tampering, so he walked past it and into the hotel, collecting his key from the desk, and going up to his room. He switched on the light, wanting the unknown watcher to take note of which window was suddenly illuminated, even as he opened it slightly.

Waiting a few minutes, he switched off the light, and settled down to wait. Door or window? Arranging pillows under the sheets to give a passing impression of a body in the bed, he crouched down in the corner against the wall, to one side of the door, and in view of the window. He checked his watch. 11.45pm.

*   *   *

By 1.00am, Gabriel realised that his expected visitor had refused the invitation. He got up and went back down into the lobby. Noticing Lucifer's key was still behind the desk, he went out into the night once more, and made his way back alongside the quayside towards the club where he had left his friend.

The place was now closed, and the interior through the windows was dark. Lucifer had obviously gone off with the girl. At least he hoped so. Nothing he could do until the morning in any case. He retraced his steps back to the hotel, and closed the window before he climbed into the bed, where he slept fitfully till morning.

*   *   *

The next morning, Gabriel was finishing off breakfast when Lucifer finally showed up, unshaven and slightly disheveled, though with a wide grin plastered across his face. "I'm glad one of us had a nice night," Gabriel complained, with a hint of wry humour. "I was followed back here after I left you."

Lucifer joined him at the table. "No one followed me. Not that I would have noticed. I only had eyes for Belle."

"I'd never have guessed," Gabriel replied sardonically.

"We walked along the beach and up along the cliffs. God, what a marvelous night it was," Lucifer enthused.

"Spare me the details," Gabriel chuckled, and then beckoned to the old woman proprietor to order a second breakfast for his friend.

"Honest, that's all we did, just walked, and walked, and walked. She told me all about herself, and she was so much fun. Full of devilment. She tripped me up and pushed me into the surf." He laughed at the memory.

"Bet that sobered you up in a hurry," Gabriel laughed.

"Gabriel, you're too stuffy. Learn to live a little," Lucifer admonished. "No reason we can't spare the time to enjoy ourselves a little while we're over here," he complained.

"I suppose not. You planning on seeing the girl again?" he asked. "I thought we'd try the estate agents, to see who has been renting out remote properties locally. Might be our best bet," he explained his reasoning.

"I'd like to, but you're right. First things first," he started into the breakfast which the old woman had now set down on the table before him. "I'm famished," he exclaimed.

* * *

Later that day, Lucifer and Gabriel met up again to compare notes. Each had had success in the few estate agents they knew of. Lucifer had remained in town, whilst Gabriel had driven into Marseilles. They cross-referenced each other's lists, noting that some addresses often appeared on more than one list. Whilst in Marseilles, Gabriel had also visited a contact of Luigi Grimaldi, and picked up some 'supplies', two Beretta's with silencers, two spare clips each, and knives.

Guns were getting more powerful these days, and more difficult for the two of them to use, with their light bone structure. The little Berettas were deadly enough in the right hands, and Gabriel begrudgingly admitted Lucifer's better skill with a handgun. He was competent enough, but the gun came as naturally to Lucifer as the knife did to himself. Stowing the guns and other supplies about their person and in the car, they returned to studying a map of the surrounding countryside.

Most likely, it was a recent sale they were looking for, and they had found one which seemed to fit the bill. A small holding had come on the market after the old farmer had died. His livestock had gone, but the property itself had been sold to a Msr Gaspard. It was nicely remote, yet within easy reach of a good road system. They would check it out from a distance that afternoon.

* * *

Three men patrolled the fields surrounding the farm. From a distance, they looked like any groundsman doing his rounds, but whereas they carried shotguns, the guns were ready for use, and not broken open across their forearm as was customary. The jackets they wore were bulky enough to conceal other weapons too. Gabriel made his assessment of the first line of defence. Inside the farmhouse would be an unknown. They couldn't get close enough to check it out for themselves, but would watch the watchers to see what their routines were, and maybe hope to question one of them before making their final attack.

"Tonight. No sense wasting time," he stated, and Lucifer nodded in agreement.

"Hit them before they get word there are strangers in the area ?" he asked.

"After last night, I'm not sure. But they certainly won't be expecting us to move so quickly, even if they do know we're here. We'll hit them as soon as it gets dark, as they're about to have their meal," Gabriel confirmed, and Lucifer nodded once more, taking the binoculars to check out the landscape for himself.

*　　*　　*

Twilight approached, and they watched the first of the outlying guards return to the farmhouse. He seemed to make no special knock on the door, or even call out, just pushed open the door and went inside, to what seemed a hallway. The photos they had of the place didn't reveal much, mainly external shots and one internal of a large open fireplace. Casiraghi, if he was still alive, was probably being held in one of the upstairs bedrooms. They had seen no movement around the barn and other outlying buildings.

The guard remained inside for about twenty minutes, then he reappeared, and headed off back towards the area he had been patrolling before. The three men had remained in their own 'sectors' during the day. Although visible to each other during the day, darkness would isolate them. Bad security, but good from their own point of view.

Gabriel went after the first guard. He made his way rapidly after him, following in the man's footsteps, moving when he heard movement, but quicker, making up the ground. The ground was hard, though small twigs were hard to spot in the gloom.

He came up behind the man as he was urinating against a tree, the shotgun propped up against the trunk. Quickly and savagely, one arm wrapped around the man's neck, jerking back the head to silence any scream, as he plunged the knife in between the man's ribs. It was over in seconds, and he gently lowered the body to the ground. A clean, but necessary death. One does not leave a live enemy at your back. He had learnt that many years ago.

Taking the shotgun, he made his way back to where Lucifer was watching the farmhouse. Scarcely ten minutes had passed since the first guard had returned from the farmhouse, when the second of them went in for his meal. He too took about twenty minutes over it, and then came outside again. "I'll take this one," Lucifer said, and began moving away in his general direction.

Gabriel remained, watching the farmhouse, and for signs of the third guard approaching. That was when they needed to move in. Keep the timing consistent, so that whoever was inside the house was expecting the third guard, and not intruders. He knew the general direction of approach the third would use, and so began to make his preparations.

Ten minutes later, the third guard approached from the fields, following a well-worn pathway back towards the farmhouse. Gabriel dropped, silently and deadly, from the branches of the old oak tree, taking him completely unawares. The butt of the knife slammed into the back of the man's head, stunning him as he fell.

In seconds, Gabriel had tied the man's ankles and wrists together with the fishing line he had brought from the car. Industrial tape went over his mouth. Unfastening the man's belt, he pulled down his trousers and underpants, and then sat back to wait for the groggy man to come around. By this time Lucifer had come back to join him, giving him the thumb's up to show he had taken care of the second guard.

As the tied man regained consciousness, he very quickly realised his predicament, threshing around on the ground helplessly. Lucifer pinned him motionless, as Gabriel then deliberately held up the sharp blade of his knife so that the man could see it clearly. Then he brought it down between the man's legs, so he could feel the cold steel against his testicles. Hard man/soft man time, and this time it was Lucifer's turn to be nice.

"I'm going to remove the tape from your mouth," he smiled grimly. "When I do, you will not shout out in any way, and you will answer my questions quickly and quietly. Do this and you will live through this night, to pass a message on to your employers. Disobey, and my friend here is going to cut off your balls and make you eat them. Do you understand?" he asked, menacingly.

The man's head nodded frantically as Gabriel hefted the man's shrinking testicles with the cold knife-blade for emphasis. Lucifer pulled the tape away from his mouth. "Please don't kill me," he begged. "It wasn't my idea. I just do as I'm told," he pleaded in a soft frightened voice.

"Where is Casiraghi? How many in the house? What weapons ? Keep it nice and simple," Lucifer advised.

"He . . . he is in the second bedroom at the top of the stairs. Two more men inside, with revolvers." He spoke very, very nervously, the cold steel against his balls held all his attention.

"No more shotguns?" Lucifer asked.

"No, just handguns," the frightened man replied. Lucifer looked to Gabriel, who nodded once simply. He was too frightened to lie, and yet he confirmed their thoughts. There was no sign of a second car parked anywhere on the farm, so the numbers would be about right. Casiraghi was still alive.

Lucifer replaced the tape over the man's mouth, and Gabriel re-sheathed his knife at his thigh. He took the man's shotgun to aid in the initial entry. Might give them a second or two's advantage when they went in. A second or two was all they needed. "Let's do it," he said simply, and the two men hurried towards the farmhouse, aware that the third man was expected shortly for his meal.

Gabriel went first, opening the large door and entering with the shotgun held casually over one arm, and the Beretta gripped in his other hand. The door creaked loudly, from hinges which hadn't seen oil in years, but Gabriel was unconcerned. The occupants must surely be expecting the third guard to come in for his meal by now. Lucifer followed behind, watching the stairs as Gabriel concentrated on the smells and sounds coming from what was obviously a large kitchen off to the right at the end of the hall.

"You're lucky Jean didn't eat it all," laughed the man who had been cooking, as he ladled out home-made soup from a large tureen into a bowl, without turning around to see Gabriel. "There's not much left, but it'll take the chill out of your bones," he promised, only then beginning to turn, and that's when Gabriel raised the Beretta, sending one silenced bullet into the centre of his chest.

A harsh gasp was all he had time for, as the bullet stopped his heart, and he fell to the floor. The ladle did the same, the noise ringing out on the stone floor, alerting the remaining guard who was in one of the other downstairs rooms. "Henri ?" he cried, suddenly stepping out into the hallway. Lucifer double-tapped him neatly, two bullets, inches apart, in his chest, and he too fell to the floor. Quickly, he followed up, dashing along and into the room as Gabriel covered him.

The ground floor was quickly searched in methodical fashion, and then the two men went up the stairs, cautious as ever, one leading, the other offering covering fire, but it was not needed. It seemed their information was correct. One bedroom was locked, the key conveniently in the lock. The other three bedrooms were unoccupied at present. Gabriel paused in one, puzzled by the feminine makeup on the dresser, and clothing visible hanging up in the wardrobe. They had seen no signs of a woman here.

Casiraghi was backed up into the corner of the room, away from the door as Lucifer opened it. Aware of something unusual going on, he had no idea it was his rescue. He had never seen either Lucifer or Gabriel before in his life. The sight of the two men, with guns in hand, unnerved him.

The thirty-two-year-old was now bearded, and his clothes were obviously the same clothes he had been kidnapped in. His welfare had obviously not been of much concern to his kidnappers. Lucifer reassured him. "Grimaldi sent us. Your uncle has missed you," he smiled, and Casiraghi suddenly realised his ordeal was over, and fell to his knees sobbing.

When the younger man had recovered himself, they gave him a few minutes to clean himself up in the bathroom, and then hurried him out of the house. The woman's clothing proved that there was at least one other member of the kidnap squad missing from the house, and Gabriel had no idea when she was likely to return. Best to be away quickly.

Lucifer had had the forethought to bring along a change of clothing for the Don's nephew, and he changed quickly, before they drove off in their rental car. It was still early evening when they got Casiraghi to drop them off on the outskirts of the village.

"Return the guns to the address I gave you in Marseilles." Gabriel advised the young man. "He will have the address of a safe house, where your own people will safeguard your return to Italy." Casiraghi looked genuinely puzzled.

"You are freelance?" he queried.

"Just friends of a friend," Lucifer admitted. With that, they bade the grateful young man farewell, and began walking into town. Behind them they heard the roar of the engine as the younger Casiraghi was keen to distance himself from the scene of his ignominious incarceration, which no doubt would need some explanation to his uncle.

*   *   *

Gabriel and Lucifer walked back into the small port, and frequented a small restaurant, where they partook of a light evening meal, as though nothing untoward had happened. Tomorrow morning, they would catch the early tide and depart. With luck, the scene at the farmhouse would not be discovered or reported until later that day, and by then they would be on the high seas, and Casiraghi would be in safe hands.

Finishing their repast, and leaving a handsome tip, the two of them returned to their hotel, intending to pack their few belongings. Once there, as they were collecting their keys, the receptionist handed Lucifer a note. He opened it, slightly puzzled, and then smiled as he read it. "It's from Belle. I'd forgotten she mentioned it last night, but there's a beach barbecue out near the headland, tonight. We're invited," he announced, obviously with the intention of going.

Gabriel preferred an early night, but was persuaded by his friend to go along. If nothing else it would help blend into the background, and pass a bit of time. The two of them went back to their rooms, and changed, putting on slightly thicker sweaters as they were expecting it to get colder as the evening wore on, with the wind coming in off the sea when the tide turned. It would be coming in now, turning again shortly before four am, as they had been informed.

They walked out past the jetty, in the direction of the headland in the distance, which was obscured by the rock promontories. They could see the flickering light of the beach bonfire in the distance, and heard the feint strains of music. They continued onto the beach, making their way towards the beach-party. Two young men were sat on one of the rocks, idly drinking beer and smoking. One of them waved, as the two men walked past, heading around the rocks.

As they rounded a large rock, they came in sight of the bonfire, which lit up a small group of men, one of whom was talking into a walkie-talkie radio. He looked like Max from the floorshow. There was no sign of Belle or any other women there. The party sounds they were hearing were coming from a portable tape-player and speakers. Both men instantly realised it was a set-up.

"*Run!*" Gabriel urged his friend, pushing him towards the receding surf-line, and the light evening mist coming in off the sea.

Lucifer needed no encouragement. Any hesitation would only let the group of men draw the trap closer, which was obviously what the walkie-talkie was being used to do. If that was Max using it, then it stood to reason that those clothes back at the farm had belonged to Belle. A classic honey-trap!

Shots rang out, and torchlight was aimed towards them as they distanced themselves from the light of the bonfire, seeking the darkness of the night to hide from their pursuers. Gabriel regretted leaving the guns with Casiraghi, but had not thought any operation of this size could be mounted against them in so short a space of time.

Gunshots echoed sporadically in the dark, but their pursuers shot blindly as Gabriel and Lucifer raced along the beach, doing their best to avoid the torch-lights. They were outdistancing their pursuers by running on the sand, their lighter bodyweight enabling them to run without sinking their footsteps into the sand so deeply.

The moon hid behind clouds, making them difficult targets in the feint mist, and they used the rocky outcrops for whatever cover they could find. "Some day, Lucifer," Gabriel gasped. "Some day, your taste in women is going to improve." Lucifer managed a sardonic grunt, more interested in putting distance between them and the group of men pursuing them.

Together, they rounded the headland, and came to a complete stop. There was no more beach. A deep inlet lay between them and safety, and it was filled with the incoming tide. "What next?" asked Lucifer. "If we try and swim it, they'll be here before we get a hundred yards." Gabriel nodded, looking around.

"Up," he pointed with his thumb, and Lucifer was quick to follow as Gabriel began to climb, almost flying up the rough rocky face of the cliff. The two men scaled the heights easily, hard fingernails finding purchase where none was readily apparent. Lucifer was almost as good a climber as was Gabriel. By the time the pursuing gang had reached the waves below, the two of them were already two hundred feet up above them, angling their climb away from the headland, and using what shadows and crevices they could find to conceal themselves from view from below.

By the time the men below had thought to look up, they were well out of sight, hidden amid the dark shadows of the overhangs. One of the men pulled out a walkie-talkie, speaking into it, hurriedly. He received a hurried response, and the group of men began retracing their steps back along the beach the way they had come.

Gabriel and Lucifer were barely out of breath at the end of the steep climb, which had taken them less than fifteen minutes. They dusted themselves off, believing themselves safe from pursuit for the time being, and wondering how to get back to their boat without attracting any further attention to themselves. Both of them were startled by the sudden feminine laughter which echoed through the darkness.

"Why, boys . . . . fancy seeing you here." Belle stepped out into the moonlight, her revolver trained on the space between the two men, ready and able to aim and fire in a second. She smiled sweetly as both men tried to cover their astonishment.

"Looks like you made quite an impression on the young lady," Gabriel grinned painfully to his friend, his fingers were beginning to move, as if nervously. Lucifer was quick to pick up on the hand-signals, and starting to move slightly away from Gabriel, making her move the gun from side to side to keep both men covered, though not making it obvious. She could only keep one of them covered at a time, and both could be just as dangerous.

"How did you know we'd be here, Belle?" Lucifer spoke to draw her attention. The girl smiled as she answered him.

"I do my homework. The dossiers provided on you two were quite thorough." Gabriel caught Lucifer's eye. This was no longer about the Don's nephew. This was personal, and that meant only one thing, if both of them were involved. "Knowing your talents, and the route you were taking, it was a simple enough deduction," she explained.

"The Church!" Gabriel accused, simply. The whole thing had been a set-up from start to finish. Knowing of Gabriel's involvement with Grimaldi, the kidnapping had been staged to draw him here. Belle nodded, and then stopped moving the gun from side to side and simply fired it, having come to a decision.

Gabriel cried out as the bullet tore through his calf muscle, and he fell to the ground. Lucifer flung himself at her before she could turn the gun on him, his attack lightning fast, and seemed to pluck the gun right out of her hand, thumb holding back the hammer as he twisted it from her grip.

A Savate kick caught him in the face, stunning him with its speed, and another knocked the gun out of his own hand, before he could use it himself, as the girl fought back with a flurry of blows, in no way intimidated by the way Lucifer had brought the attack to her. Lucifer backed off, sensibly wary of her obvious combat skills.

"Why, Belle?" he asked, preparing himself for her next lunge. He sidestepped, trying to keep his body between her and where the gun had fallen.

"Orders are orders," she smiled, her white teeth flashing in the moonlight. "They want him alive. With that bullet in him, he won't be going anywhere in a hurry. You, they unfortunately consider expendable," she stated. "They said you were good. Let's see if they were right. I'm pretty good myself," she grinned. Drawing back the side of her slit skirt, she pulled a knife from a thigh-sheath, and instantly the sharp point was dancing towards him, slashing and jabbing, as Lucifer leapt back, trying to avoid her attack.

From the ground, Gabriel cursed. The bullet had merely grazed the muscle, but he was still in shock from the sudden wound. He saw the dance of death taking place in front of him, watching and instantly aware of the skill the woman was showing with the knife. It was all Lucifer could do to avoid it, and he was allowing her to force him back, with lightning fast moves, perhaps deliberately so, to draw the fight away from Gabriel and give him some time to recover.

Then he noticed that the woman wasn't keen to follow up too quickly on her attacks, and the glint of the blade in the bright moonlight drew his attention to its shape. That was a handmade knife, and 'handmade' meant only one thing. She could use it.

She was trying to put distance between them deliberately. "Close her down!" he warned his friend, though Lucifer didn't seem to recognise the danger he was in, or what the girl was trying to do.

"Easy for you to say!" cursed Lucifer, as the blade danced in front of him. "Shit!" he cursed, as he felt the blade nick his arm. For his every move, she seemed to have a counter. She was more than good. Gabriel forced himself onto his feet, as the flow of blood eased. It still hurt like hell, and would for some time yet. As good as his healing metabolism was, it had its limits. He had to move, and move now, despite the weakness and pain in his leg as he put weight on it.

Belle's hand moved the knife so fast, Lucifer was losing sight of it in the darkness, as she angled it from side to side. It would catch the moonlight for a second, and then the edge turned and seemed to disappear, and that was when it would suddenly be coming at him from a different direction, slash, slash, thrust. A quick change of hands caught him by surprise, and he discovered how ambidextrous she was to his cost, as the blade ripped open his shirt and left a bloody streak across his stomach. "Ahhhhh . . . ." he cried out, and Belle responded with a cruel laugh, her white teeth again catching the moonlight.

Both of them had lost sight of the gun now, and Gabriel hadn't seen where it had fallen. He looked around but could not see it in the darkness. All down to the knife then, and the girl was using it well. She had drawn blood three times now, and Lucifer's left arm was bleeding badly.

Back and forth, Gabriel watched them dance, the moves fast and frightening, for he could see how this dance was going to end. As good as Lucifer was at unarmed combat, the girl was better, and she was armed. Every attempt to block ended in spilt blood. Lucifer was tiring.

She forced him back, back, deliberately letting him put some distance between them as he was weakening and needed a breather. Now was the moment she had been waiting for.

Her teeth flashed once in a wicked smile as her hand came up. She took a small step back, and then her arm snapped forward, sending the knife flying across the gap between them, straight for Lucifer's heart, and he knew she was not going to miss.

The perfectly balanced blade turned once, twice in the moonlight, closing the distance in less than a second, and Lucifer could only gasp at the speed and the skill she had shown, when Gabriel lunged, and an equally fast hand literally plucked it out of the air.

Two mouths now dropped open in surprise as Gabriel's nimble fingers hefted the blade. It's perfect balance had enabled him to judge just when to be able to grasp it. "Nice knife," he commented once, before his hand flicked out sideways, in a sudden blur, sending the blade straight for the girl's throat. "Catch!" he smiled cruelly.

Belle had time to gasp a second time, at the realisation that the death she had tried to administer to Lucifer was now being returned to her. She flung herself back, trying to avoid the deadly blow, and her training almost saved her. Instead of burying itself in her pretty throat, as Gabriel had intended, it sank home in her shoulder, spinning her around with the force of the impact.

So close to the edge of the cliff, one foot slipped on the shale, and she went over the edge. Both men stood helplessly listening to the long single scream, and finally, a splash from the waves below.

Lucifer turned to help up his friend, who had fallen once more, his bleeding leg had given out. "You're right. I have a lousy taste in women," he forced himself to joke.

"It's the same with me and blondes," Gabriel agreed, still limping, and allowing Lucifer to help support him. "They'll be the death of me yet," he grunted, forcing a joke as he put weight on the injured leg again. "Let's get the hell out of here. This place will be crawling with gendarmes by morning."

The two injured men made their way along the cliff-top, keeping to the darkness and away from the pathways, as they knew the men from the beach below would soon be searching for them. Time to catch the evening tide.

Chapter Nine

1958 Italy

Ryan had received the request from Cardinal Zola personally. Laura's assistance was required to infiltrate a Mafia don's villa. An inside 'man' was required to assist in a planned raid to recover stolen Church treasures, which had been lost since the war, 'liberated' first by the Nazis and then later by the Mafia. Laura's looks would enable her to ingratiate herself into Don Morricone's good graces. While frowning upon Laura's use in this regard, it was still a request from Zola himself, and so he put the mission to her, explaining that she fitted the physical profile for the type of women who appealed to the old Don.

After some deliberation, Laura agreed to it. She had a low self-esteem after many years of trying to blot out the pain of a second stillborn baby, seeking new relationships in an effort to drive Gabriel's face from her mind, but nothing worked. His face still haunted her, despite throwing herself at other men, and the relationships never lasted. Disgusted with herself, she would end the affairs quickly once her mind was made up, with no remorse. Becoming an old man's mistress to serve the Church's ends was only a minor irritant, in the scale of things. She would endure. No pain was worse than what she had already suffered.

Morricone frequented a strip-club called the Pomme D'Or every weekend, where the Church had influence over the manager, who kept them informed of the Don's visits. It would be an easy matter to substitute Laura for one of the regular girls, so she could catch his eye. Nature would do the rest.

The hardest part was arranging to lure Morricone's head enforcer Luigi Grimaldi out of the city. Grimaldi had a lot of influence on Morricone, and would insist on a thorough check-up of Laura's background before allowing her to be installed at the villa. They could provide her with a good background even at such short notice, but not good enough to stand up to Luigi Grimaldi's thoroughness.

In the weeks that followed, once installed, Laura had the run of the estate, though Morricone's men always seemed to be watching her. She flirted with them, and acted friendly enough, to ease any suspicions. To them she was just another floozy after an easy life with a rich old man.

The intended raid on the villa was time to coincide with other raids across the city, for maximum impact, and so that none of the dons in residence would be forewarned against such an eventuality. The Church would recover all their property in a single night. Unfortunately, things did not go according to plan.

*　　*　　*

Laura regained consciousness to find herself bound hand and foot, lying on the bed, whilst some of the Mafiosi cleaned up the room around her, wrapping Don Morricone's body in a sheet. A belt had been used to bind her arms behind her back, and someone's tie used to fasten her ankles together. Her face and body still ached from the beating she had taken, but already she could feel herself healing. She felt guilt over the old man's death, despite the way he had treated her since she had become his mistress.

The drug was supposed to put him to sleep, not cause a fatal heart-attack. His men had swarmed into the room as he'd pressed the alarm button, overpowering her before she'd had a chance to give the signal to the Solomon team waiting to infiltrate the building to recover the stolen Church treasures.

Even worse, they'd caught her with the signalling torch in her hand, and knew she was up to no good, but just what, they had no idea. She knew they would be interrogating her shortly, and she wasn't looking forward to it.

The men were in a foul mood. The old man's death would reflect badly on them, and doubtless his nephew would vent his wrath when he was finally informed about his uncle's death. Meanwhile, they had sent urgent word to Luigi Grimaldi, the Don's most trusted lieutenant, to get to the villa with great urgency to handle this situation.

Grimaldi had been in the south for the last month, and had been furious that the Don had installed another mistress in the villa in his absence, without him being able to check her out for himself. He would not be pleased at the turn of events. His business for the Don concluded, he was already on his way back to the villa.

The Don's mistress was obviously working for someone else, perhaps another rival Don, for this was not unheard of. She had poisoned the old man, and had been caught in the act of attempting to signal someone in the overlooking hills. Security had been stepped up in the grounds, and would remain high until Grimaldi himself arrived to take charge of the situation.

The old man always listened to his dick instead of his men, where his women were concerned. Laura had moved into the villa some 3 weeks ago, after the Don had met her at a wild party in one of the more exclusive strip-clubs in Rome.

A rare change from the usual class of woman the old man found to play his kinky little games. Such women did not needlessly degrade themselves for their men. But that was the only way the Don could get it up these days. A spy from the very outset, then, and they must learn for whom she was spying.

Gianni could see the woman was awake now, though still pretending to be unconscious, lying there with her eyes almost closed, watching what was going on in the room as they cleaned up the scene. Her sheer nightdress was rucked up around her thighs, the big breasts almost spilling out of the low cut bodice. He admitted to himself, he had been jealous of his padrone, but then he was still alive, and his padrone was dead.

He found it strange, as he ran his eyes over her bound body. He had seen the fight she had put up, when they had found her. She had not panicked, and had fought hard to get away. Fought well, in fact. She had known how to fight. She took quite a beating before being subdued, and so did more than one of his men. He expected the bruising on her body to be worse than it was.

Paulo came back into the room. Stepping aside as another two men carried the old man's body away. "Time to make the bitch talk!"

he snarled. Gianni watched as he walked over to the bed, and grabbed a handful of the woman's long golden hair.

"Ahhhhhh! You're hurting me!" Laura screamed, as the angry Italian pulled her off the bed and onto the floor. He grinned as he kicked her in the stomach, and Laura went white as the wind was forced out of her lungs. She lay there gasping, her knees drawn up, trying to protect herself as she fought to regain her breath.

Paulo stood over her, his face contorted with rage, as he fought to control his anger. He needed information more than revenge. Revenge would come later. "Take her down to the cellar," he ordered his men, and Laura was forced to her feet, still gasping. Her ankles were untied, and then she was frogmarched out of the bedroom.

"Would it not be better to wait for Grimaldi, my brother?" asked Gianni. Paulo sneered derisively, shaking his head.

"Grimaldi will want answers. I intend to have them." He scowled, and followed the other men out of the room.

* * *

Outside, in the wooded copse on the overlooking hillside, a small group of men were noting the increased security in the villa's grounds. Their plans had obviously gone wrong. Their inside agent had somehow given the game away, and been captured. This raid would have to be called off. Across Rome and further south, a co-ordinated series of raids were taking place tonight, as the Church made a concerted effort to get their stolen treasures back out of the clutches of a number of the mafia Dons.

One of them spoke into a field-radio, to his superiors, relaying the evening's events. Their agent must be presumed lost, or compromised. He stood by for confirmation of orders. Long minutes went by, when the radio crackled into life once more. He eventually turned to his men, to relay instructions. "Maintain your positions. We cannot abort. The agent inside is one of the Chosen, and we must not abandon her," he quickly explained. His men looked concerned.

"But they are doubling security. See for yourself," he pointed. "We are only a small force. How can we get inside the place now?" he asked, expressing the concerns of all of them.

"We wait for another operative to assist us," he explained, his face giving away nothing of his own emotions, but he shivered plainly as he revealed the name of the operative who was even now being diverted to this location. "Some of you may have heard of her. Her name is Belladonna."

*　　*　　*

"Get your hands off me, you animals!" Laura screamed as they tore at her nightdress, laughing as they grabbed and fondled her now bare breasts. This was the prelude of things to come, she knew, for she had been made aware of how the Mafia operated. Things would get much, much worse, until she talked, and then they would probably kill her.

"You stuck-up whore!" accused one of her assailants, as he shoved a hand in between her thighs. Laura swore, and tried to kick out at them, but they were prepared for that, keeping to the side of her as they assaulted her, tearing at her nightdress. "You've lorded it around this villa for long enough. Time you learned your place!" he laughed, ripping the flimsy material.

Naked but for her silk panties, Laura was dragged down the lower stairs by the laughing hoodlums. The men had openly lusted after her for the last few weeks, as the old man had been fond of showing her off to his men. Now they finally had their opportunity to sample her obvious charms for themselves, and were eager to take advantage of her present situation. She had no friends in the villa. All of the men had been devoted to their padrone, and she had been found with his dead body.

Behind the struggling woman, Paulo and Gianni followed the screams down the staircase. Gianni was not looking forward to what he knew would happen. He knew his own brother's disposition towards sadism. A shame Grimaldi was not here to take charge. He stepped over the remnants of the woman's nightdress.

*　　*　　*

The old army motorbike roared through the night, the sound and smell of its exhaust the only signs of its passing, for the rider rode it with the headlight covered with dark cloth, wrapped thoroughly around so as to show no light. Belle's night vision was excellent, a match for any other bird of prey on a night as dark as this.

Though momentarily annoyed at the relayed orders, she had to admit that her presence at the other raid was superfluous, and it would go off successfully despite her absence. Changing targets like this added to her excitement, a drug she craved more and more as she honed her skills.

It sounded like trouble at this other villa, a well-planned raid gone wrong, and one of the Chosen in trouble. The Holy Church looked after its flock, but none so well as their Chosen. Blood of Christ was given to few of their agents, their most prized assets. It had never been offered to Belle, a fact which rankled her.

Already one of the Sword of Solomon's best agents, Belle was still at the tender age of 18, more than a match for agents that were twice her age. Her strength and skill were incredible for a woman, even more so considering she was so young.

The villa was still some twenty miles away. A good half hour, or more, to travel. Belle could only hope events at the other villa were not advancing too quickly. She knew the way the Mafia operated too. Information first, by torture or coercion. They were good at such things. One of the Chosen would last a long time under torture. She was tempted to reduce her speed.

It brought a wry smile to her face, that one of their Chosen was in trouble, and it was up to Belle, an un-'blooded' agent, to attempt to save her. She gripped the handlebars tighter, enjoying the feel of the throbbing engine between her thighs as she rode through the dark night.

*   *   *

In the cellar, half a dozen of the men who could be spared were gathered, to assist in the humiliation and eventual torture of the spy in their midst. Gianni didn't fool himself that torture would be necessary to get the information they sought. This Honey Trap had been well-prepared. Whoever had prepared it had known they were going up against the Cosa Nostra. No one did that lightly. This woman would either know nothing, or everything. Either way, he knew his brother would delight in prising that information from her.

There was a gap between the long racks of wine, where a space had been cleared. It had obviously been used before, for there was a small sturdy chair there, bolted securely to the stone slab floor. It was going to be used again, shortly. The air was rank with the sour smell of old wine. But other smells lingered as well. Unpleasant smells, the kind you didn't let your mind linger on, lest it conjure up visions of just how those smells had been produced in times past.

Laura cried out as they threw her about between them, from one man to another. Roughly they pulled her to them, running their hands up and down her body, and forcing kisses on her, laughing as she tried to bite them. "Beware! The bitch has sharp teeth," laughed one of them, coarsely, throwing her to one of the others.

Paulo watched the proceedings carefully, judging how far to let the warm-up continue. Laura screamed as thumb and forefinger savagely twisted her nipple, guttoral laughter her only response, as more indignities were forced upon her, hands raining hearty slaps on her pantied buttocks as they passed her back and forth between them, too fast for her to attempt to kick them again. It was all she could do to keep her balance. The belt was cinched tight behind her back, just above her elbows.

Then on a signal from Paulo, Laura was dragged over to the old wooden chair, which had been bolted to the stone floor. She cried out as she was forced down into it, her bound arms behind the back of the chair, and a length of rope used to tie her ankles to its legs. She shivered helplessly as the men stepped back from her, for she knew worse was to come. "I didn't kill him," she said suddenly, only too aware of her own vulnerability.

"What was that?" Gianni asked, mocking as though he hadn't heard her words.

"I didn't kill him. He had a heart attack," she tried to explain, as she fought to regain her self-control, get her breath back. Paulo scoffed at her claims.

"You were found standing over his body, with a powerful torch in your hand, and the lights switched off even though there was nothing wrong with them. I don't believe you, Signorina," he sneered. "Who are you working for?" he asked. "You were trying to signal someone. Who was it?"

"Talk! Tell us what we want to know, and it will go easy on you," Gianni cautioned her. Paulo walked around behind her, and Laura felt his hand playing with her long blonde hair, lifting it and sifting it through his fingers.

"You are a very beautiful lady, Signorina." He let the hair slowly run through his fingers as he complimented her. "It would be a shame if we had to destroy that beauty," he warned. Laura was hyperventilating, her senses swimming as she tried not to panic, remembering the cover story that had been developed for her, details, names, half-truths that could partially be confirmed.

"Our doctors will confirm the heart-attack, if such it was, if that part of your story is true. For now we are more concerned with who you work for, than revenge against you," Gianni tried to reassure her. "Whoever planned this attack on our 'family' will pay for their rash judgement," he promised.

Paulo's hands continued to caress her, moving now to her shoulders. "It would be well for you to tell us everything, Signorina. My men have watched you with the padrone for the last two weeks. They do not see many pretty ladies. They would enjoy your beauty if they could. If I tell them they can," he threatened.

Laura looked up at the grinning thugs, as they sat around on other chairs, one of them pouring wine for the others. They were looking forward to the 'entertainment', running their eyes over her naked breasts, which Paulo's hands now cupped as she shivered, squeezing and hefting them casually. "So beautiful," he droned on. "Talk to me, Signorina. Tell me what I want to know, or I will force you to talk, and then if you are still pretty enough, perhaps my men will be interested in playing with you before you die."

"Ravanelli," she blurted out. "I work for Ravanelli." she gasped, as his fingers squeezed, unable to control her trembling. "I needed money, and he said it would only be for a few weeks." She tried to sound convincing. Laura's fear was quite real, for she had heard of Paulo Frattenzi's reputation as a sadist.

"Basta!" one of the men cried out, on hearing the name of one of the other Dons, a rival whose greed was notorious. Such inter-rivalry between the Mafia families was not uncommon, and was certainly plausible. Ravanelli would of course deny such claims, whether innocent or guilty. Her claims would certainly increase friction between the two families.

Paulo left Laura for a moment to converse angrily with his men. Laura could still feel his finger-marks on her bruised breasts. Two of the men disappeared back out of the cellar, to start making inquiries. Then he rounded on Laura once again. To forestall his intentions, she blurted out more of her cover-story. "I was signalling to a small party of men who were to come in and steal the old man's ikons. Ravanelli wanted to add them to his own collection," she explained hurriedly. "I gave him a drugged glass of wine, but it was only supposed to make him sleep soundly. I didn't know about his heart condition," she explained. "Then I was to open the bedroom window and let them in. I knew the combination of the wall-safe. It was to have been a quick easy job." She slowly got her breath back as she talked. "His death wasn't my fault. It could have happened at any time with his poor health."

Gianni and Paulo looked at each other for a moment, then Paulo turned to Laura once more. "I want names, Signorina!" he warned. "Who first put you up to this, everyone you know in their organisation, telephone numbers, signals, as much as you can tell us."

"Ravanelli will pay for this insult!" Gianni warned.

*   *   *

While Laura was undergoing interrogation in the cellars, Belle covered the last few miles to the rendezvous in the overlooking hills, and a small party of black suited men made themselves visible at her approach. Belle was similarly garbed herself, having been ready to go in with the other infiltration team. A small map was scanned with the aid of a torch, taking care that its light not be seen from below, then Belle borrowed some binoculars to view the revised security arrangements herself in the villa grounds. There were never more than a dozen men on the estate at any one time, from the notes scrawled on the rough map. 4 men and 3 dogs on view, meant at least 8 more men inside the house. Servants did not stay on the property overnight. The groundsman had his own little house, towards the rear of the estate, and he would be staying inside it while this commotion was going on. She could discount any interference from him.

The dogs first then, she decided. They were running free, and would pick up any movement long before the human guards. Taking charge, Belle gave instructions, clearly, concisely, and some of the men in the group found themselves amazed at the way this slip of a girl was taking charge. They could find no fault with her strategy, or her own self-belief that she could rescue this operation.

The small party started down towards the rear of the villa. They still had a couple of hours before dawn, and the men in the grounds would be feeling the worse for wear after patrolling all night, feeling more secure that the danger was over now that dawn was approaching and the knowledge that they had seemingly forestalled a raid on the villa. They would not be expecting that raid to continue regardless.

*   *   *

"Again. Tell us again," taunted Paulo, pulling Laura's face up by her hair. "I think you are lying to us!" he grinned.

"It's the truth." Laura gasped against the pain. It felt like her hair was being pulled out by its roots as he forced her to look him in the eye.

"A very clever story, Signorina. You've worked on it well. Such a shame that Pierluigi Batistuta died in a car accident over a week ago, so you could not possibly have been in contact with him unless it was by a séance, no?" he spat fully in her face, and Laura tried to recoil. The palm of his hand quickly followed, slapping against her cheek forcefully. Laura cried out, fearfully. Inwardly she cursed her ill-fortune. Batistuta had been set up beautifully for this operation, and now a chance of fate had killed him, and looked like killing her as well. "Now we will get to the truth Signorina!" his eyes gleamed as he fished in his pocket for a lighter.

He took it out, holding it in front of her face as he flicked the top open, thumbing the wheel till the spark caught the wick, and a long flame burned brightly as he adjusted it, then began moving it from side to side. Laura found her eyes following the flame, as though he was hypnotising her, which indeed he was, with fear!

"Such a beautiful little thing, this flame." He ran his fingers lightly through the flickering flame, too quickly to really feel the heat. Laughing, he moved the flame closer to Laura, till she could feel its heat. "So simple, and yet so effective," he chuckled as he used the flame to illuminate Laura's exposed body. "Such nice breasts! It would be a real shame to hurt them, would it not?" and he moved the lighter closer, so that she gasped as it neared her nipple. Laura screamed, long and hard, her screams echoing off the cold stone walls of the cellar. They could be heard coming up from the ventilation grilles in the grounds of the villa.

*   *   *

Belle and her party heard the screams, and where the men wanted to rush in, she bade them wait, and stick to her plan. "Don't worry about her. Worry about me if you disobey my orders. She'll still be there when we get inside. She's a Chosen, remember. They don't die easily," she laughed, scornfully.

She leapt to the top of the wall, astounding the men with her, for it was fully ten feet high. Crouching low on top of the wall, she surveyed the scene inside the grounds. Searchlights lit the house, but left the perimeter in darkness, which would work to their advantage. She had already decided on her point of entry. Vines covered the wall at the rear of the house. They would be strong enough to take her weight, and she was a skilful climber. The bedroom window would be no problem for a sharp knife, and Belle was very good with sharp knives.

Belle fastened a grapple to the top of the wall for the rest of the men to scale, and then she dropped inside the grounds. She took out a dog-whistle from her close-fitting tunic, and put it to her lips. She blew once, the noise pitched too high for the human ear to hear, yet she knew it would bring the three dogs running. Taking out an automatic pistol, she began screwing the bulky silencer onto the end of the barrel. Hiding in the dense shrubbery, Belle turned at the sounds of running paws on grass, seeing the first big dog coming at her. She waited till the running dog was almost close enough to leap, then she fired one single, silent, shot, taking it in its head as it charged her. The head shattered, and the dog fell. Belle turned instantly to deal with the second dog, finding the third close behind. They had been well trained, attacking in silence.

She fired from the hip at the closest dog, seeing it fall, and then threw herself to one side as the other dog leapt at her, turning and shooting as the animal's body passed over her. Both dogs fell dead to the ground. Preoccupied with those two kills, in quick succession, the last dog was on her before she realised it, and Belle barely had time to jam her forearm into the creature's jaws as it went for her throat and she fell back beneath the beast, her gun falling from her grasp.

Two of her men had scaled the wall by this time, and had drawn their guns, trying to get a clear shot at the animal as it attacked her. One of them dropped down, and made to run to her position, when Belle suddenly rolled clear of the dog, which now lay still on the grass. She reached down and withdrew the commando dagger from its ribcage, the blade having pierced its heart.

The entire escapade had taken place with little noise. The screams from the cellar, doubtless attracting the most attention from the guards still above ground. Belle examined her arm briefly. Sore, but still useable. The blood-flow would cease shortly, she knew from experience. She picked up the gun, and quickly reloaded, and fitted a new silencer. She re-holstered it under her arm.

As her men gathered around her, they were aware of the sounds of an automobile pulling up at the main gate. "Quickly now, we haven't that much time before they miss the dogs," Belle warned, and led the assault on the rear of the villa, leaping and climbing up the clinging vines like a human fly as her men watched from the ground.

Attaching a grapple to the balcony, she quickly turned to use her knife on the window frame, springing the window open in seconds, and entering silently, not waiting for her men to follow her. The upstairs seemed deserted, and Belle made her way to the master bedroom, identifying the wall-painting that concealed the safe as two of her men followed her.

"No time for niceties. We blow it open. Set the charge for five minutes. The rest of us will take care of any opposition downstairs. I'll find the Chosen. Meet me later in the woods. Go to it!" she ordered, and strode purposefully out of the room to take charge of the rest of her men. Behind her, the two men began unpacking the small charge of gelignite.

*   *   *

At the main gate, Grimaldi berated the few men who had remained at their posts as he drove through. "Where the hell is everybody?"

he raged. As they broke the news of the padrone's death, a cold rage overcame him, for he was charged with security here. His absence from the villa, not his decision, he had thought adequately covered by Paulo and Gianni, two trusted lieutenants, though it seemed he was wrong.

The old man frequently installed women at the villa to cater for his sexual appetites, but Grimaldi had always had the women checked out, in case of just such an eventuality. He trusted few men, and even less women. Now that guttersnipe Casiraghi would take charge of the family, and where would that leave Grimaldi? Probably blamed for the whole damn mess!

He heard the screams from the cellars, and cursed. That damn Paulo! Brushing aside a couple of the men, he stormed into the house, determined to cut short the sick bastard's party.

*　　*　　*

Laura screamed as her long blonde hair went up in flames, her head turned into a human torch for a few painful seconds, as she threshed helplessly against her bonds. Paulo laughed hysterically as he applied the flame of the lighter to ignite the woman's beautiful locks. She flailed uselessly in the chair, screaming endlessly as the flames from her hair flicked at her face. The sickly stench of burnt hair and blistering flesh filled the cellar rapidly.

One of the other thugs, mercifully, at a signal from Gianni, poured a bottle of wine over her, dousing the flames. Laura gasped and sobbed helplessly, tied to the chair, as the wine ran down her body. Her hair, her beautiful hair . . . .

"Bastard! You bastard!" she cursed, gasping. "I told you the truth. Please believe me. The truth!" she sobbed. Most of her hair was gone, and what was left was plastered to her blistered scalp with the wine, making her look almost bald.

"You lie so wonderfully, Signorina," Paulo chuckled. "A pity you are not enjoying this as much as me, but we still have some more hair to burn!" he reached down between her legs, shoving his hand down into her silken panties, and ripped them from her as she screamed anew. Gianni turned his head away, hearing the footsteps on the stairs.

Grimaldi stood there, filling the stairwell, an impressive figure despite his age. Paulo and the rest of them turned towards him. "You sick fuck!" cursed the older man, as Paulo stood up from the tethered and obviously terrified woman. "We do not make war on women. Not while I am in charge here!" he raged. His nose rankled at the smell of burning hair. Paulo Frattenzi diplomatically shrank away, as the older man came forward to examine the woman. He did not recognise Laura in her present state, so dishevelled, and so many years ago. He had aged, and she had not. Laura had never seen him before in her life, as far as she could recollect, yet knew he was responsible for the end of her suffering. "Untie her, you bastards! One of you, take her to a doctor. I assume you have gotten enough information out of her by now?" he glowered at Paulo. Gianni answered, trying to deflect Grimaldi's wrath away from his brother.

"She says Ravanelli was behind it all. But there were 'inconsistencies' in her story. We needed to be sure," he went on. Laura slumped forward in the chair as her arms were finally unbound. Another of the men went to untie her feet. She groaned in pain as she tried to raise her head. Grimaldi turned again to say something else to his errant lieutenant, when he was interrupted by the sound and reverberations of an explosion from somewhere in the villa above.

Gunfire rang out almost simultaneously, and the screams of wounded or dying men soon followed. "Back upstairs! Quickly you fools!" Grimaldi screamed. "Bring the woman!" he ordered, and Laura found two of the men helping her to her feet.

Grimaldi led the charge up the stairs, and Laura felt herself being half-carried along towards the increasing sounds of gunfire. Gradually, she was taking more notice of what was going on around her, the gunfire getting louder. Her strength was returning slowly.

A dead body lay on the floor, blood still pouring from a chest wound, as the men exited the cellar stairs. More gunfire came from outside in the grounds. Grimaldi quickly re-assessed the situation, splitting his men. "Leave her! Get out there and help our men in the grounds," he ordered, and Laura felt herself thrown roughly onto a small sofa in the reception hall. "The rest of you, follow me!" He started up the stairs to the upper levels, where more gunfire could be heard.

A fusillade of bullets stitched holes in walls and bodies, as they met resistance on the staircase. Grimaldi and his small band returned fire, forcing their way up the staircase, step by bloody step. A slim rope suddenly dropped into view in the stairwell, from one of the higher levels, and a small, obviously feminine, figure slid down the rope, firing a silenced automatic pistol into the backs of the attacking Mafiosi, as she descended. The silent shots were deadly, and men fell one by one, their fate a secret from the men charging ahead of them, for she took the last man first, and the deadly bullets worked their way up the crowded staircase, with cool precision, taking out four of the men before the rest had any idea what was happening.

The figure dropped to the ground a few yards away from Laura, and she knew the woman must be one of her own organisation, though she did not recognise her. Quickly, she came over to Laura, assessing the damage, though quick to see Laura was still mobile. "Cute hairstyle! Hope the scumbag that did this is one of the ones we've killed." She flashed a cold smile. "Come on, I'll help you walk." She knelt and began to help Laura to her feet.

Just then, behind her on the stairs, Grimaldi was being forced to retreat under heavier fire from above. Only he and two of his men were still standing. As they were forced back, his eyes caught movement from below, and he saw the black-clad figure standing over the naked woman. His gun-hand came up quickly, firing as he turned, and although Laura screamed out a warning, Belle could only half turn, the bullet slamming into her shoulder as she fell back.

The gun fell to the floor, and Laura went after it, as Grimaldi fired again. Grimaldi's second shot missed, and Laura had time only for one. The bullet took him in the side of the head, and he fell like a stone, dropping out of sight.

One of the other men was felled by a shot from above, and the last of them ran out of the main doors into the night, where more shots could be heard. Laura turned her attention to her would-be rescuer, who was struggling to sit upright, nursing her arm gingerly. "I owe you," Belle grimaced. "Looks like you Chosen aren't as inept as I thought," she forced a smile. "Better find some clothes, and we can get out of here," she suggested.

Chapter Ten

After more than a week of seeming inactivity, which was not really fair, for Laura knew Gabriel was constantly on the phone or e-mailing his contacts, she was becoming increasingly frustrated at the lack of progress. She felt she could make much more of an impact there on the ground herself, making her own enquiries. After all, she reasoned, no one living knew she had betrayed the organisation. Ryan and his accomplices were all dead. Gabriel's Mafia friends had disposed of the bodies, and it could only be assumed by her former associates that hers was among them. Until she actually showed her face, she would be believed dead. True, when it was realised that she wasn't dead, people might put two and two together, but she still thought it worth the risk.

Laura determined to give Gabriel another couple of days, and then if nothing came of his enquiries, she would act herself. She had to get to Belle before Gabriel talked to her himself. He wouldn't understand or forgive what she had done, been forced to do as it happened. The circumstances were irrelevant. She had killed one of his best friends.

Lucifer's personal effects were still in some of the rooms in the villa. Laura had found one of many passports in one of the desks, all made out in various names. She had studied the photographs. With her hair cut short, and no makeup, she might even be able to pass herself off as Gabriel's brother, whom the world at large did not know was dead. She took one such passport on a whim. Gabriel had organised an American passport for her under the name of Davis, which was as good a forgery as anything she had seen the Church provide, yet, always the good agent, she preferred to have a number of identities to hide behind, if circumstances warranted it. Her code name of Chameleon had been well chosen.

*   *   *

Upstairs in the villa, Gabriel brooded over a cup of coffee. He studied the printouts of reports from his various contacts in Rome. How many of them could he really trust? How many of them remembered him ? Most of them only knew him by reputation, respected enough that it was. Omerta didn't mean much these days, even in Italy, and it was hard to be loyal to someone to whom you were not personally known.

Ryan's disappearance would be accredited to Gabriel. Yet for all that, the Sword of Solomon were quiet these last few months, as though regrouping their resources. As far as he knew, they were not actively seeking him out at the moment. He covered his tracks well. He knew though that they had a long memory, and that their network of informants would be seeking him out just as he himself was now seeking his daughter.

The more people he involved in this, the greater the chance of a leak. Double-agents were not unknown. He must be sure before bearding the lion in its den. Unless he was really lucky, he would have to go to Rome himself to meet his daughter. A long overdue meeting, hopefully on better terms than the last. He hoped when she learnt the truth, she would find it in her heart to forgive him for what he had done.

*   *   *

In Rome itself, in a small rundown office overlooking the Via Candia, one of Gabriel's informants, Carlo Inzhagi, wrestled with his conscience. He knew that Gabriel was a confidante of some of the higher echelons within the Mafia, and a standing instruction was to offer the man called Gabriel any such assistance he required, as and when he required it. The name Gabriel had seemed to exist since before Carlo was born. He was sure he had heard his father refer to the man, when he himself was but a child. Whoever this operator was, he must be someone special. Someone the Dons spoke of as one of their own family. He had gathered the man (if man it was) was not Italian, yet that only made the awe in which his name was held, in even higher esteem. For the Dons to offer such assistance and reverence to a foreigner was unheard of.

Carlo was a private investigator, who was not affiliated to any of the families, except by distant marriage. He remained on the fringes of the organisation, occasionally contacted and asked to run errands, which he did, grateful for the money such errands brought his way. It was hard bringing up three children and a fat lazy wife by earning an honest wage in modern day Italy.

He knew of the Mafia's blood-feud with the clandestine organisation within the Church, though not its details. He had heard some of the priests mention this Gabriel's name, to his own informants. These priests sought information about the man called Gabriel, and it was rumoured they would pay well for such information. Perhaps the same inquiry could generate money from both sources.

If he handled this right, the Mafia might end up paying him for information on the nun being sought, and the priests might be persuaded to pay him for revealing that she was being sought by the man they were after themselves. The mysterious Gabriel.

He took his hat from the coat-rack, and left the office, locking the door behind him. Time to go cruising along some of the seedy bars, frequented by the lower life-forms of the Italian underworld. There were nuns aplenty in Rome, but to find one particular nun under all those voluminous robes would take some doing.

*   *   *

Throughout Rome, other eyes and ears were soon scouring the city, and nuns were scrutinised ever more closely, as the word went out on the underworld grapevine. More sophisticated checks were run by some of the hackers in league with the Mafia, funding their legitimate jobs by moonlighting for the Cosa Nostra, who if truth be told, lurked in the shadows of big businesses all over Italy.

Access to social security records, and birth certificates was a matter of public knowledge, even concerning men and women who eventually joined the Church. They were not born into it, after all, but started life as ordinary men and women. Mirabelle Cannucci was one of thousands of possible names that came up on their hit-list, for Gabriel could not afford to be too specific in his descriptions, or tell them what he was really looking for. Keywords only, and dates from the Second World War to modern day, pulled up a lot of information, and it would take a long time to sift through.

Gabriel knew how identities were created, and had to be 'adjusted' over the years to disguise longevity, for he and Lucifer had done this for centuries. It was going to be a long hard struggle to sift through such information, and he hoped to have quicker success looking through the many photos the Mafia were collecting for him, for he remembered Belle's face only too well.

*   *   *

There was much corruption in Rome these days, and the police often despaired. Once such policeman was Michaelangelo Bonetti. He couldn't believe what two of his informants had now just revealed to him, having dismissed the first informant's story as too crazy to be believed. "The Mafia is looking for a nun?" What in God's name was going on? Puzzled, he asked one of his colleagues to run the description and nom de plumes through the Crime Computers, and two days later, one of his subordinates came up with some interesting case reports, though no known photograph was found to exist in their files. A few artists impressions showed a dark-haired woman, which could have been anyone from Sophia Loren to his own mother (as she would have been some thirty years younger).

The name Belladonna had been used over the last thirty years or so, in connection with a female assassin or terrorist. It was hard to describe consistently some of the crimes listed as being connected with her. Murder, theft, and a possible two bombings, though that seemed out of sorts with her usual modus operandi. Fifteen separate murders had been attributed to a female assassin matching her description, ranging from as early as 1958, to as recently as 1995.

Obviously not the same woman, then, so a code name of some kind, assigned to a lone female operative, but for which organisation? A daughter, carrying on where her mother left off, perhaps? Predominantly preying on the Mafia, so the police in their wisdom had not been actively pursuing her activities, letting criminal prey on criminal as long as no member of the public got hurt, and now the Mafia seemed to think this woman was a nun? It was a strange world, but not that strange, surely? Such things were for comic-books. Bonetti felt his interest increasing as he read more details, and he determined to ask his informants to try and gather more information about this matter.

*　　*　　*

The woman that most of Rome was now looking for was currently living under the alias of Maria Caldone, and the six roomed flat she occupied when in Rome was comfortable, though not exactly affluent. It was owned by the Church, but at her permanent disposal. Only her superiors in the Sword of Solomon kept any other keys for the place, and so she treated it as her home base. Her tastes didn't run to the exotic or even to the expensive. They were just 'her tastes', and the décor was simple yet functional.

Her neighbours thought of her as a model, a misconception which Belle was keen to feed, as it explained her frequent absences and the strange hours she kept. In truth, she had done some modelling for one of the Fashion Houses, but the same face on too many magazine covers too often would raise some suspicion, so she had faded away from the spotlight of the catwalk, preferring relative anonymity.

She sat now in her 'greenhouse' as she called it, the room which she used to store her little indoor garden of exotic and deadly plants. Cultivating the little garden was a hobby of hers, and the Church arranged for her cleaning lady to carefully water the plants when she was away.

Half of the room was given over to the garden, with plants arranged in troughs down either wall, so that it did give the impression of being in a rather unique jungle. A water fountain humidifier was kept on whenever she was in the room, adding to the effect. The soft subtle lighting was on a timer, to vary its brightness and direction. A tall bookcase filled the third wall, containing books on exotic flora and fauna, and others which dealt with toxins and poisons, another interest of Belle's, though this time a professional one.

Running her fingers inside her shirt, Belle fingered the recent tattoo on her left breast. Her own design, which the tattooist had copied onto her skin. Belladonna, such a lovely yet deadly flower, and her namesake these days. She had laughed when she had first heard the nickname, but it had stuck and seemed appropriate enough.

She enjoyed this room, the strange smells of the plants. The night view of Rome out of the picture window was breathtaking, which more than made up for the view during daylight. Brought up on a farm, concrete edifices were not considered things of beauty. Eternal City it might be, but most of Rome paled when compared to the architectural delights within the Vatican City.

Belle also had an office/apartment beneath the Vatican, which she used occasionally, when called back for consultations and mission briefings. Sister Belle was an oft-seen figure walking the echoing corridors of power beneath that city. Away from the Vatican itself, Sister Belle ceased to exist. She did not keep any of her clerical attire here, and save for the crucifix she kept above her bed, there were no other trappings of the Church here to lead anyone to believe she was inordinately religious, which she was indeed not. Certainly, not to the extent of a true nun anyway. Her beliefs were more practical.

She had been brought up to believe that as one of God's chosen agents on Earth, it was her job to act against the agents of the Devil, who ranged from the Mafia to anyone the Council so defined. They would point and she would act, with finality.

Over the years, her authority within the organisation had grown, and Alonso Borgia had taken her under his wing, so that effectively she answered only to him, and Alonso Borgia now ran the Council. When not being called upon to do his will, her time was her own, and on occasion, many weeks would pass before the Church had need to call upon her special skills.

During such times the only constraints the Church placed on her movements was that once a month she would give blood at the Church's own medical facility beneath the Vatican. She had learnt over the years of her unique physiology, and now understood the strange nature of her own blood. For many years before this understanding, she had heard of and resented the Chosen amongst the hierarchy, the ones who had been given the Blood of Christ, to prolong their life-spans. She now understood why she had never been offered, what she had thought at the time, a priceless gift.

She had since been taught that only few beings were ever born with this unique gift, this rarest of blood-groups, and that the Church sought to replicate it scientifically, and that was why she was asked to give blood each month. Her own recovery from a knife wound, and a bullet-wound, had amazed her, and once she had grown to full adulthood, physical signs of aging ceased. The death of her parents was thus regretted by the Church, as one of them must undoubtedly have passed on the rare blood-group to their daughter, before Belle had administered her own brand of justice to her abusers.

She passed in front of a mirror, sweeping back her black hair, and paused to admire herself. She was more than sixty years old, yet had the outward appearance of a woman in her mid twenties. She had asked the scientists if they knew how long she would remain like this, and their simple answer was that they just didn't know.

Looking back over her life, she wondered just how much of it there was still ahead of her. She could still remember her childhood, her life on the farm, before the day when her life was turned upside down. After that it seemed as though her life had been predetermined. She had allowed the Church to rescue her from her own hell on earth, and she now repaid them with her loyal service. She had killed men and women, saved the lives of others, in line with the Church's whims.

She had known men, and women, had some as friends, others as lovers over the years. None of the relationships lasted. Some turned sour, and others she had to end when permanent youth was commented upon by an ageing partner. It was a lonely life she led at times, and yet she threw herself into her work for the Church with vigour, enjoying and excelling in the varied missions.

She had carried out every assignment to a satisfactory conclusion, except one. And that one still rankled in her memory. She blamed inexperience, and insufficient character briefing for that single failure, against the man called Gabriel. Since then she had made it her business to learn as much about him as she could. She had not been told of his age, and obvious experience when she had been sent against him, else she would have been far warier in her dealings with him. Truth to tell, the Church did not know his real age, though they readily accepted he was well over a century old.

She had asked many times what had happened to him over the preceding years, but no one within the organisation seemed able to give her the information she sought. Their paths seemed destined never to cross, yet she was surprised no one had ever arranged a 're-match' between her and the terrorist.

She knew she was second to none within the Sword of Solomon, and she now had nearly forty years more experience than she had done the last time they had met, but then again, so would he, for he was also a benefactor of having the same unique blood-group. She had then to assume he had been killed, either accidentally, or by someone else who had got extremely lucky.

She had wondered about the uniqueness of her blood-group over the years. Just how rare was it? How many people around the planet were likely to have it? The Church surely couldn't know them all. She had gotten hers from one of her parents, but she had killed both of them herself, painfully. But what of her relatives? Had the Church sought out the other Cannucci's? Why would no one tell her of this?

She had toyed with the idea of launching her own enquiries, doing some genealogy research on the internet. Belle didn't know if she could bring herself to revisit old familiar places, even though she knew the farm had been sold out of the Cannucci family. Probably every one of the relatives she had known as a child was now dead, but the ghosts would still linger, and they would not be pleasant. Ghosts were one of the things you couldn't kill.

The relationships she had found herself in over the years had suffered as a result of her abuse by her father. Jessica remained the one 'real' love of her adult life, though others had almost come as close, and time had doubtless robbed her of the vengeance she had plotted against her murderess Angelica. She still felt an empty space inside her from time to time, and she still kept those earrings to remind her of her lover, though once she had intended a better souvenir to be Angelica's heart, encased in silicon, and used as a paperweight on her desk!

What would she be now, even if still alive? A doddering old crone whom Belle would likely pass in the street and not recognise. Time was a healer, or so they said, but time had never healed this particular wound. First loves are remembered forever, so they say. Belle didn't know how long she was likely to live, but knew she would put that particular saying to the test.

Belle was feeling melancholy, and went through to the lounge to pour herself a drink. She took the bell-shaped bottle of dark Pusser's Rum from the wine cabinet, and searched for a glass. A tall one, she decided. She added ice to the cut-crystal glass, and unstoppered the bottle, scenting the heavy aroma of the rum as she did so. She poured, and the dark liquid just about covered the ice, which crackled in protest. Belle added coca cola to the glass, filling it up just over halfway.

She left it on the coffee table while she put some music on her hi-fi. The Corrs . . . . an ideal choice for her mood, and as the Gaelic music filled the room, she settled herself back on the sofa, and brought the now misted-up glass to her lips, taking a deep swig, and enjoying the harsh bite as it filled her mouth, slowly swallowing it down.

Chapter Eleven

Alonso Borgia brooded in his opulent private apartments. Things had not gone well of late. The failed mission to capture Gabriel in England had cost him one of his best operatives in Father Ryan. The only other known Angel, Michael, must also be assumed dead, or reunited with Gabriel and Lucifer, his long-lost love. The Blood of Christ was too rare a commodity, and after all these years, their scientists still had not managed to replicate it.

Even the Angel-child, Belle, who unknowingly gave them a pint of her blood to experiment on each month was not enough, for her blood did not have the strength of her father's, at least that was the excuse those damn scientists had given for their latest failures. Greater potency with age, they had finally theorised, but it still sounded like an excuse. Plus she was technically a half-breed, even born of a mother given the Blood.

He had long dreamed of draining Gabriel dry. Supplies taken from Michael, the only other pure source, would not last forever. Michael could only be assumed dead, after his sudden disappearance in England.

It was imperative that Gabriel be taken, but just how? The man was too good at covering his tracks. For all Borgia knew, he might even have the audacity to live in Rome itself, right under their noses.

Should he try the fire-walled e-mail address once more? Sometimes the messages were answered, and sometimes not. They had tried to by-pass that fire-wall many times, but Gabriel's computer system seemed just as inviolate as the Vatican's own network. He bounced signals off satellites far too frequently to even begin to track him down via his internet usage. How then should he go about handling this?

The girl Belle had once been used in an attempt to secure Gabriel, and how Borgia had fumed when he had heard that she had been sent against him.

It had been learnt that Gabriel's aid was being sought by the Mafia, and other council members saw an opportunity to snare him. Borgia had been away from Rome, and was thus not consulted on the operation. Guillaume and Romanus had been duly chastised upon his return.

The girl herself did not know of her true parentage. What would happen if she found out? Whose side would she take in the ongoing enmity? Still, it might prove useful leverage in drawing Gabriel out. If he could be made aware that he had a daughter, surely he would seek her out? Perhaps he already knew. If he found out, would he believe? He would at least seek to make sure. It was not a strategy Borgia liked to consider, but as a last recourse, there might be no other way.

It had amused him to make the girl his mistress, knowing her history as he did. An Angel-child of his own to play with. The girl herself found the arrangement of mutual benefit, for she rose rapidly within the ranks of the organisation of the Sword of Solomon, and was also kept in the lap of luxury when not 'on assignment'. She was free to go as she chose, yet Borgia had indeed grown fond of her.

Borgia's Machiavellian mind was going through all the possibilities. The Donovan woman had borne the child, but had not known of its survival. If she had mentioned it to Gabriel when they had finally met, would he guess the child might have survived? Was she herself still alive, or killed with Ryan? The Church had received no information at all after Ryan's last transmission. Local sources could discern nothing. The Mafia must have helped Gabriel against his own men, and cleaned up all traces of the conflict. They were good at such things.

The red wine tasted, *thin*, was the only word that readily came to mind. It only looked like blood, and was nowhere near as sweet. Yet, he could not afford to gorge himself too readily. More pressing matters were the evening's meeting of the Council, and how to deal with the treacherous Achille Ratti's plans to oust him as leader. He was being blamed for the failure of Ryan's mission and more importantly the loss of Michael.

As powerful as Borgia was, the rest of the Council could indeed oust him as leader, if they all voted against him. The loss of Michael must be compensated for. Meaning Gabriel must be taken. If that meant risking the girl, then so be it. Blood was so much thicker than water, after all, and tasted all the sweeter.

*　　*　　*

Inzhagi's enquiries were getting him nowhere. No one had ever tried to count the number of nuns in Rome, and no wonder. His underworld contacts were getting nowhere, or so he thought. One positive thing that had come out his investigations, was the fact that the clergy had come to hear of them, and it was really of no surprise when Carlo was contacted by the Church.

Father Marco Falcone looked younger than Inzhagi, and Carlo always wondered at the priest's continued good health, for he knew he was actually younger than the good father, though it was certainly not obvious when you compared the two of them. Falcone had performed his own marriage ceremony many years ago at the Church of St Bartholeme. As a more or less good Catholic, Carlo had gone to confession every week. Well, almost every week.

After Carlo had made his confession, and received the usual absolutions from the priest, Falcone began instigating a new line of conversation. "I hear you have been seeking word of one of our sisters, Carlo?" Inzhagi stiffened within the confessional. He had not expected any reaction from the Church, and especially not so close to home. "Might I ask why you are making these enquiries? We are quite solicitous of our good sisters, and would not wish them to come to harm," he explained.

Inzhagi cleared his throat. "Well, Father, I make these enquiries on behalf of a friend of a friend," he started to explain. The good Father obviously had his own contacts, else he would likely have not learned of his own investigations. Which of course meant that he was now in contact with the more darker inner circle of the Church, that few knew existed. "These sort of favours take up a lot of my time, and my time is expensive," he went on. "I have a family to support, as you know, Father." He heard a soft chuckle from the adjoining cubicle.

"There is a small possibility that I may be of assistance in your enquiries, my son," Falcone continued. "We may be able to help each other."

"These expenses, Father," Carlo started to continue, when Falcone interrupted him.

"Whether the Church may help in that regard, will depend upon the name of your 'friend', Carlo. We must help each other in these troubled times," Falcone explained. "It may be possible for me to put you in touch with this particular sister, as long as I am sure your friend means her no harm. There is a long lost relative, with whom she has been trying, herself, to get in touch, but without success. If you can confirm his name to me, we may be able to bring about a joyful reunion."

Inzhagi listened to the priest's words, and realised the good father wasn't quite telling him the whole truth, for he had heard enough fabrications from various informants in the past to be able to tell when he was being fed a line. Still, as long as the priest was willing to pay for the information.

"I believe his name is Gabriel, Father," Inzhagi admitted, and heard the soft intake of breath through the perforated screen, and the priest's head nodded in the darkness.

"Very well, I will consult with Sister Belle, and if she is willing, I will put you in touch with her. Go with God, my son." Falcone blessed him as he left the confessional. Nothing for it but to wait, then, thought Inzhagi, and he put on his hat once more as he walked toward the front of the Church. At least he now had a name to go on. Sister Belle.

*   *   *

Borgia smiled as he received Falcone's news. So, Gabriel did know. Fortuitous, indeed. This would make everything so much easier. Yet now the web must be spun to catch the fly, and Borgia had been spinning such webs for centuries. Belle would be the bait to draw Gabriel into Borgia's clutches, yet he must prepare the bait carefully, for she was no fool, and neither was Gabriel, he knew from personal experience.

Twice before, their paths had crossed. Once he had almost had him. Almost. But Gabriel had escaped him, with the aid of the Devil's own luck. Gabriel, who knew secrets about Borgia that even the

Council didn't know, for he was careful to conceal his true nature from even them, his 'oldest' friends, if he could call anyone friend. Gabriel had been there at his re-birth into the world. Coincidence, or divine intervention? Borgia had always wondered.

*   *   *

1457 Italy

Strange how the memory was so vivid after all these centuries. Pope Callixtus III, he had been called in those days, and his entourage had camped for the night in the deep woods, on an overnight tour of the outlying provinces for one of the many summer festivals that were held every year. Borgia had killed and bought his way into the Church, mainly at the behest of his family, but once installed as Pope, he had begun to see the benefits of such power. He had even done some 'noble deeds' in his time as Pope, but he had also assured his own family's wealth at the same time, along with his own of course.

His last night as a human was spent at first in prayer, as he and his entourage enjoyed a simple meal, and then he had retired to his tent, where he enjoyed a glass of wine before retiring for the night. He snuffed out the candle, and settled down for a peaceful night's sleep, though that wasn't what transpired.

Outside the tent, in the trees overlooking the small clearing where the tents were encamped, cold eyes were watching. The figure melted into the dark branches and foliage, invisible from the ground. Tethered horses began to become restless and very unsettled, as the moving breeze carried the scent of death to their nostrils. The figure chuckled once, amusedly, as he waited for the last of the candles to go out.

*   *   *

Earlier in the day, a lone horseman travelled through the woodland path. His crimson doublet and padded breeches marked him as one of many mercenary soldiers who plied their trade in the provinces during these troubled times. The wars between the nobles seemed incessant, and there was always work to be had for a skilled swordsman.

Gabriel preferred the adventurous lifestyle to that of the merchant, chosen by Lucifer. His friend was making a success of his business in Florence, buying and selling fine wines and bolts of cloth. Florence seemed to be the centre of the world at the moment, and this was where Gabriel was now headed, having recently finished one campaign, albeit unsuccessfully, and was returning to Florence to seek out fresh adventure and employment. He hoped to be reunited with his friend for a few weeks, while he was there.

The woods were dark and dangerous places, even during the day, for robbers and footpads often attacked lone travellers. He hoped his bright clothing, and prominent rapier would deter anyone from accosting him on his travels, for they could see he was no helpless merchant. The few people he met, either greeted him cordially, or just moved out of his way as he rode past on his horse.

Gabriel was aware of the horse's skittishness as the light grew more scarce through the thick treetops, but he forced it onward regardless. He had many miles to go to reach Florence, and detouring around these woods would add days onto his journey. He would need fresh provisions to last him, and had not much money left to buy them at the moment, for his last employer had been slain on the battlefield before Gabriel could broach the matter of owed wages.

He had ridden long this day, with only a brief pause for a midday snack and to feed and water his horse. With luck, he would reach the other side of the woods before nightfall, and then find somewhere to spend the night. Two more days should see him in Florence.

His journey was interrupted by a rope noose which suddenly dropped from above, encircling his neck before he could react, and the cries of the ruffians who had planned the ambush echoed around him as he was jerked out of his saddle.

The five footpads whooped with glee at their easy prey, appearing now from out of the undergrowth where they had concealed themselves, laughing as they watched him jerk, his legs kicking, fingers frantically trying to prise the rope free, before his struggles finally ceased, and he hung there, quite motionless, as the footpads chuckled with the ease with which they'd caught their prey.

Two of the men chased after Gabriel's horse, eager to rifle his saddlebags, whilst the remaining three lowered him down to the ground to strip him, and take his purse and weapons. As the three ruffians closed in on him, Gabriel suddenly lashed out with his poniard, sinking nine inches of cold steel into one man's belly, and spilling his intestines onto the ground. The other two cried out, as he sat up, pulling the noose from around his neck as he got to his feet. Gabriel's lighter than average body-weight had saved him from a snapped neck. His playing possum had lulled them into lowering their guard.

Drawing his rapier with his other hand, Gabriel cried out as he deflected a dagger blow from one of them, lashing out with the longer blade of the rapier, and impaling a second man. Letting go of Gabriel's horse, the other two men joined in the fight, each of them rushing at Gabriel from both sides, daggers raised to strike, to help their comrade overcome him.

Gabriel parried one blow, jumping against one of the men, and turning him to accept the plunging dagger his friend had meant for Gabriel's back, and he cried out once as he died. The remaining two men stared at their three fallen comrades on the floor. Not so easy pickings after all. The swordsman handled the rapier and the poniard familiarly, obviously no stranger to a fight.

The two men kept their distance, circling around him as he fought to watch both of them at the same time. The ground was now dark with blood, and getting slippery underfoot. The two men were no novices either, having worked together before. At a nod from one, the other charged forward, sword slashing down at Gabriel, who parried, turning the blade away, and then only just managing to avoid the second blade, which plunged through his doublet, and he cried out as the blade sliced his side.

Gaining in courage, the two men pressed him harder, as he made pretense that the wound was more serious than it actually was. He let them beat him back, and made a couple of weak ineffectual attacks himself, which he allowed them to easily parry. Gradually, the point of his rapier was lowering, as if he no longer had the strength to raise it.

"Now! Run him through!" urged one of them to the other, who quickly ran forward recklessly as Gabriel pretended to stumble. The long cold blade projected a foot out of his back before he had time to realise his error, as Gabriel lunged from a kneeling position.

The last man took stock of the situation, as Gabriel was freeing his sword, and ran for his life. If five men couldn't kill this demon, then what chance had one such? Gabriel decided to let him go, more interested in the whereabouts of his horse, but he stripped the men of what little coins they carried. It would do to purchase food before the delayed journey was over. Cleaning his blades on the clothing of one dead man, he set off in the direction his horse had bolted, hoping the stallion hadn't gone far.

*   *   *

Hours later, long after darkness had fallen, Gabriel cursed the skittish horse. Alone and on foot in the middle of the woods. Without a horse it would take a week to reach Florence. He walked on, following the pathway as best he could in the feint moonlight, determined to put as many miles behind him as he could before he tired and tried to find somewhere to spend the night.

The glow of a distant campfire was a welcome sight. A bit of warmth, and perhaps some food and drink would not go amiss, and so he headed for it.

*   *   *

Borgia had not known what it was that had woken him, for he had not seen the shadowy figure creep around the back of his tent, and use one sharp fingernail to slice down the canvas to make an entranceway. Small and wiry, the figure was stood over him as he opened his eyes, momentarily puzzled. "Giuseppe, is that you?" he mistook the figure for one of his man-servants, for the briefest of seconds, and then the figure leaned closer, red eyes transfixing his own, jaws opening, and those teeth, those hideous teeth, getting closer and closer.

Borgia had time for one scream, loud and terror-filled, before those teeth fastened on his throat, and he knew the agony and the ecstasy he had dreamed about all his long life.

"Ware the camp!" came the cry, as the dozing guards came alert at the sound of their master's scream, and more torches were lit as they tried to understand what was happening. Clerics and many man-servants began appearing from their own tents, which were lit up as flint-boxes were used to relight their night-time candles.

One tent remained in darkness, and they realised with growing horror, whose tent that was. Guards and priests alike rushed for the tent, and more cries went up at the sight of a bloody-mouthed demon from hell that erupted from the tent, hissing once at the frozen guards, and which then turned and ran for the woods, with a few of the more braver guards in pursuit after they had regained their composure. The rest of them entered the tent with the priests, and they found Borgia lying there, amid blood-soaked sheets, barely alive, his breath hissing out through his savaged throat, and blood on his own lips. He was dying.

*   *   *

Gabriel had heard the cries from the distant campfire, and was momentarily considering whether he should show himself at this time, when a small figure came rushing out of the darkness straight towards him. The figure paused, snarling at the sudden surprise, and allowing Gabriel to see the full horror of its appearance as it transfixed him with those blood-red eyes.

Naked and begrimed, the creature, for Gabriel could not find it in himself to call it a man, stood almost five feet tall, hunched over, with its chest matted with drying blood. Sharp white fangs, like those of a ravenous wolf, showed in its open mouth as it snarled at him. Nails like talons hung from its long fingers, flexing slowly, as it debated its actions. The two of them stared at each other for mere seconds, though it seemed much longer.

Then, the sounds of pursuit behind the creature provoked it to attack, and it leapt at Gabriel, covering the distance between them before he had time to draw his rapier. Gabriel screamed as he flung himself back, horrified, rolling and grappling with the thing as its talons sank into his doublet, ripping the stuffing from it as it sought his flesh.

Those long teeth snapped at his throat, and Gabriel feared for his immortal life, for this was no human thing he fought. Managing to get a booted foot between them, he managed to kick the beast back, away from him, and pulled his rapier as he rolled away from the thing, finally feeling a bit more confident as the thing came at him a second time, seemingly oblivious to the long blade.

Gabriel thrust home, skewering the thing, which then unbelievably ignored the cold steel running through it's vitals and sank it's talons into Gabriel's neck, dragging itself forward and forcing even more of the rapier through itself as it sought to sink it's teeth into Gabriel's throat.

Crying out, Gabriel fought for his life, kicking and punching, man and beast rolled around on the woodland floor. His hold on the rapier loosened, and he dragged free his poniard, stabbing again and again to no effect. The thing would not die!

Closer and closer came those sharp fangs to his throat, as Gabriel made one last frantic effort, driving the sharp steel into the side of the thing's neck, hard enough to come out the other side, and he sawed hard, working the blade back and forth. The thing cried out at last, pausing in its attack to try and defend itself, as Gabriel forced it back at last.

Though bleeding from dozens of small wounds, Gabriel knew that he had to continue the attack. He had finally found a way to hurt the thing, and he must give it no quarter. Light grew and torches approached as he forced the thing down on the ground, straddling it. The men at arms cried out encouragement as they saw that Gabriel was fighting the beast.

With a last tremendous effort, Gabriel finally sawed through the thing's neck, beheading it, and,with a final gout of hot blood which covered the grass, it lay still. Gabriel shivered, before wearily getting to his feet, and being instantly attended to by the men at arms as he almost collapsed from the exertion.

"Well done my friend, you will be rewarded well," one of the men promised. "That thing attacked Pope Callixtus!"

* * *

Back at the camp, the clerics and priests were doing all they could to save Borgia's life, though they quickly realised it was hopeless. The savage wound on his neck had been bound, but he had lost too much blood, and his skin was almost white. He was dying. Two of the priests talked together hurriedly, knowing they did not have much time. Borgia would be dead before sunrise.

The Blood of Christ was carried with the Papal procession as part of religious ceremony. Contained in an embellished jewel and gold ikon, it was never actually used, merely revered, but it *was* true Blood of Christ, with the life-prolonging powers that only a few of the inner circle of the Church knew about, and even fewer were allowed to actually imbibe.

The two priests were part of that inner circle, though Borgia as yet was not. They finally nodded in agreement, reaching the decision that would have a marked effect upon the rest of Borgia's life. One of them went to fetch the ikon, while the other herded all the man-servants and clerics out of the Pope's tent.

When he returned, the two of them went into the tent, to say prayers over the dying man, and one of them poured the contents of the ikon down Borgia's throat as the other gave a blessing. Borgia drank as they bade him, and then his body began to feel afire. He wrestled on his pallet, pulling weakly at his nightshirt, as within his body, something unknown and never before heard of was taking place. Both vampiric parasite and Angel-blood now coursed through his veins, mixing, and to a degree, fighting each other for dominance. It felt as though boiling oil coursed through his body.

The two priests were in awe, as they witnessed what they thought of as a holy miracle, for the colour began to come back into Borgia's flesh, and he soon sank into a deep sleep. On hearing the renewed commotion outside, the two priests left Borgia to sleep, and went to see what was happening.

*   *   *

The master at arms lead the way back into the encampment, carrying a grotesque head impaled on a pike, held high to catch the firelight. "The thing is slain!" he pronounced. "How goes it with his Holiness?" he asked, concerned both for the Pope's safety and his own. For he had set the guard about the camp. The guard who had failed to protect his Holiness. With disdain, he threw the head into one of the watch-fires, where it instantly began to spit and bubble as it caught fire, and turned to present Gabriel to their eminences. "This man slew the beast as we watched," he announced, as a weary Gabriel raised his head, half-carried in as he was by two of the guards, for he was too weak to walk unaided.

"See that he is given rest and succour," one of the priests announced in gratitude. "His Holiness lives, though has been savagely injured.

With God's grace, he will survive." Gabriel was lead away to a nearby pallet, where his wounds were tended to by one of the clerics, and food and fine wine were brought to replenish his strength.

Repasted, and his wounds bandaged, Gabriel at last fell asleep on the pallet, where he remained undisturbed until the next morning.

*　　*　　*

He awoke to find the camp awake and busy. Much activity was taking place around one of the largest tents, which he had gathered belonged to Pope Callixtus. Men at arms showed him where he could wash, and relieve himself. This done, he was plied with food once more. Freshly roasted boar was being turned over the open fire. He washed it down with water, refusing the wine being offered.

He talked with the guards of the Papal Procession, and was promised a horse in return for his intervention last night. Those that had seen the fight with the beast had repeated the tale to the others, and Gabriel was held in high regard. His weapons had been brought, and cleaned, and then returned to him.

He replaced the rapier in his scabbard, still remembering that he had run the thing through, with no effect whatsoever. What kind of creature could ignore what should have been a fatal wound? Some kind of berserker? He had heard of some pretty ferocious and tough animals in his time, but this one had been human, at least once. What sorcery had turned a human being into something like that ?

*　　*　　*

Later that day, Gabriel was brought before the Pope, who had wanted to personally thank him for his efforts of the previous evening, and so it was that Gabriel and Borgia first met, the latter propped up on his pallet, his voice still hoarse, and his throat still bandaged.

Gabriel introduced himself as a mercenary, en-route to seek employment in Florence, giving his real name, for he thought of no reason why he should not do so. The name meant nothing to Borgia at the time, and Borgia even went so far as to bless him. Although not religious, Gabriel accepted the blessing as was expected, for he saw no reason that men should not be allowed their own beliefs, whatever they were.

With a new horse, and well-provisioned saddlebags, Gabriel left the camp behind. Florence remained two days away, and a reunion with Lucifer awaited.

Chapter Twelve

Borgia smiled as Belle arrived for her assignation in his apartments, dressed in her surplice and habit, as was her wont whilst walking the corridors of the vast underground network. She had her own key, and Borgia awaited her in bed, naked below the silk sheets. His large barrel-chest was matted with grey hair, and despite his age, he had the look of a well kept man in his fifties. Belle could attest to his vigour.

"Missed me?" she smiled seductively, yet also wantonly, and she slowly began to raise the long skirt of the habit, as Borgia watched appreciatively. Higher and higher it went, revealing ever more inches of bare leg, and then finally a dark swatch of hair at the juncture of her thighs, for she wore no undergarments. "Mmmm, I can see you have," she chuckled at the movement of his flesh under the silk sheet.

Smiling, she held her skirts high as she clambered up onto the bed, and as Borgia threw back the single sheet, she lowered herself slowly onto his erect manhood, moaning herself, as under her, Borgia groaned with pleasure.

"Ahhhhhhh, my little Angel," he chuckled at his own joke, reaching up to fondle her big breasts under the thick material.

He could shred her garments in seconds if he so wished, yet it was his pleasure to continue the charade, and the two lovers continued to lose themselves in each other. He used the rosary beads to pull her head down towards his own, and raped her mouth with his eager tongue.

Belle responded in kind, riding him harder and faster, her juices wetting his loins.

*   *   *

Afterwards, as the two of them lay there in the large bed, Borgia cradled her in his arms, for he was indeed fond of her. "Have you grown bored in Rome, my precious?" he asked. "It has been a while since you have been required to carry out any missions for the Council."

Belle stirred against him. "One can never get truly bored in Rome, Alonso," she mused, though after so many years she had seen everything worth seeing in the city, and the new modern architecture was never as good as that which it replaced as buildings came and went. "Perhaps some change might do me good," she suggested. It was never good to remain in one place too long, lest people with long memories remembered her face as it had been, and as it should not have remained. She could not stand the confinement that the members of the Council suffered, restricting themselves to their apartments under the Vatican, when not out and about in the city.

Borgia at least had his outside interests, his opulent and lavish nightclub, which for some perverse reason he used to seemingly draw attention to himself, whereas the other members of the Council shunned it. He frequented the club at least twice a week, occasionally with Belle on his arm, though not wearing her habit and surplice, but then again that would not have really seemed so unusual at Borgia's, for decadence was a by-word at that establishment.

Some of the Council were suffering from failing health these days, for as she understood it, the more Blood of Christ you imbibed, the less effective it became, and some of these Council members were older even than Borgia, which only served to highlight the differences between them.

There had been rumblings and rumours that Borgia had secured a more effective artificial substitute for Blood of Christ, which he kept for himself, and was the reason for his continued good health. If so, he did not share such a secret even with her.

"Remember Marseilles?" Borgia asked, seemingly nonchalantly. Belle's attention picked up, and she roused herself from her post-sexual torpor.

"You know I do," she stated, brushing the hair out of her eyes, and raised herself up on her elbows. "It was many years ago, but why mention it?"

"There may be an opportunity arising whereby you may be able to blot those unpleasant memories from your mind," he smiled, casually. "This man Gabriel has heard about you, as your reputation has grown," he explained, lying skillfully, an art he had mastered over the years. "He is a proud man, this Gabriel, and his pride may be his downfall. It would seem as though once he learned you did not die from that fall into the sea, then somehow he put a face to the name Belladonna. We have found out that he is making enquiries about you. Obviously, he is now determined not to leave unfinished business." Borgia cautioned her out of seeming concern. "You must be very careful, my dear, but with careful preparation, we may use this situation to our advantage."

"We draw him in, and then take him?" she understood the strategy immediately. Borgia chuckled.

"Yes, but carefully. We need him alive. We do not want your pride to interfere with our end objective. I don't want him killed. I know you've dreamed of killing him for many years, but be practical. Dead he is of no use to us. Defeating him, the great Gabriel, should be enough of a salve to your pride."

"As you say," agreed Belle, her hand reaching for him under the sheets. "The Blood is more important than my pride. Defeating him will suffice," she agreed, her hand working him beneath the sheets, though he needed little encouragement to get hard once more.

Borgia chuckled, more at the success of his act than her own. He had his own reasons for wanting Gabriel alive, and they had nothing to do with letting the other Council members use him as their own personal blood-bank.

*   *   *

Father Falcone called to see Inzhagi at his home, and Carlo dutifully invited the priest inside, surprised by the man's prompt follow-up. After accepting the customary glass of wine, and socialising with Carlo's wife and two children, Carlo and the priest conferred in private, Falcone handing the man a colour photograph of a nun, taken discreetly it seemed, for the nun was not looking into the lens.

A pretty woman, Carlo thought. Inwardly, he was always disappointed to see so many pretty nuns. It wasn't fair to deprive the rest of the male population of such women. Let the ugly ones serve God, and the pretty ones serve Men, was his own personal ideas on the subject.

"Sister Belle asks that you send this photograph to her uncle Gabriel," Falcone explained, and with the photograph, he also handed over a thick envelope. "For your expenses," Falcone explained, though he didn't have to. Inzhagi felt the thickness of the envelope. That should indeed more than cover his actual expenses.

"The Church is very considerate, Father." Carlo thanked him, and then took the envelope and went to lock it away in his desk, before his wife became aware of it.

"The Church looks after its children, Carlo, as it has always done," Falcone smiled, though with a hint of faint menace behind his eyes. "You may tell Uncle Gabriel that you have found the girl. She visits my Church daily in fact. Do not give any details, just tell him she's here, and you will put him in touch with her when he arrives," Falcone warned.

"Do you wish me to advise you when he makes contact, Father?" Inzhagi asked.

"But of course, and then we will let the good Sister and her Uncle get together, eh?" Falcone smiled, knowing Inzhagi didn't believe his story, but then Falcone didn't believe Inzhagi's either. Still, as long as the man was prepared to carry out his part of the bargain . . .

His own men would be watching Inzhagi, and would know the second Gabriel showed up. They would also have his phone tapped, in case the contact was by phone, both here at his home and at his office.

"Another glass of wine, Father?" Inzhagi asked, but the good Father declined.

"Best be on my way. I have a Mass to conduct tonight. It has been a long time since I saw you at Church, Carlo," he commented. Inzhagi looked guilty.

"I do not come as often as I should, Father, but I always sit at the back. You may not have noticed me," he avoided the priest's eyes.

"I don't miss much, my son," Falcone smiled coldly, and inwardly, Inzhagi shuddered. "Good day." He fastened his overcoat as Inzhagi saw him out the door.

*   *   *

Laura went into Gabriel's study, after Manuel Estevez dutifully carried down the evening's latest printouts, responses from Gabriel's vast network of informants. Only his master would have a chance of ferreting anything useful out of such a mass of information. He left them on a tray in the large study, as he usually did. Gabriel would eventually collect and sift through all the information, more usually than not discarding it.

Purely by chance, the topmost fax was from Inzhagi, and it contained a photograph which caught Laura's eye as she walked past. She picked it up, staring fixedly at the faxed image. Belle, without a doubt. She scanned the text message quickly, reading Inzhagi's story.

Gabriel was in another part of the house, and she quickly folded the fax, slipping it inside her blouse and bra, the paper nestling under her breast. She had to seize the opportunity, and went quickly up to their bedroom to collect a few things, including her passport, and others which even Gabriel did not know she had had made. Once Gabriel had introduced her to some of his contacts, it had been a simple matter to have a few 'extras' made. Her codename within the organisation had been Chameleon, and it was a name well-earned.

She had not had the same high-profile as had the woman called Belladonna, but listening to rumours, it had been common knowledge that she had been sleeping with one of the Council Members. His name had been Borgia, she believed. Laura had done things in her past she was not proud of, but she had never slept with someone to further her chosen profession. Other reasons, that Gabriel need never know about, but not that!

She had her own contacts in Rome, and as long as no one knew about her change of allegiance she felt confident she could contact her daughter. Inzhagi was as good a place to start as any. Borgia was another, if she could find him.

She called out as she went down the stairs, shoulder bag in hand. "Darling, I'm taking the car. I'm going into the city to do some shopping." From above, she heard Gabriel's faint voice replying, as she put on her jacket.

"Don't be late back. Manuel's preparing dinner for seven," he reminded her.

"Okay, I won't," she lied. "Love you." Gabriel came out onto the balcony only in time to see the front door closing behind her. He shook his head, and then slowly walked down the stairs and into the study to check through the latest reports Manuel had left for him.

Laura did indeed go into the city, but straight to Ezeiza airport, where she knew there was an Air France flight leaving for Europe that afternoon. Pausing only to purchase some clothes and a single suitcase, she did some quick packing so as not to look too unusual a passenger, and then booked a ticket using the credit cards recently supplied by Gabriel. By the time Manuel began preparing dinner, she was already 36000 ft above the Pacific.

*　　*　　*

When Gabriel finally began to make enquiries about her non-appearance, his contacts within the local police reported the whereabouts of his car in the airport car-park, and Gabriel cursed aloud. He guessed Laura's intended destination, and asked Manuel to check the flight manifests.

What had caused her to take off like that? True, she had not quite seemed herself since seeing Juliana, but he assumed it was just impatience with the slowness of the investigations. Then, turning, he noticed the half looked at pile of latest printouts. Going upstairs, he took them to his computer, and began scouring through the latest receipts in his Inbox, comparing them to the hardcopies Estevez had left for him.

One item was there that wasn't in the pile, and he printed it out, complete with photo. Laura had seen this and took off like a brooding bird that had lost its chick. She now had at least a day's head start on him. "Laura," he spoke to himself. "I hope you're as good as you think you are." Picking up the phone, he dialled a number in Rome. Time to call in a few favours.

*   *   *

Donatello Grimaldi was very pleased to hear from Gabriel, whom he remembered as being a very good friend of his uncle Luigi. His uncle's reputation with the Cosa Nostra had helped him build his own, and Gabriel had been a friend to him after Luigi's death. The Grimaldi clan owed the man a lot, and they knew a few of Gabriel's secrets, such as his longevity, though the secret of it had never been explained.

Donatello had been co-ordinating Gabriel's inquiries here in Rome during the last couple of weeks. One of those inquiries had obviously had positive results. He didn't need to know just why Gabriel had been interested in tracing this nun, but he was keen to offer his assistance in tracking her down.

He took down Inzhagi's name and details as Gabriel explained he wanted surveillance only on the man, and surveillance on anyone else who might be watching him. He didn't give Laura's name, just a loose description, for she would be a fool to return to Rome and not change her appearance. As a former Solomon agent, she would have no friends among the Mafia. Donatello Grimaldi then went on to discuss Gabriel's arrangements to enter Italy, advising caution, for he knew of the Church's enmity towards him.

He would fly into Malta, where a fast boat would have him in Sicily in a few hours. From there, by car and ferry into southern Italy, and from there he would make his way north to Rome. He had used the same route before, secure in the knowledge that Sicily, being the birthplace of the Mafia, he would have plenty of allies to assist him in illicitly entering Italy.

With a couple of clicks of the mouse, he forwarded Inzhagi's fax to Donatello, so that he would have the photo to aid him in watching out for Belle. The Mafia certainly had the manpower for such an operation. Finding one particular nun in Rome would be like looking for a needle in a very big haystack. Inzhagi's help would be invaluable, if it could be trusted. Gabriel would make his own assessment when he met the man.

He hoped he could get to Belle before Laura made contact. Hopefully she would see the attention Inzhagi was going to be getting from Donatello's friends, and be very wary of making contact. He needed to see Belle before Laura did, to try and explain who he was, and why he had tried to kill his own daughter that dark night on the cliff-top.

Could she forgive him? Would he even get the chance to ask? She had no idea he was her father, only an enemy of her precious Church. If she got the opportunity to kill him before he could explain things, he had no doubts she would likely take that opportunity, for she knew him only as an enemy.

*   *   *

Belle's initial part in the operation, was to become highly visible for the next few weeks. Once a day she was to walk the two and a half miles from the Vatican to Father Falcone's Church of St Bartholeme, and then back again. Wearing her normal nun's regalia she would be inconspicuous to everyone but the people seeking her.

Sword of Solomon agents would be taking part in the sheperding, watching her back, and watching the watchers. She would be in charge of the team, in constant communication by discreet radio communication. The habit was bulky enough to conceal the wires and transmitter so that she could maintain voice contact with the other team members, some of whom she knew, having worked with them before.

Nothing would happen until Gabriel showed up, and when he did, Belle smiled to herself. Then we shall have our rematch. She had her pride too, as Borgia rightly accused. It came before a fall, so the saying went. She had taken hers off the cliffs above Marseilles those many years ago, and was damn lucky the tide was coming in at the time, else she had been smashed on the rocks below. This time it would be Gabriel who would fall from grace!

*   *   *

Laura had used her head-start on her lover well, flying into Charles de Gaulle, and switching identities as easily as she changed clothes, then booking into a small hotel for the night to catch up on overdue sleep, for she could never manage to get proper rest on a plane. Even the comfiest seats couldn't compare to a proper bed. Not that the bed in the hotel was anything like a proper bed, either, but it at least enabled her to sleep.

Refreshed, the next morning, she changed clothes. She checked out of the hotel as Laura Davis, and took a taxi back to the airport to catch yet another flight for Leonardo Da Vinci as Louise Tackett. She had thought her plans through on the transatlantic flight. If Inzhagi could put her in contact with Belle, she would be able to arrange an accidental meeting.

They had worked together once before, on that ill-fated operation at the mansion, though at the time neither of them knew the other. They had not met since, but both knew of the other's reputation within the organisation. She would need to sit her down and explain their estranged relationship, reveal herself as the girl's mother, and tell her of her father. Most of all, she needed to explain the strange workings of fate which had kept them apart for so many years, and emphasise the need for her secrecy over the death of Grimaldi.

It was only after her recovery from her ordeal in the mansion that she had been told the identity of the man she had killed to save Belle's life, but that would not make it any easier to explain to Gabriel that it had been her bullet that had killed one of his best friends. Far better, if he never found out. She did not know how such a disclosure would affect their newfound relationship.

Now that she had found him again, after so many years, now that she was on the verge of finding a daughter she had never known, she didn't want anything to spoil her chances of happiness.

It felt as if she were juggling with a house of cards. Just one mistake was all it would take to bring it all crashing down around her, and her nerves were on edge. Could Fate be so cruel to her? It had been, so far, with her life, she reminisced, as she settled back in the rear seat of the taxi. Twice she had found happiness, and twice it had been snatched away from her. She would not permit that to happen a third time, even if that meant taking on her former allies and friends in the Sword of Solomon.

Chapter Thirteen

It took two days for Gabriel to enter Malta, via England, where he took a holiday excursion flight with dozens of other tourists, all keen to enjoy their break in the sun. Alcohol was served on the flight, and liberally dispensed among the pleasure-seekers, but he merely asked for a half-bottle of wine to go with his meal, after all, it would not be suitable for a man of the cloth to appear to be drinking too much.

Father 'Patrick Ryan' parted company from the main bulk of holidaymakers after they decamped the plane, and went to the Hertz desk to rent a car for the journey north of the island, to where he had arranged to be picked up by boat. The name on his false passport was innocuous enough, yet a personal joke which he was sure the Vatican would approve of, had they known about it. When in Rome, what better way to blend into the background, than by appearing to be just another faceless priest? He would just have to make sure his own side didn't shoot him first by mistake.

*   *   *

The high-speed boat skimmed across the waves, leaving the rocky shoreline of northern Malta behind them. The Mediterranean was calm this night, and they made good time, their large white wake spread out behind them, luminous with disturbed plankton in the moonlight. Gabriel would have preferred a moonless night for such a crossing, but the timing was taken out of his hands by Laura's rash departure.

He settled back against the bulkhead, letting his body rise and fall with the swell, and feeling the surge of the two massive engines which drove the craft forward. He had never met the two men who had hailed him on the rocky shore, but they answered his signalling torch with the agreed signal. Likewise, they had never met Gabriel before, and would probably forget about him by tomorrow, for they were used to being sent on such errands, delivering anonymous persons to anonymous destinations under cover of darkness.

Once he got to Sicily, he would pick up the car and the supplies Donatello had arranged for him, complete with the cellphone and names and phone numbers of Mafiosi foot-soldiers already staking out Inzhagi's apartment, and under instruction to follow any and all orders given them by the man called Gabriel. The ferry left early tomorrow morning for mainland Italy, and by tomorrow night he hoped to make Rome.

*   *   *

The meeting of the Council was getting quite heated, with accusations flying back and forth across dark mahogany table. "Yes, it was my proposal," admitted Borgia, restraining the urge from reaching out and snapping Ratti's neck like a dried twig. "But you all approved the motion, did you not? Ryan suggested we use Michael as backup, and we have grown to put much trust in his judgement. He has been one of our best agents for many years, even before his conversion," he explained, staring them all down.

"His judgement was obviously faulty, else he'd be here now to explain his own failings," Ratti pointed out. "The girl remains our only source of any form of the Blood of Christ, however weak. It is another risk, and look how the last one turned out."

"It is Gabriel who has made the opening moves here," Borgia explained. "He is the one actively seeking the girl, and it is an ideal opportunity to draw him into our clutches. He must be aware of the risks in coming here, yet that is what he will do. Somehow, he has found out about his daughter, and we can use that against him. Here, we *control* Rome." He waved his arms about him, emphasising the power these council member had over the workings of the Church, and thus the people who followed it. "Once Gabriel sets foot inside Rome, he will not set foot outside it again," Borgia promised.

"The city is set to be a battleground," protested one of the others. "You know he will have help from the Cosa Nostra?"

"And we have our own agents in place. In a one for one battle, our own men are far superior to these Mafiosi. We control the situation, whereas they can only react, and that will be too slowly," he went on. "The girl will be well-protected, watched whenever she is outside the Vatican. Gabriel will not be able to approach her without my men's knowledge. Then the trap closes, and we take him. If the streets run red with Mafiosi blood, then so what? The police will assume it is just more gang warfare breaking out, or blame it on those Red Brigade fanatics. There will be no repercussions," Borgia promised.

"There is always the danger of the unknown," Ratti went on. "We all know the man's resourcefulness, and he took on Ryan and his party, including Michael, all by himself," he pointed out. "That operation was carried out in England, where his resources will doubtless have been limited. Here within Rome, as you readily admit, he will have help from at least the Grimaldis, if not some of the other families. I like it not," he scowled, the sagging spotted jowls made his bald head look much like a brooding vulture in the candlelight.

"You think I would risk the girl in this enterprise without taking all possible precautions? Our relationship is no secret. Some of you have lusted after her yourselves. She is mine, and I would keep her," Borgia admitted.

"She is not your only paramour. Does the girl know of her rival? Perhaps you tire of her?" another accused. Borgia rounded on him.

"My affairs are my own business. You would do well to ensure they stay only my business!" he warned.

"Perhaps our good Alonso likes a threesome from time to time, eh?" another joked, trying to lighten the mood. "That nightclub of yours has made you decadent."

"I have *always* been decadent," Borgia laughed, joining in the good humour. Ratti was his main protagonist here, as always. The rest of the council were in his pocket. Ratti had been the last Pope to have been accepted onto the Council of Vampires. A move Borgia had resisted. Whilst alive, Ratti had discovered much of the workings of the underground Church, and it was in an attempt to subvert him to their cause that the vote had been taken. Borgia was all for just killing the man before he made too much of a nuisance of himself, but the others would have no papal murder on their conscience.

Ratti had been offered and accepted the Blood of Christ, though Borgia had seen to it that the blood he received was the weaker strain from Belle, thus his health was not what it should have been. He saw admittance into the underground Church as a way of getting it back to its original aims of furthering the good works of the Church.

Since then, Ratti had been a constant foil. A sharp thorn in Borgia's side. He was trying to eat away at Borgia's power-base, disagreeing every time he thought Borgia was trying to progress his own private agendas. Borgia liked power, had always liked power, was *born* to power in one of the most powerful families in Italy. Ratti was not long for this life, if Borgia had his way. There were ways and means, despite the wishes of the rest of the Council.

Borgia enjoyed both revelling in, and flaunting his power, and his nightclub was a suitable stage on which to do it. Some of the other council members had visited the establishment on occasion, but most preferred to maintain their privacy. For with the signs of advancing age, they stood out in the crowd of mostly younger revellers.

Ratti's comparatively poor health was the cause of his greater animosity lately. He it was that had accused Borgia openly of having a successful artificial substitute for the Angel-blood they all depended on, for he simply could not understand Borgia's continuing apparent good health.

Borgia had truthfully told him that his scientists had been unsuccessful in replicating the blood, but he did indeed have a substitute, and it was anything but artificial. Nothing could replicate the taste of fresh warm human blood, and he had an inexhaustible supply of it.

*   *   *

When Borgia had first been converted by the vampire's bite, the strange hunger horrified him, and he fought against it. The strange parasite in his now converted bloodstream struggled to exert its dominance. But at length, he had given in to his dark craving, and frightened himself by his own savagery, as he sank his teeth into the pale soft neck of one of his many paramours as he lay beside him one night, who awoke screaming to find Borgia feasting on his blood.

The catamite's screams had brought men at arms into the Papal bedchambers, but by then Borgia had regained enough of his composure as to convince the men the boy had gone mad and injured himself. Such was his influence that the boy was taken away, and returned to his family, sworn never to repeat what had happened there that night, upon pain of death.

Borgia gradually came to realise what he had become, for he was a learned man, and had read the 'other' books which the Church kept from the public's view, those that dealt with devils, demons and vampires.

The Angel-blood in his veins enabled him to control his cravings, sufficiently to go without blood for many nights, whilst he continued his own research into his condition. Strong light now hurt his eyes, though he found he could still walk in the sun without burning up. Either the Angel-blood helped regenerate his tissue faster than the sun could destroy it, or the notion was just a fallacy.

He had no reaction to the sight of a crucifix, or other holy symbols. He still enjoyed garlic with his food. Holy water had no effect on him either. He laughed at the notion of actual shape-changing, but spent many hours concentrating, trying to will it to happen, but nothing did. More time was spent with a captured rat, staring at it, willing it to do his will, but the rat just ignored him and scurried about the room. Nothing mystic therefore about his transformation then, just the craving for blood, and the immense power he now felt in his body.

Lore maintained that it was possible to pass on this 'dark gift', which was obviously true. If an attack resulted in actual 'death', then that person would rise again as a newly converted vampire, once the parasite had time to assert itself. This Borgia thought undesirable, for he revelled in his newfound power, and he wished no rivals. Others must exist, like the one who had created him, and these he decided to make his prey. He would hunt them not out of necessity, but for sport, for the sheer pleasure of it!

This he did, over many years, prowling the dark city streets of Rome, till eventually Borgia remained the only such creature of the night. Other vampires feared what was in Rome, and stayed far away.

Years passed, and Borgia's continued good health and youth were causing comment among the clergy who remained unaware of the Clandestine Council which effectively ran their lives in the world above. It was time for a papal 'death' to be arranged, and white smoke to be burned, so that Borgia might take a place at the Council Table. Pope Callixtus must eventually die, so that Alonso Borgia could be reborn, properly.

*   *   *

Achille Ratti had his own suspicions about Borgia's continued health. He had personally interviewed their scientists to verify Borgia's claims. If they were telling the truth, then how did Borgia look so well when the rest of the Council looked withered and older with each passing year?

He too had read the 'other' books, which the Church kept secreted away from the general public, and his enquiries of some of the older council members had revealed vague details of the circumstances in which Borgia had received the Blood of Christ. He kept his suspicions to himself though, not daring an out and out confrontation with his arch enemy. If his suspicions were correct, challenging him outright would be a fatal mistake. Yet, there were more ways to skin a cat.

*   *   *

Borgia's reign as head of the Council had not been without his setbacks. Gabriel in particular had been a thorn in his side, as he had sought to castigate the Church for its age-long relentless victimization. Michael was the latest and last angel to be lost to his machinations. Before Michael, Matthias had died in Spain, and two of the former council members had died with him as a wrathful Gabriel and Lucifer had decimated one of the Church's laboratory facilities in Spain.

Now only the Angel-child Belle remained, apart from Gabriel himself. If Borgia lost her because of his schemes to snare Gabriel, his reign would be over, and Ratti would have the backing of the rest of the Council against him. Also, if the girl was lost, then their only remaining source of Blood of Christ would be lost with her. Such a dilemma. Damned either way, he brooded. He needed to consult with

Falcone. Solomon's best remaining operative had a particularly bright mind, and a fresh insight would prove useful as he mulled over the best way to take advantage of the current situation.

Borgia had been goaded once in the past, to seek out Gabriel himself, and it had ended in failure, and had been received with mixed feelings among the rest of the council. Some of the fools lauded him for making the attempt singlehandedly. Others, amongst Ratti's cadre had openly criticized his rashness and eventual failure. Results were everything. It didn't matter how close you came, if you didn't achieve success it was all for nothing.

Borgia was a proud man, and his pride could be used against him. Yet he learned by his mistakes, and he would now, doubtless, use his pawns to achieve the endgame he desired. Unless, someone else took a turn at moving the chess-pieces.

*   *   *

Inzhagi went about his daily routine, unaware of the team of Solomon watchers that were slowly being put in place around him. The bulk of the team would concentrate on maintaining cover on Belle, as she made her daily walkabout to the Church of St Bartholeme and back. A team of four would switch regularly in pairs, maintaining round the clock surveillance on him. Sooner or later, Gabriel would make contact, and a simple radio call would close the net.

There was a chance he would use the phone, but a simple phone-tap would alert them should that be the case. Gabriel was no fool, and would know it also. He would seek to make contact some other way, possibly by means of a proxy so as not to alert them. That was why the bulk of their group kept close to Belle, on Borgia's orders. Not many people disobeyed Borgia and lived to tell of it.

*   *   *

The sea journey from Malta to Syracuse had tired Gabriel. Whether it was the constantly throbbing engines or the sea air he couldn't say. But once on Sicily, he slept for most of the day, planning on taking the evening ferry across from Messina to Reggie di Calabria on the mainland.

From there, it was an overnight drive almost 500 miles to Latina, just to the south of Rome, where his friend Donatello Grimaldi had his estate. Less people about at night, and he would make better time on the motorways. Up through Cosenza, Salerno, then stick to the coast road to Latina. The car was nothing ostentatious, just a small Audi, in line with his cover as a priest. Still the engine was finely tuned, and he expected to reach Latina before dawn.

The ferry crossing had been uneventful. He had felt no unseen eyes on him, and if there were any, they seemed to pay him no more attention than the other ferry passengers. Pulling away from the docks, and heading towards the motorway, he noticed no cars keeping up with him. His disguise was light, and not enough to fool any determined watcher who had a recent photograph. But priests and nuns were ten a penny in this damn country. Hiding in plain sight was more to his tastes than merely scurrying along and making slower progress, frightened at your own shadow.

As evening wore on, Gabriel was driving leisurely up the western coast of Italy, automatically planning his route off the main roads, adding time to his journey, yet satisfied of the arrangements Donatello Grimaldi was making in his absence.

Slower to respond than the Solomon agents, Mafiosi were now being made aware of his search, both for the nun and one particular person who might be searching for her herself. Gabriel had only made vague references to Laura's identity, aware that she might already be known by the Mafiosi as a Solomon agent herself.

Inzhagi was the key, and the Mafiosi would keep him safe until he could see the lie of the land for himself. If Laura were spotted, then she was merely to be kept under surveillance until he got there, unless she attempted contact herself, and Donatello had given his men orders to switch their surveillance to her, in that eventuality in the hope that she would lead them to Belle, and offer her protection against any Solomon agents who would doubtless be in the area.

Borgia was baiting this trap well. Yet Gabriel had no choice now but to take the bait. Belle remained the unknown quantity, doubtless brainwashed since birth by the Catholic Church. By her reputation, she was one of the Church's most accomplished assassin's. Was she now beyond redemption?

He didn't understand Laura taking off like she did. Certainly, motherhood was a new feeling to her, and doubtless emotionally damaging under the circumstances. Yet her sudden disappearance complicated things. He now had two women to worry about. Laura had never revealed much of her time with the Sword of Solomon under Ryan's tutelage, and obviously felt confident in her own abilities, yet she was intending to go head to head against her own former organization. He had learned to respect them over the years.

Rome was the stronghold of the Catholic Church, even aided by the Grimaldi clan, it would undoubtedly get messy, with too many players to keep track of. He would need as much backup as he could get to come out of this alive.

*   *   *

As Gabriel made his way north, Laura herself was already in place, having made the most of her head start. Her known contacts had revealed Inzhagi's address, and she was already watching the watchers, driving past in one of two hired cars she had rented. After a couple of tours of the neighbourhood, she had spotted the two men.

There was a coffee bar down the street, which allowed her to keep one of the stakeout cars in sight, if not Inzhagi's office itself. She would maintain a discreet surveillance from there, whilst her own informants would dig up what they could on the man's background and known movements.

Laura had not made the mistake of contacting her former organisation once she had re-entered Italy. Like all good agents, she had cultivated her own allies and informants over the years, people who knew nothing of her activities for the Church, and knew nothing of her supposed death. Not many in number, they were thorough in their work, and had never failed to deliver for her in the past.

Later that afternoon, as Laura returned to her small rented apartment, there was a manila envelope waiting for her at the reception desk. She took it up to her room before opening it, and learnt a little more about the private eye called Inzhagi.

An average investigator, Inzhagi made more than his wife knew, and kept an uptown apartment where he stayed overnight on odd occasions during the week, where he was known to take other women.

Some he was known to pick up in bars, where he was known to stop off on his way home for a nightcap. Making contact was going to be easier than she thought. All she had to do was take care of the surveillance in a way that would not raise suspicion, which was easier said than done. It was no good making contact, if that contact was known about. All surprise would be lost, and as good as she felt herself to be, she had no illusions that she could go against a full Solomon Hit Squad. She knew how they worked, and they were damn good.

Time for a little shopping, before Inzhagi finished for the day. Laura went back downstairs and out into the fading afternoon sunshine. There were one or two boutiques along the street that would have the sort of clothing she was after. Evening wear to go.

*   *   *

The information in the Manila envelope was proving very reliable. She would have to slip Mario a bonus for doing such a good job in such a short time. As she watched from her rental car, Inzhagi parked outside Le Chat Noir, and his watcher then parked his own car not too far away, but on the opposite side of the car-park. He would have to follow Inzhagi in, for the interior could not be seen from outside the establishment.

As Laura watched, Inzhagi locked his own car, and walked across to the entrance, where he was greeted familiarly by the doorman. The Solomon agent followed at a discreet distance behind, and Laura saw him enter the establishment, and then take up a position just inside the lobby, where he could watch, yet remain unseen himself by those within.

Locking her own car, Laura fastened her handbag and turned to walk across the car-park towards the waiting doorman, the click clack of her stiletto heels rang out across the distance between them, and the doorman turned an appreciative stare in her direction. Such women of the night were not infrequent visitors to the establishment, and she knew she was giving just the right impression. Tall and leggy, as her slit dress revealed a lace stocking-top, her full breasts bouncing as she walked confidently towards the doorman

He forced a smile, along with an appreciative stare, as he opened the door for the unknown hooker. "Grazi . . . ." she smiled a dazzling smile in his direction, and his heart skipped a beat, but then she turned away, and disappeared inside. Sighing, the old doorman allowed the door to close behind her, contenting himself with the sweet fragrance that still lingered momentarily in the air.

Laura waltzed past the Solomon agent with barely a glance, no one she knew, swinging her ass deliberately as she felt his eyes on her. He looked her up and down, and dismissed her without a second glance. Just another hooker. An expensive one, no doubt, but a hooker nonetheless.

Inzhagi was secure inside. His back up was watching the fire-escape at the rear, and he himself covered the only way out. If anyone of Gabriel's description made an appearance, the two way radio in his pocket would quickly call assistance. He lit a cigarette and leaned against the wall. The waiting game was a boring one, yet necessary.

Inside the bar, Laura spotted Inzhagi sitting on a bar-stool at the half-crowded bar. Still early, there were over a dozen people in the establishment. Inzhagi was talking to a woman, a hooker if Laura guessed correctly, though not one of the more expensive variety. Both of them looked her way as she crossed the floor and came to the opposite end of the bar.

She ordered a whiskey sour from the grinning barman, leaning casually against the bar-rail, as she took a drink and surveyed the room. More than a few of the men were looking in her direction. Her short slit dress revealed an awful lot of leg, and her low-cut bodice advertised her wares quite openly. Most of the men just looked, and wished they had more money in their wallets, sighing as they resigned themselves to just enjoying a drink.

She cast an eye in Inzhagi's direction, and he caught her stare. So did the woman he was with, who glared at Laura, face reddening indignantly, as the blonde attempted to muscle in on her trick. The shorter stockier woman approached Laura, intent on making her territory clear. She leaned forward, whispering in an agitated manner, and gesticulating in a typically Neapolitan manner.

Laura accepted the whispered tirade calmly, and then leaned forward to whisper something herself to the younger woman. The whisper was low, and heard only by the woman herself, who stiffened noticeably. Ashen-faced, she turned and quickly left the bar, watched amusedly by Inzhagi and some of the other patrons. Laura merely smiled sweetly as the woman left, meeting a few of the men's stares with a calm disdain. She again flashed a smile in Inzhagi's direction, and the half a bottle of red wine he had imbibed gave him the courage to return Laura's smile.

With envious eyes on him, Inzhagi got down from his own bar stool, and made his way over to the end of the bar where Laura waited, nursing her own drink. She took a sip from her glass, and turned towards him, red lips wet and moist. She smiled, a warm and seductive smile this close up.

"My name is Carlo," Inzhagi introduced himself. "And you are?"

"Anna," Laura introduced herself. "I am so pleased to meet you, Carlo," she smiled, holding out her hand for him to take, and he kissed it in a romantic gesture which she found mildly amusing.

"Would you like some company, Anna?" Inzhagi asked. "Rome can be such a lonely city, despite its diversities."

"You are right. Such a big city, yet so full of boredom. My office job bores me to tears, and I like to get away and have some excitement now and then," she explained, allowing him to lead her away from the bar and into one of the secluded booths. Inzhagi snapped his fingers to the barman, ordering more drinks.

*　　*　　*

Outside in the lobby, the watcher took note of Inzhagi sitting with the blonde whore. Lucky bastard, he thought to himself, and then lit another cigarette. Must earn more than me to be able to afford such a good looker.

*　　*　　*

Inzhagi and 'Anna' were getting along like a house on fire. They had moved from the bar, to a more secluded booth. She laughed readily at all his jokes, and seemed to match him drink for drink, though her tolerance was obviously higher. Laura had quickly switched to vodka and tonic, as soon as Inzhagi had joined her, and was drinking more tonic than vodka, after a discreet talk with the barman, who was used to hookers indulging in such tricks to sucker their customers.

Inzhagi professed to being single and keeping a large cosy apartment in town, the description matched the one given her by Mario. An ideal location to question him further, once she took care of the watcher. She gave a friendly giggle as Inzhagi's hand massaged her thigh, fingers tracing the pattern on her lace stockingtop revealed by her dress's slit side.

"So, how much is tonight going to cost me?" Inzhagi chuckled. Anna chuckled with him.

"That depends on you," she giggled. "A blow-job, a quick fuck, or something more versatile," she teased. "I'm game for anything you have in mind, but nothing is for free," she wagged a finger. "Why don't we see how the evening goes, and discuss money in the morning?" she smiled.

Inzhagi chuckled at her wanton demeanour, and he slid his hand under the slit in her dress. 'Anna' moaned as she allowed Inzhagi's hand to grip her tightly between her legs, his fingers clutching the damp G-string. "Naughty, naughty . . . ." she chided, though made no move to make him remove his hand.

Grinning wantonly, Anna plucked the sidestring of the black G-string, and pulled it away from her hip, in plain view as Inzhagi removed his hand. Inzhagi chuckled as he took hold of the string, and as she wiggled seductively on the seat, Inzhagi pulled down, and the tiny G-string slid down her thighs.

She grinned brazenly into his face, as she allowed him to pull the tiny piece of black silk down her legs, lifting her ankles to allow Inzhagi to remove them completely, and he held them upto his nose, inhaling her musky odour and groaning loudly, as she chuckled mischieviously. "Getting you hard?" she giggled amusedly, and reached down and poked the bulge in his crotch. 'Anna' smiled seductively, as if approving of the hard lump down there. "For the right price, I'll do anything you want. You'll find I'm a very broadminded girl," she chuckled throatily. Inzhagi liked talking dirty, for she could see the affect of such language on his swollen crotch. The wine made him pliable, and the talk made him horny. Time to make a move. Dislodging his questing hand, Laura stood up and went to move past Inzhagi. "Got to pee," she grinned, and clutching her handbag, she made her way across the room, swaying a little deliberately on her high-heels.

Acting more drunk than she was, she attracted no undue attention to herself as she slipped past the watcher and entered the toilet immediately behind him. Switching out the light once she was inside, she entered a cubicle and stood on the seat. Cautiously peering out of the window, she could see into the back-alley behind the club. The second watcher was there, as she knew he'd be, and he would remain in position as long as he thought nothing was wrong. She would have a couple of hours if she worked it right.

Switching back on the light, she flushed one of the toilets, and took the small cosh out of her handbag. She then came out of the door, brushing down her dress self-consciously, keeping one hand behind her back, clutching the small cosh out of sight. The watching man suspected nothing, his attention held by the scene within the bar, as Laura slid up silently behind him, taking him quickly from behind and slamming the cosh into the back of his head.

He went down instantly, collapsing to the carpeted floor, and Laura looked around worriedly as she struggled to half-lift him and pull him back into the toilet. Getting him inside was a struggle, and stripping off his trousers and underpants was even worse.

She shoved them down into the cistern of the adjacent toilet, where he would not readily find them. Quickly searching him, she found his radio, and snapped the small aerial. Then she took his wallet, and keys, making it look like a mugging. With a bit of luck, he would be too embarrassed to report what had happened. Stripping him would delay him in attracting attention to himself, or getting his fellow watcher in here. Struggling anew with his dead weight, she managed to prop him up on one of the toilet seats.

The small bottle of chloroform came out of her handbag, and she used bunched up toilet tissue to soak and hold to his face, till his breathing grew shallower. She held her breath for as long as she could and then flushed the soaked tissue in the bowl. He was now deeply unconscious, and good for an hour or two before he came around. She replaced the bottle in her handbag, along with the cosh.

She came back out of the toilet, smoothing down her dress calmly, and entered the interior of the bar again with a smile on her face. Inzhagi grinned stupidly as he waited for her.

Chapter Fourteen

Eve Maggio was a rare sight around the precinct these days. Heads turned when the gorgeous redhead turned up, and Bonetti knew of her arrival by the wolf-whistles that heralded her. This was her second year at the precinct, and she had been transferred from southern Italy because her face was getting too well known by too many Sicilians. She could best be described as a part-time lover, for her work in Narcotics meant she flitted in and out of his life all too infrequently, sometimes away for months on some case or other.

But her absence made their reunions all the sweeter. Bitter sweet on occasion, but when they were sweet, they were sweet indeed. The woman had won his heart when he thought himself done with women. His estranged wife had seen to that. After the bitch left him and took his kids, he hated women for a long time, and then this one just walked into his life. She had a certain something 'extra', which most women did not have. Their little secret, which would forever remain just between the two of them.

Reminiscing, he had had no time to think it over. She had his pants off on the first night they met, giving him the best blow-job he had ever had. She was ever a one for making instant decisions, and she had obviously decided she wanted him in her life. Bonetti was in love with her, surprising himself, and he openly admitted it, though Eve herself would not speak of her own feelings for him. But hey, she was with him, so that must mean something, he told himself.

Truth to tell, their relationship was often stormy, with Eve often just satisfied to go out with a meal for him and then back to her own apartment. Bonetti, being a red-blooded man, often wanted more, and it hurt his pride when she 'wasn't in the mood'. She could sometimes be 'not in the mood' for months on end, frustrating the hell out of him, and then he would take a drink or two, to help while away the lonely hours. Then all of a sudden she would turn up, often after he had had too much of a drink to perform adequately, and expect him to make love to her. What was he supposed to do? Say no? Any reluctance soon vanished when she melted into his arms.

Chances happened all too infrequently these days, so he made the attempt, and more often than not failed to satisfy one of them, for she was never happy unless he came too, and sometimes he put so much effort into pleasing her, that he was too tired to climax himself.

It was alright for women. Most of them just lay there and let the man do all the work, and tiring work it was too at his age of 49. Pleasant, but tiring nevertheless. Police medicals were getting harder to pass each year. Lack of exercise with this desk job was what he blamed for his bulging waistline. He didn't overeat or over-drink, just enjoyed life in moderation. Sex was a great exercise too, and one he wanted to perform, but Eve all too often was unavailable. Still an attractive man, he was not without other offers from women of various ages. They didn't have the same 'attraction', and he was nothing if not faithful to Eve. Trouble was he didn't know if she remained faithful to him during her absences.

The slightly askew nose was the only vague mar to her beauty, and her body was to die for. Those tits needed no bra. He could see the way his own men acted around her, and his relationship with her was an open secret within the precinct. How then did she handle all the attention when on assignment elsewhere? It was best not to dwell on it, he thought. All the men in his department fantasised about her. If they only knew, chuckled Bonetti to himself.

"Damn it's good to see you." He embraced her, hugging her to him. Eve responded momentarily, and then broke away.

"Good to see you, too, but not in public. You know I don't like other people seeing us together." It was a response he was well-used to by now. She always had to be in control of this relationship, and at times he found it hard to take a backseat and let her do all the driving.

"Christ Eve, everyone knows we're seeing each other. Who cares? You're single, I'm separated," he complained.

"Our bosses might not like it," she admonished, then blew him a kiss by way of apology. "I'm back in town for a week or two. Rumours of some of the Mafia's hard-men moving drugs. Millions of tourists, and Billions to be made getting them hooked on heroin and crack."

"You free for dinner tonight?" Bonetti asked hopefully. Eve smiled.

"I may be," she answered coyly. "So what are you up to lately ? Anything I can help with? It'll be a day or two before my assignment's fully mapped out. Until then I'm more or less a free agent," she admitted.

"This forthcoming Nato Summit. Falco has volunteered me to head up the security arrangements. The bastard!" He pulled a face.

"Look at it as his way of expressing his confidence in your abilities," she chuckled.

"Confidence my ass. You know he's just looking for me to screw up so he can fire my ass. He and I have never seen eye to eye."

"You have to give a little. Remember Confucius," Eve suggested, sitting on the edge of his desk so that her skirt rode up a little to reveal one curvaceous thigh, which Bonetti couldn't help but notice. His mind started wandering again, remembering the detail of the snake tattoo, which seemed to crawl out of her pubic hair. "A snake in her Garden of Eden", was how she described it, and that was just what it looked like. Eve, the temptress who had corrupted Adam, with a little help from the snake. It seemed appropriate somehow. The tattooist must have gotten quite a shock when she had shown him where she had wanted the tattoo, and what he found in the undergrowth.

"Your boss can't be as much of an asshole as Falco," Bonetti chuckled.

"All bosses are assholes. Just some are bigger than others," Eve agreed chuckling.

"Come on then." Bonetti put his coat on and then started walking her out of the building. "Over dinner I'll tell you about this terrorist I'm trying to find."

"I can't wait," smiled Eve, taking his arm, and walking with him to the lift. Envious eyes followed the couple out of the building.

"Bet he'll have a smile on his face when he comes in tomorrow morning," chuckled one of them.

"Make a welcome change," another of Bonetti's men complained.

*   *   *

Falcone nodded to a few fellow priests on his way to meet with Achille Ratti. Answerable to the full council, Falcone's first loyalty was to the man who had made him a Chosen, offering him the precious Blood of Christ which had kept him in the best of health, looking no more than a man in his early forties, though in fact he was over eighty. Ratti, it was, that had made the decision, and it was to him that he looked upon as his patron.

He had been a trainer at one of the many diverse Sword of Solomon camps in the north of Italy. His wartime service for the American OSS had been of benefit, enabling him to pass on his many clandestine skills to would-be Solomon recruits.

The aged walls rang with the slap of leather on stone as he walked the many underground corridors to where Achille Ratti maintained his chambers. Aware of his aged appearance, and wary of Borgia and his machinations, Ratti kept himself quite removed from the everyday hubbub of life in the secret city.

Cctv cameras followed his movements along the corridors as he neared his destination, yet he still needed to pass a retinal scan, before the final door would open for him. Ratti was extremely careful of his security, even among his so-called friends and fellow council members. Falcone agreed that he was wise to fear Borgia, The man gave him the creeps.

He took the opportunity to clean his glasses whilst he waited for the door to unlock, and then replaced them before entering the darkened chambers. In truth, he no longer needed them, since becoming Chosen, but wearing them was a habit he found difficult to break, and so had resorted to changing the lenses for plain glass. "Good evening, your Eminence," he greeted Ratti.

"Ah, Marco. So prompt, as ever. What would I do without you?" the older man chuckled throatily. Falcone refrained from commenting on the obvious goad. The old man sometimes liked to play word-games with him, for he remained suspicious even of his friends. Borgia's constant antimony towards him was unnerving. They had almost come to blows a few times in the middle of council meetings.

Ratti was indeed fearful of his rival, yet it was as though something inside him just could not remain quiet in the face of Borgia's such insolent disregard for the views of the other council members. "I take it you are involved in Borgia's latest scheme?" Ratti asked, although he already knew the answer.

"Excellence, you know I must follow the wishes of the Council, and you yourself were there when the vote was taken."

"I was indeed, and your involvement could be indeed auspicious. For you know well the risks Borgia is taking to save face?"

"Yes Excellence. I know of her bloodline, though she herself does not. It was explained to me before I agreed to participate in this operation. It is of the greatest importance that her life be maintained if we do not capture Gabriel. She is our only remaining source of Blood of Christ now Michael is gone," he admitted.

"You taught the mother, I believe," Ratti commented almost nonchalantly, though the nuance hinted that he knew more of their relationship.

"Yes Excellence. I said a prayer for her when I heard the news of her death. She was a fine woman, and a good servant to the Church," Falcone commented.

"Yes, a pity," Ratti agreed.

"Do you think Gabriel has indeed found out that she is his child, and that is the reason he seeks her out?" Falcone asked. "The mother herself knew nothing of her child. She was told it was stillborn."

"It would seem so. Although we have told her it is his pride at finding out a supposed dead foe still exists that causes him to seek her, the child is not stupid. She is after all, one of our best operatives. Next to yourself, of course." Falcone bowed his head in quiet acknowledgement of his own standing in the Sword of Solomon.

"If it pleases you, Eminence." Humility was a game played all too well within these dark chambers.

"Indeed it does, Falcone. Indeed it does." Ratti poured himself a glass of wine, and a second for Falcone, which he took gratefully. The old man sipped pensively. "Although her blood is basically the same as her father's, Belle's blood is seemingly diluted by her age. The older the source, the more efficacious it seems, and Belle is younger than you yourself. Our scientists remain hopeful of replicating it, nevertheless. While we have a steady supply of it, it will supplement existing stocks. But if it should be lost to us, and Borgia blamed . . . ." he smiled strangely, as his words sank in with Falcone.

"But Eminence, if it lost, it is lost. What will we do when stocks run out ? They are already severely depleted. Gabriel remains the only source," he asked, bewildered by the old man's strategy.

"I will explain." Ratti continued, and he talked long into the night.

* * *

Belle soaked in the bathtub in her apartment, sipping from a glass of iced rum as she let her toes play with the ornate taps, and mused over recent events. She had enjoyed the walks to St Bartholeme's over the last couple of days. She had followed instructions, taking her time, and keeping to the one route. The team of agents in place were all avidly listening in constantly on the discreet throat microphone she wore. The battery wasn't too big, but powerful enough for the duration of the walk, and nestled discreetly under her habit.

She often stopped for a cappuccino at a street-side bar as part of her routine. The days were hot, particularly so when wearing the restrictive clothes of a nun. She had made sure to choose an establishment with only one way in and one way out, so as to be easily covered by the team of watchers.

She didn't know how long she had to act as bait, but if Gabriel fancied his chances, then he would be in for a warm welcome. Surely he wouldn't dare beard the Church in its own lair? Yet looking at his file, daring audacious moves like this were one of his trademarks. She had made one mistake in her last encounter, and had thought about it time and again over the years. She had underestimated the speed of his healing factor, had not expected him to regain his mobility so quickly, and distracted by the fight with Lucifer, who was no easy mark either, he had surprisingly interfered at an inopportune time, seizing the initiative, and using it before she could react.

She swallowed the Pusser's rum slowly, taking it neat this time, wanting to savour it as it slowly slid down her throat, burning its way down. Alcohol itself was a poison, few people realized. Depending upon the dosage, it could be as fatal as say arsenic. Yet many poisons were pleasant enough to the taste, and some taken in small doses could prove beneficial within certain conditions.

Since that day on the farm, Belle had taken a perverse and intense interest in poisons, reading and experimenting with many chemical concoctions, and natural poisons in snake toxins, plant extracts etc. She considered herself an expert, and often carried a few of her latest favourites around with her, along with an antidote or two. Truth be told, she was trying to develop a universal vaccine, not so much as a benefit to mankind, more for her own convenience. She often mused with the idea of publishing some of her findings in the scientific and medical journals under a nom de plume.

She took another sip of the dark rum, enjoying the bite as it trickled down her throat. She had left the large picture window opened, and the night-time sounds of the city floated in through the bathroom door. People's voices drifted up in vague snatched from the streets below. Engines raced, and horns blared loudly occasionally. In the distance the odd police siren could be heard.

Rome was one of the finest cities in the world, yet it shared its vices with most of the others. A thin veneer of culture needed only the scraping of a fingernail to reveal the harsh reality under the surface. Belle was familiar with both those worlds, yet she had stopped thinking of herself as wholly human the morning they dragged her out of the sea near Marseilles. That time she should have died.

The bullet wound recovery was miraculous enough, though not a fatal wound, but that knife missed its target by centimeters, and the fall itself was enough to kill most people. Yet she had survived.

Unconscious, she had floated on the tide, finally rescued by her fellow agents, and hospitalized prior to Ryan arriving on the scene, spitting blood because he had been too late to supervise the operation himself. He looked upon Belle as the daughter he had never had. Always taking an interest in her 'career', and putting his influence to work to assure she rose rapidly through the ranks to a position of influence within the clandestine organization.

Had he known what she had become? Had any of them? She had not formally been given Blood of Christ. She was not Chosen, born with a unique blood-group. Over the years, once she had reached maturity, all signs of ageing had ceased.

On these quiet evenings, Belle thought a lot about the world, and her place in it, the things she had done at the behest of others. Faith was one thing, but blind faith could sometimes be misplaced. She was tired of this constant war between the Church and the Mafia. Yet who else could serve the Church in the same capacity as herself? They had given her so much. Could she really turn her back on them?

The in-fighting within the organization was getting so irritating. The Devil's Nun, and Helle's Belle, they called her behind her back, these days, jealous of her influence and relationship with Alonso. She kept the worst of the insults to herself, though refraining from administering her own brand of justice. She could be just as cruel as Borgia in her own way. She had gone as high in the organization as she could go. What remained as a challenge for her?

Best not to think of such as things whilst she was busy with this present mission. Such thoughts could wait until after the great Gabriel was laid low. Payback was a bitch, and she owed him.

*　　*　　*

Laura and Inzhagi came out of the Chat Noire arm in arm, laughing and giggling, as the doorman called for a taxi. The cab pulled up at the kerb, and the old driver leaned back to open the rear door. Laura went to climb into the back of the cab, squealing loudly as Inzhagi's hand went up the back of her dress, and she fell into the rear of the cab as Inzhagi and the cab driver laughed coarsely. The cab driver was well-used to chauffeuring Inzhagi and his whores.

Inzhagi got into the back of the cab with her, whispering something to the driver that caused more loud laughter, and closed the door. The black cab pulled away, with the sound of more raucous laughter coming from inside, which the doorman could still hear, as it went off down the street.

Inzhagi was all over her, hands roaming freely as he pressed his lips to hers eagerly. Laura returned his clumsy embraces, though not keen on putting on a show for the grinning old timer who adjusted his rearview mirror to keep an eye on what was happening in the back seat.

"Easy, tiger," she chuckled, trying not to struggle too hard, not wanting to dissuade him from what he thought was going to be a night of passion. "Ohhhh!" she gasped, as Inzhagi's hand freed one bare breast from inside her bodice, and his hot mouth went down to suckle on her turgid nipple. Embarassed, she glared at the grinning wizened face in the rearview mirror. He was getting a good 'tip' tonight, that was for sure. She hoped he would pay at least some attention on the road ahead.

The driver was indeed finding it hard to concentrate on his driving. The leggy blonde getting felt up on the back-seat was a real looker, much higher class than he usually had in his cab. Lucky bastard had his hand up her dress now, and then quickly he corrected his steering, only slightly brushing the kerb.

Inzhagi forced Laura's hand down to his bulging crotch, and she feigned passion, her breast wet in his mouth, as she massaged his swollen length through his trousers. "Ohhh baby, such a big one . . . ." she faked her enthusiasm, fingers squeezing.

*　　*　　*

When the cab eventually pulled up outside Inzhagi's apartment building, the passengers got out, Laura smoothing down her evening dress, and wiping the back of her hand across her mouth. Her lipstick was a bit smudged, and she smiled wantonly at the old cab driver, who chuckled at her brazen attitude. The apartment building was right out in the sticks, obviously chosen to be as far away from his office and his home as possible. His wife would not be very likely to drop by unannounced even if she did know about it, which Laura doubted.

Inzhagi pulled out a wad of lira to pay the old man, and then handed over the black silk G-string as a tip. "Keep them," he laughed. "She won't be needing them for the rest of the night," he added, laughing. The old man held them up to his nose, and he inhaled deeply, and then sighed as he hung them from his rearview mirror.

Not a bit nonplussed, Laura sidled up to the open window. "I might want them back later. It gets draughty under here," she chuckled, raising her dress slightly to get the old man's attention. "Hang around for an hour or so," she whispered hurriedly, so Inzhagi couldn't hear. "Give me a ride back into town, and I'll give you a better ride in the back seat." The old man chuckled, nodding eagerly, and then pulled away before Inzhagi could quiz him further. "Let's go, baby," Laura smiled, taking his arm and ushering him towards the building. Inzhagi allowed her to help him keep his feet, as the night air sobered him up a little, and he managed to remember the door code successfully, punching in the right numbers which made the electronic lock open. In they went, and took the lift to the seventeenth floor, enjoying a passionate embrace on the way, as Inzhagi couldn't keep his hands off her.

His keys opened the door to his apartment, and the two of them went inside. Not too shabby, Laura thought to herself. If his wife knew how much of his salary he ferreted away to lavish on this pussy-palace she'd probably kill him. The view out the large picture window gave a good panorama on the nightlights of Rome.

Inzhagi was taking off his coat, and Laura went over to the bed, sizing it up, nice and large, metal frame and headboard. It would do for what she had in mind. "Get undressed, baby. Party time!" she giggled as she first put her handbag down on the dresser table, and then reached behind her to unzip her dress.

Inzhagi's eyes widened as Laura allowed the dress to fall around her ankles, standing there naked but for her hold up stockings while he admired her. She was gorgeous, and no matter how much she charged him in the morning, tonight would be worth it. He pulled off his clothes hurriedly, as Laura raised one stilletoed foot onto the bed as she began to slowly sensuously roll down one of her silk stockings, smiling sweetly as he watched her.

He was in good shape for a middle aged man, stomach still reasonably flat, and big powerful chest matted with hair. His cock stood up proudly between his legs, and as he pulled off his trousers, he reached for her eagerly. "Easy, baby." Laura took hold of his throbbing member, gave it a few friendly jerks, and then walked him towards the bed, pulling him by his dick. "Let's do things my way. How about a little bondage?" her eyes flashed, and she held up her silk stockings. Laughing, Inzhagi was quick to agree, and lay back on the bed as Laura tied one end of a stocking around his wrist, and he held out his arm as she fastened the other end of the stocking through the metal railings of the headboard.

"I'm gonna enjoy this," he chuckled. Laura took his other arm, tieing the silk stocking tight on his wrist.

"Not as much as me," she smiled knowingly, and then fastened his second arm securely to the headboard. She stepped back from the bed, amused at the sight of him laying there, arms outstretched and tied securely. His cock waved about as he tested his bonds, amused at how securely he was held.

Men were just so fucking *easy*, there was no other way to describe them. A modern woman enjoyed living in a 'Man's World'. Let them call it that if they wanted, if they wished to delude themselves. They had passed laws to protect women from overly masculine men, unknowingly castrating themselves in the process. Women were the true predators in today's world. Most women, even the uglier ones, could get all the cock they wanted, while most men had to beg for just a little pussy. "How about a little music?" she suggested, going over to Inzhagi's expensive-looking hi-fi.

She bided her time looking through his CD collection, and eventually chose some heavy rock music. The sound echoed off the walls as she played it, and then adjusted the sound slightly. She didn't want to disturb the neighbours, just drown out any screams from Inzhagi.

"Come on, Anna. Don't make me wait any longer, please." Inzhagi cackled. "Give me some of that sweet pussy," he urged. Laura walked slowly and deliberately back towards the bed. Her smile should have told him something was wrong, but he was still too inebriated with the wine to catch on.

"You'll wait for as long as I want you to wait," she smiled, sadistically, and Inzhagi groaned, flexing his nylon bonds in frustration. She went into the bathroom, and was delighted to find Inzhagi kept a straight razor there. Which meant she wouldn't get blood on the switchblade she'd brought in her handbag. She walked back out into the bedroom carrying a can of shaving cream and the razor. Her face was still smiling, but all of a sudden the smile on Inzhagi's face disappeared as he saw the razor in her hand. "Time now for another handjob!" she announced merrily, reaching for his dick which was wilting rapidly as Inzhagi pulled frantically at his bonds, finally realizing that something was wrong.

"What the fuck are you doing?" he started to panic. The silk stockings were extremely strong, holding him fast, and she sat alongside him where his legs couldn't reach as they flailed about helplessly. Then he became suddenly still as the razor approached his manhood.

"Now I'm going to give you a shave," Laura smiled sweetly, "and just how close a shave you get, depends on the answers you give me. Understand?" Inzhagi nodded, eagerly, terrified. His manhood began to shrink visibly, even before she pressed the aerosol, and covered his testicles with cool menthol shaving cream.

Interrogation was a skill she had learnt over the years in the Sword of Solomon organization. Persuasion always yielded better results than force. All you had to do was convince people you were serious and ready to use that force. Inzhagi had never been more nervous about a shave in his life. Italian men were oh so macho. A few deft strokes of the razor, and he was begging to tell her everything she wanted to know, though for amusement, Laura kept on using the razor.

By the time she had learnt all she needed to know, his foreskin and testicles were bald as a baby's bum. Let him explain that to his wife, she thought to herself. Just one little nick had drawn blood, at the mention of Falcone's name. An unwanted complication, and best avoided. Falcone had been the conduit used by the Church, and had advised him of Sister Belle's frequent visits. How convenient. She knew the way the Sword of Solomon worked.

Her decision was made for her. She would need to contact Belle between the Vatican and St Bartholeme's. One thing she agreed with Gabriel, was that speed was of the essence. You could wait and plan in cases like this, where a sacrificial goat was left out just waiting for the predator to come take it, in the hope that the hunters would grow bored and provide an opportunity. Or you could strike quickly, before the hunters had settled into their hides, and more hunters would be arriving the longer she waited. These hunters were staked out, waiting for one predator, unknowing that a second predator was loose in the jungle.

She had the morning to stake the place out, but she must contact her when she appeared. Inzhagi had said she took her time, pausing for a coffee. The coffee bar then was the logical place. It would be watched, but speed was her ally, and they would be watching for Gabriel, not her. If she knew Gabriel, he wouldn't be far behind her. He had his Mafia friends to help him, but they were no friends of hers.

Grimaldi had been a good man. She had recognized his kindness to her when he had rescued her from the wine cellar, but during the shooting, she had only time to aim and fire. She was given no choice at the time, not knowing whether his target had been Belle or herself. Regrets were wasted. Gabriel's memories of him were better than her own, and the knowledge that it had been her finger that pulled the trigger must be withheld from him, if their newfound relationship was to survive. She didn't see any other way she could have handled this. She must be the one to find their daughter first!

Using the chloroform, she put Inzhagi out, cautioning him not to say anything about this evening to anyone if he valued his life. Inzhagi believed her. Retrieving her stockings, she cleaned up in the bathroom, and then got dressed. Checking the street below from the window, she was pleased to note the taxi was parked down there at the kerb, waiting for her. It would save having to get the rental agency to collect her car from the car park. The less loose ends she left, the better. She took the blonde wig from her handbag, and left it deliberately in the bathroom. Disinformation to confuse Inzhagi, if his curiosity got the better of him.

Letting herself out the front door, the cabbie looked up at the noise, and a broad grin split his features. "Didn't last long, did he?" he chuckled.

"No stamina," Laura agreed and climbed into the rear of the cab once more. "Take me back to Le Chat Noir," she instructed."

"What about my 'fare'?" the old man chuckled, leaning back over the seat. Laura smiled back at him.

"Once we get back into the center of the city, find somewhere secluded. Then come join me back here," she smiled. Chuckling, the old man pulled away from the kerb. Laura's black G-string was still hanging from his rearview mirror. It looked a lot damper than when she had last seen it, and she wondered what the old man had been using it for.

Ten minutes later, the cab turned into the yard of a deserted warehouse, old timbers crunching under the wheels, and the old man got out. He was already unfastening his trousers as he opened the rear door. Laura smiled as she lay back on the seat, raising her dress, and then raising one leg invitingly. The old man eagerly dropped his pants altogether, exposing himself and clambering eagerly into the rear of the cab, as she beckoned him between her legs "Come on, big boy, I want that whopper inside me!" she chuckled eagerly. The old-timer struggled to position himself on the back seat, groaning at the feel of the silk stocking against his aching balls. "Go on, put it in me," Laura urged, giggling.

The old man gasped as she moved under him, reaching up to embrace him, but then her two hands came together on the sides of his head, popping his eardrums violently with the sudden concussion, and he screamed, threshing about. Laura connected with a solid right hook as she threw him off and then rolled him beneath her, and he lost consciousness. Her knuckles would be a bit sore in the morning.

The last of the chloroform was used to good effect, and she left him asleep on the back seat as she took the wheel herself, and drove the rest of the way to Le Chat Noir. The G-string could stay where it was. A small enough price to pay for the information she had obtained, and the only 'fare' the old man would have for the ride back into town.

Circling the place twice, she did not see anything that looked untoward. Either the Solomon agent was still wondering where his clothes were, or his friend had somehow helped him from the building. Her car was still there, and she parked the cab next to it, transferring quickly, and driving away into the night. She needed to get some sleep before morning and still had some planning to do.

Chapter Fifteen

All roads looked the same in the dark, especially the many motorways, thought Gabriel. The traffic was consistent all over the world. Only the makes of cars changed. Some went too slow, some went too fast, and some thought they owned the road, lorries and HGV's in particular. Well, he wasn't going to argue, not unless he was driving a Sherman Tank at least.

Plenty of time to think, on nights like this. Was he really heading back to beard Borgia in his own den? Last time he had barely escaped with his life. It had only been dumb luck that had stepped in and saved his life. But Belle was his daughter, and Laura his wife in spirit if not yet on paper. He could not simply abandon either of them, and certainly not both.

After the debacle in Spain had resulted in Matthias' death, Gabriel had brooded, and decided to travel to blot his failure and guilt out of his mind. Furthering his interests in engineering and technology, he took a series of jobs around the world, to gain practical experience.

*   *   *

It had started in Jakarta in '79, having taken a job as a consultant for Black & Veatch International, who were building a large power station in Pluit, on the Muara Karang peninsula, which overlooked the well-named Sea of a Thousand Islands. A nice name, and it looked gorgeous, but the site itself stunk, being situated on the estuary where one of the many open sewers spilled black water, soiled with sewage, into the sea. High tide often flooded the site, and more than once he and the rest of the workers had had to swim off the site itself when they couldn't get the buses on. A hot shower and clothes in the bin followed shortly afterwards.

Jakarta back then had still been ruled by Sukharno, and all foreigners had to use the military airport, because of civil unrest. Not that Gabriel saw much of that, as it was restricted to the outlying districts and suburbs, and not downtown Jakarta, Blok M and the like, where most of the ex-pats congregated.

There was always the feeling of being watched in Jakarta, one of the noisiest cities that Gabriel had ever experienced. There was an underlying feeling of resentment among the locals towards the foreigners with their money, cars, and more importantly jobs which the locals saw as theirs by right, though Gabriel supposed that many nationals across the world felt threatened by more skilful labour being used where lack of local skills could not be overcome. A lot of Third World countries expected to be able to compete with the rest of the world overnight, and it just wouldn't happen. Ever!

Such countries must learn to walk before they can run, and some of them were so far behind the rest of the world that it would take them a long time to catch up. Thirty years or so of experience could not be imparted in less than thirty years. No matter how much they deluded themselves. Fast-track or no fast-track.

Gabriel had taken the job for practical experience more than the money, which truth to tell he had no need of. Many investments made over hundreds of years had built up more capital than both he and Lucifer could ever have hoped to spend. Apart from a permanently topped-up account of £10, 000, 000 pounds, all the rest of his vast fortunes were invested in a variety of companies on the leading edges of technology, or otherwise donated to a selection of ever-changing charities.

It was a good life for the ex-pats here in Jakarta, and the locals benefited from all the money that was spent by them locally by the foreign workers. The Indonesian women were beautiful and oh so graceful, and they naturally flocked towards the English, the Dutch, the Italians and the Americans because they could offer them far more than their own men-folk. A way out of poverty was all they wanted, and yet they were resented by their own kind when they took up with a foreigner. Gabriel did his best to stay away from temptation. It was extremely difficult.

One night, he had allowed himself to get drunk, blind drunk. A knock on his door at two in the morning was greeted with dismay. John, the Instrument Engineer who lived across the hall in the Garden Hotel, was known to drink at all hours, and liked company. Gabriel did not want any more, and so pulled on a pair of briefs and opened the door, prepared to give him a verbal volley.

Gabriel was greeted by one of the bellboys, muttering something in Indonesian, which he hadn't yet mastered. He had tried lessons, but there were over two hundred different dialects of Indonesian, and all of them seemed to be currently in use in Jakarta. What you learned from one teacher, was unintelligible to the next person you met on the street. Fortunately, most spoke English, Dutch or Spanish.

Unsteady on his feet, he supported himself with a hand braced against the wall while the bellboy kept on muttering, and then when he finally finished, Gabriel ungraciously told him to "Fuck off", in plain English, and closed and locked the door. Eager to climb back into that lovely warm bed, Gabriel stripped off his briefs and started to crawl under the sheets, when he was stopped by a feminine giggle. There was now a naked woman in his bed.

Just how she had slipped under his arm while he was arguing with the bellboy he never knew. He recognized her finally as Yeti, a barmaid from another hotel that he used to drink at, but could not remember inviting her to his room. Not wanting to insult the woman, he did what a man was expected to do under the circumstances, though very quickly afterwards cooled the relationship. He wanted no entanglements. He was just grateful it had turned out to be a real woman, and not one of the many banshees who operated out of Jalan Kendal, who preyed on unsuspected foreigners. Any chiffon scarf, thick wrists or Adam's apples was usually always a dead giveaway, but all cats are grey in the dark, so to speak.

After working out there for three months, complicated visa arrangements required him to leave the country and fly to Singapore, where he had to apply for another visa from the embassy. It took three days to process, and so Gabriel set out to explore the famous Lion City, so different from Jakarta.

He soon fell foul of the taxi scam, which required the first customer to pay for the daily permit that allowed a taxi into the city center. He took it in good heart, and just put it down to experience. At least that was preferable to the cab drivers in Jakarta, who took unsuspecting foreigners miles out of their way if they thought they didn't know their way around. The city literally sprawled along. No sign of beggars anywhere, which was a welcome relief from some of the hideous sights in Jakarta. He had felt sorry for some of the misshapen wretches until he found out that most of them had had themselves deliberately crippled, as organized begging was one of the few 'jobs' that the locals could hold down.

If he thought the Indonesian women were graceful, then these Thai women were in a class of their own. Walking out in public without getting a severe hard-on took tremendous willpower.

The roads were so much cleaner. The taxis kept driving in a straight line as they drove under flyovers, and not zigzagging because they spotted a bare brown arse sticking out over the edge. Public toilets were virtually unknown in Jakarta, and the locals just relieved themselves wherever they felt that it was convenient. Shitting on foreigners in their cars was a popular pastime.

On his first walk along the famous Orchard Road, Gabriel literally bumped into Jimmy Edwards, a well-known English comedian in his day, who was now in the twilight of his career, and touring abroad in the third world. Sweating profusely, the portly comedian with his trademark moustache was walking back from the supermarket, a plastic shopping bag in each hand. Lots of fading stars eventually ended up touring the Middle East and Far East circuits, as the big hotel chains sought to compete with each other and strived to cater to their foreign visitors with familiar faces providing evening entertainment.

The pavements themselves were so clean in Singapore, as there was a hefty fine for dropping litter, and heavily enforced. Gabriel was looking forward to enjoying three days in this wonderful city.

It must have been his passport, he thought, looking back. Something to do with his passport had alerted the Church to his whereabouts. Either some computer trace had been run, while he was out sightseeing, or the Church had an agent within the embassy, and his luck had just plain run out. He had the feeling of being watched as he left the embassy on the third day. The feeling refused to leave him all the rest of that day.

It was in the Raffles Bar that he saw him. Thickset face grinning over a dry martini, on the far side of the room, and an attendant Thai beauty at his side, but the face was looking at him, not her. A face that stirred memories, memories that fought to surface from the depths of his memory. The man was there one minute, and gone the next. So was the beauty with him.

Gabriel had to get up early in the morning to catch his flight back to Jakarta, and so he could not stay long at the famous nightspot. The face plucked at his memory all night, the burning eyes coming back to stare at him.

He paid his taxi off outside his hotel, collected his key, and took the elevator up to the eleventh floor to his room. The key slid in the lock and turned easily, but his senses were alert before the door was halfway open.

Blood, lots of blood. The thick scent filled his nostrils, and his hackles rose immediately. Rising on the balls of his feet, he was instantly wary. Listening, and framed against the light in the doorway of a darkened room, he was instantly vulnerable, should anyone inside have targeted him. Yet all within was silent. Deathly silent.

Making his mind up, he entered the room swiftly, eagerly slamming the door shut behind him to drown out any backlight, and rolling to one side as quickly as he could. He came up hard against the wall, letting his eyes adjust to the light, or lack of it. Still quiet. Gabriel's acute hearing caught no sound of anyone taking so much as a breath.

Slowly, he rose to his feet, following his nose in the direction of the bed. In the dark shadows, he made out the shape lying there. Scraps of torn clothing littered the floor. The woman was stretched out on the bed almost ceremoniously. She had been raped, and then murdered. Her throat had been torn out, and the sheets were soaked with her blood.

Gabriel got closer, careful not to get his suit messed up. The girl's throat had been savaged, ripped open as though by a wild animal. And then Gabriel started, as he recognised the girl, as the one he had seen with the man with staring eyes earlier that evening.

His mind was trying to make sense of it all when the sound of police sirens infiltrated his brain, a sound that was getting louder and closer, the more he stood here, looking down at the dead girl in HIS bed. It was too much of a coincidence.

Whirling from the bed, he pulled open the wardrobe, intending to grab his case and immediate personal effects, and get the hell out of Dodge. He paused, surveying the space where he knew he had left his case. A quick check of his bedside drawer revealed more of his personal effects had been taken. No time to ponder further. The sirens had paused, obviously outside the hotel lobby. It didn't take a magician to determine which room the police would be coming to.

Quickly, out onto the balcony. No fire escape, but only two floors to the roof. Closing the picture window behind him, Gabriel quickly balanced on the railing against the faint breeze which plucked at his clothes mischievously. Powerful leg muscles propelled him high enough to get a grip of the next balcony above him. He pulled himself up as quietly as he could.

The curtains drawn, but lights and music from within. Repeating the acrobatics, he leapt for the top floor balcony. Swinging himself up, he noted the darkness within, and tried the window, only to find it locked. Nothing left but the roof, where he could at least find access to a fire escape and hope the police hadn't had the forethought to block it off before they found out they were dealing with a brutal murder, and the location of the room it had taken place in.

His hands gripped the parapet, muscles jerking as he raised his body over the edge and onto the flat surface. A number of rectangular aluminium vents projecting through the roof gave off steam from the floors and kitchens below. Up here he could hear more street noises. He could also hear someone breathing, lightly, calmly. Someone was waiting for him.

Gabriel whirled around, and saw him, leaning casually over by the roof exit to the internal stairwell. The fire escape was also a short distance from his position. The burning eyes fixed upon Gabriel once more, and the grinning mouth opened in a grin that Gabriel had only seen once before, exposing long wickedly sharp canines.

* * *

"I believe the name is Gabriel?" the figure announced. "It's been a long time, but we *have* met before," the man chuckled. "Although I go by a different name these days, you understand. Callixtus doesn't really trip off the tongue in this modern world we find ourselves in, does it?" he smiled mirthlessly.

"I remember you," Gabriel admitted as the memory came flooding back.

"Good," smiled Borgia. "If you remember me, then you must remember what I became on that fateful night."

"A vampire!" Gabriel accused. Borgia nodded, smiling once more. "But you work for the Church, right?"

"Dear boy, I don't *work* for the Church, I *am* the Church these days!" Borgia chuckled. "You have been a thorn in our side lately, and it seems if you want a job doing, well, I'm sure you know how the rest of the proverb goes."

Gabriel was sizing him up. Big and powerful, thickset, with long powerful arms. The only other vampire he had fought had been a tiny skinny thing, and it had been extremely difficult to kill. He had no weapon. The roof was bare, apart from a few television aerials. It would not be bare for long, for the police would be up here sooner rather than later.

"Did you have to kill the girl?" he asked, edging closer to the fire escape.

"No, I didn't have to kill her. I wanted to. Her death was enjoyable. I am sure you could never understand just how it feels to drain someone's blood like that," Borgia stated. "Her death was useful in that it served to get you up here," he smiled mirthlessly.

"The police will be here soon." Gabriel moved closer, and then stopped as Borgia stepped towards him, surprisingly light for one so large.

"Indeed they will, so let us commence," his mouth opened wide, as did his arms, and he moved to take Gabriel in his dark embrace, rushing him quickly.

Fast as Borgia was, Gabriel flung himself back, quickly somersaulting and rolling to get distance between them. Landing close to one of the aerials, he snapped off one of the aluminium rods, slashing back and forth at Borgia, using it like a sword. Borgia simply laughed, though he was wary of Gabriel's extended reach.

The two of them circled each other in silence, waiting for the opening that they both knew would come sooner or later. Neither of them could wait too long for the police. Borgia too, decided to break off one of the rods from one of the aerials. "En garde!" he proposed, snarling, and came at Gabriel, showing a remarkable degree of expertise with a 'sword'.

The rattle of aluminium on aluminium was hardly the same as tempered steel on tempered steel, but neither of them could afford to relax their guard. The metal rods became a blur, as they rang back and forth.

Gabriel made the first mistake. Eventually treating the aluminium rod as though it was indeed a sword, and expecting Borgia to do the same, he relaxed his guard after parrying Borgia's strike. But instead of withdrawing to strike again, the stronger man whipped the aluminium rod to the side, slamming it into Gabriel's upper arm with enough force to break the hollow bone, and Gabriel cried out in pain as he gave ground, swapping the thin rod to his other hand, and trying to put distance between them as he fought to deal with the pain.

"I did my homework, Gabriel!" Borgia chuckled, as he pursued slowly yet relentlessly. "We have had enough of your brethren in our keeping over the years. We have dissected one or two once they became worthless to us," he snarled, long arm whipping back and forth, as Gabriel tried to parry. "Strong and muscular, yet your hollow bones are a decided disadvantage in a close-quarter fight, if your opponent knows your Achille's heel." He laughed, and pressed his attack, Gabriel giving ground once more.

Borgia was right, and he was too powerful an opponent in these circumstances. Gabriel needed to escape. He simply couldn't win if he stayed here. Desperately, he thanked his own ambidextrousness as he fought on against Borgia's deft and powerful strokes.

"You're right Borgia, my hollow bones can be a weakness, or a strength. It depends how you use them," he smiled back harshly. "Follow me if you dare!" and with that, he hurled the aluminium rod at Borgia to give himself a moment's slight breathing space, and then turned, running for the edge of the roof.

Borgia ran after him, eager to close the distance, expecting him to whirl and make a stand, but Gabriel kept on going, to the edge and beyond, as he flung himself into space, one arm held into his side, the other stretching out and trying to clutch at the clouds, as he soared off the roof, and out into thin air, as though trying to fly without wings.

Borgia cried out in frustration as he thought Gabriel had chosen suicide over facing him, and then again in rage as he reached the edge himself and watched the arc of Gabriel's fall, angling down over the patio beneath, his hollow bones having given him enough of an arc for him to miss the hard concrete beneath. The loud splash from the swimming pool below was evidence of his survival

There was no way Borgia could duplicate such a feat, and avoid serious injury, and he would shortly have the police to contend with. He watched in frustration as Gabriel slowly pulled himself out of the pool, so far below. The bastard even managed a weak wave with his good arm.

Pulling a small torch from his pocket, Borgia signaled the helicopter which was holding position a half mile to the south of the hotel roof, and it came in and dropped a small rope ladder to him. By the time the police reached the roof, Borgia had already made the interior of the cockpit, and Gabriel had hid among the security of the streets.

*   *   *

South along North Bridge Road, heading into the center of the city, and quickly finding an all-night banking outlet, Gabriel used his American Express card to draw out some money, a lot of money, before the police tracked him down. He was now on the run, both from the police and the Church, and he was a long way from home. First he needed medical help, and then a place to hole up for a day or so, and let his broken arm mend. Then he had to get out of the country, and not by any legal means, for both sides would be watching for him.

He needed to go south once more, avoiding the main streets where possible, but needing a cab to take him most of the way. The Empire Docks had many boats, and a sub-culture of their own. One of the small boats would get him offshore, and onto the Malayan Peninsula, or back onto Indonesia. He would be un-trackable on the open sea.

His arm needed urgent treatment first, though, and he flagged a cab down with his good arm, holding the other one stiffly against his side, careful not to damage it further. "Doctor! You take me to doctor, yes?" Most of the cab-drivers spoke reasonable English, and the driver nodded as Gabriel climbed into the rear. Once his arm was properly bound up, he would make his way towards the docks while it was still dark.

*   *   *

The night rolled by, the sky lightening somewhat to the east. Latina was still an hour away. He stopped at a filling station, and topped up his petrol tank, and used the opportunity to use his cell-phone to call ahead to Donatello, and advise him of his progress. He was looking forward to a peaceful sleep, resting whilst Donatello's men did the groundwork for him. Best he keep out of the way until he had a good idea of what he was facing.

*   *   *

The estate was still well lit-up around the high wall. Donatello took his security seriously, with internal feuding still a problem with the Families, not to mention the rare attacks by the Sword of Solomon. Gabriel had changed out of his disguise at the filling station. The sight of a priest arriving at the gate would have caused a stir, so it was his more normal face which he presented to the security camera as it rotated around and zoomed in on the side window as he wound it down.

He smiled calmly, and a bit wearily into the lens, waiting for the operator to compare his face with his records. A click announced the opening of the large wrought-iron gates, which opened inwards on their mechanisms. Gabriel drove through, and followed the meandering lane through the trees, which lead to the large country house he could see across the lawns in the distance.

Despite the late hour, half the house was already roused, and he was pleased to see Donatello himself there to greet him as he pulled up outside the place and parked his car. Donatello came down the steps as Gabriel exited the car. "Gabriel, my friend. It is good to see you again." His arms came out to embrace Gabriel, well used to this Neapolitan familiarity by now.

Two of Donatello's men came out with him, and Gabriel nodded to each, their faces known to him, and the men who themselves recognized the recognition. They were not unknown lackeys to this man, who always made a point of remembering their names. It meant much to these men.

One of them began removing luggage from the boot of Gabriel's car, whilst the other man slid into the driving seat, and then moved the car to the secure basement garage, down the ramp at the side of the house. "We have a nice room made up for you. I daresay you will be tired after such a long drive, but I have made the arrangements as you wished. No doubt you will want to go through them before you turn in." Donatello was familiar with Gabriel's methods by now, and Gabriel nodded in confirmation.

He followed Donatello into a large ornate study, where papers and photographs were already strewn across a large leather-bound desk. Donatello ordered coffee, and then the two of them sat down in the armchairs, in front of a warming log-fire, which Gabriel enjoyed, slipping his shoes off and toasting his feet in front of the flames.

"I have twenty men. They took up their positions today, photographing anyone who seemed suspicious. My lieutenants are going through the photos overnight, comparing faces to known agents of the Church." Donatello explained, and Gabriel nodded. "We have some photos of the girl. I thought you'd want to see those personally," he explained, and got up from the chair to bring a wad of photos from the table. He handed them to Gabriel.

Belle, his daughter. Looking as beautiful as the day he'd tried to kill her. He leafed through the photos whilst he savoured his coffee. "Any sign of the woman I mentioned? She may attempt contact with the nun. I want to know when she does, and I want her covered by your men, against any interference by the Church. Follow her if you can, and see where she goes. Then I will need that information myself, so I can arrange to make contact with her."

"None of my men has reported any blondes paying the nun any attention," Donatello replied truthfully. "Nothing suspicious about the way the Church are playing this. Nothing overt. The nun just walks to and from St Bartholeme's. Keeps to the same route," he explained. "One more day of close surveillance and we'll be able to identify all their operatives."

"I don't like waiting, even though I agree, we need to take the time. They're already in place, and it's their killing-ground."

"You think they'll risk open war on the streets of Rome?" Donatello's eyes widened. "The Eternal City hasn't seen anything like that in many years."

"They know I'll be seeking help from the Families. On my own I'd stand little chance. They want me alive, but your men will be shown no mercy once they get involved. I hope you've explained that to them all."

"My friend, my debt to you and my friendship is well known by all my men. There was no shortage of volunteers when I explained things, don't worry on that score," he reassured Gabriel.

"It's my fight. I need help, but I don't want to get anyone killed," Gabriel explained.

"We are looking forward to it. We owe those Solomon bastards for past spilt blood. They killed my uncle, as you know. If the streets of Rome run red with blood, it will be theirs, not ours," he promised.

*   *   *

Laura was up early the next morning, giving herself a good two hours to familiarize herself with the layout of the streets around the coffee bar. The night had given way to one of her strange dreams, sometimes prescient. Falling rose petals like rain, that eventually turned into raindrops of blood. She didn't know what it meant, though she was used to such strange dreams by now.

She wore a headscarf around her blonde hair as she left the hotel. Laura hadn't been to Rome in years, and didn't think anyone of the Solomon team who would be watching Belle would recognize her. Falcone operated out of St Bartholeme's, and she had no intention of going anywhere near the place.

A typically hot Italian day, and she dressed accordingly, in a plain white business suit. A small Beretta fit snugly in a thigh holster, accessible quickly via the slit in her skirt. She carried a more powerful Walther in her handbag.

She knew the drill on operations like this, and knew which of the typically innocent passersby were most likely agents. Men and women, not too young and not too old, fit and wearing loose clothes to conceal weapons, like she herself was wearing. They weren't looking for her, but for Gabriel, and as long as she kept moving, not drawing attention to herself, they would likely ignore her.

The Mafia watchers were a different proposition, and Laura did not know they were in position, already called up by Gabriel. They had been told to expect the nun, and other watchers. Gabriel wanted photos taken of the other watchers. Anyone who remained or returned to the area was to be photographed discreetly. Some overlooking apartments had been commandeered. Others moved from street to street, knowing the route the nun was to take. The Solomon agents remained on the ground. Mobility and instant reaction could be required at a second's notice. No one underestimated the man called Gabriel.

Laura behaved as a typical shopper, flitting from shop to shop, and making purchases, though keeping a careful eye on her watch. When it was within a half hour of Belle's scheduled appearance, she made her way to the coffee bar and took a spare table, ordering a late morning breakfast to take her time over. She sat back to wait. She was unaware that her photo had already been taken by one of the watching Mafiosi.

Excited by the prospect of finally meeting her daughter, and yet apprehensive as to how the meeting would turn out. How would she react if a strange woman, looking no older than herself, claimed to be her mother? There was no way to tell. She just had to play it by ear and hope for the best. First, she had to take care of the watchers and to do that she enlisted the help of one of the waiters, whom she found talkative enough.

"I'm here to meet my sister. She hasn't seen me for years, since she joined the Church. I should have been here a few days ago but my flight got held up. Has she been in? We'd arranged to meet here, and I haven't been able to contact her."

"Si, Signorina. A nun has called in the last two days. She just has a coffee, and she did indeed appear to be waiting for someone," he confirmed.

"I wonder if you would do me a little favour?" Laura asked, smiling sweetly, using that smile that all women use when they want something from a man. The downward tilt of the head, the coy look up to catch the eye. It almost invariably worked, and this time was no exception. "Could you pass her this note?" she said, handing him a slip of paper.

"I'll just sit over here and watch her reaction, before I let her see me. It's a private joke from when we used to live together," she smiled.

"But of course, Signorina. It will be my pleasure," the waiter smiled back, and placed the folded paper in his pocket. Laura sat back against the wall mirror, her back to the entrance, taking in the reflections. It couldn't be long now. Nervously, she kept checking her watch. Anxiety was starting to take over. Planning for the moment was a lot different to living it. After a while, she caught the reflection in the wall-mirror, as the nun entered the coffee bar, and took a seat behind her.

Laura's breathing was shallow, as she forced herself to remain calm, forced herself not to watch the woman's reflection in the mirror. Be cool, be calm, she told herself. The nun then politely ordered an espresso from one of the waiters, which was soon brought by the young man Laura had spoken to earlier. In the reflection, she saw him pass the note to Belle along with the cup and saucer. The man winked casually to Laura as he walked back to his position behind the bar. Laura watched from under the brim of her hat, at Belle's reflection, the curious expression on her face as she opened the folded piece of paper.

*   *   *

Belle was suspicious as soon as the waiter passed the folded note over to her. She took a quick look around the coffee bar as she opened it. The note was short and to the point, and said simply 'Switch off the microphone.' Again, she cast her eyes around the room. No one there even came close to Gabriel's description. A conduit then? Some friend of his to arrange a meeting? Surely he must suspect the Judas Goat strategy? How then would he attempt to draw her out, away from the watchers?

Only one thing for it, she decided, and reached under the wimple to disconnect the throat-mike. "Don't be alarmed. I'm going off air for a few minutes. Maintain your positions," she whispered into it, before switching it off, and placing it on the table in full view of whoever it was that was discreetly watching her. To casual eyes, it appeared just like a pair of walkman earphones. Belle took up her espresso, and sipped patiently.

A tall woman stood up from one table, and came over to sit at the next table to Belle's, bringing her coffee cup with her. Their eyes met, and a hint of recognition suddenly dawned on Belle. It took a few seconds to place the face. "You're not part of the team," she blurted out, puzzled by the appearance of a woman she knew to be a Sword of Solomon agent.

"I'm not part of the team at all these days, Belle," Laura started, and then paused, unsure of how she should continue the conversation. She hadn't thought it would feel so awkward, to be sat here like this, face to face with a woman who looked her equal in age and experience, yet was her own daughter.

"I haven't seen you since that night at the villa," Belle explained. "Did you leave the organization?" Belle remained calm. They were in a public place, and the knife she had in an arm-sheath could be accessed in less than a second, if the need arose.

Laura cleared her throat, before she went on. "As far as Solomon is concerned, I'm presumed dead, and that's how I'd like it to stay." She took a sip out of her cooling coffee.

"So why are you here?" Belle asked, puzzled. "Why show your face, and interfere with this operation, if you wanted to remain anonymous? I don't understand," Belle said truthfully.

"'I have a personal interest in this operation," Laura went on. "A *very* personal interest," she emphasized.

"What's Gabriel to you?" Belle asked, for if she knew about the operation, she obviously knew it's objectives. "Do you want a piece of him too?" she smiled coldly. Laura shook her head.

"Take a look in that mirror, Belle. Take a good look, and then take a deep breath when you look at my face again," she suggested. Belle turned to the mirror, looking at her own face, hair masked by the close-fitting wimple. Then she turned again to look at Laura, whose own hair was masked by the headscarf she wore under her broad-brimmed hat. She did indeed catch her breath!

"My God, we could be sisters," she realized the striking resemblance, the bone structure was so similar, and the eyes looking back at her were her own. "I never realized that night we met. The resemblance is uncanny!" she admitted.

"Belle, what do you know of your parents?" Laura asked.

"You're a Cannucci?" Belle asked, exasperated at the thought she still had a living relative, though such a strange coincidence that two members of the same family would end up working alongside each other in such a clandestine organization.

"No, I'm not," Laura answered truthfully, "and neither are you," she explained. "My real name is Laura Donovan. I'm your real mother." The words came rushing out, before she could control them, let alone subdue the effect. Belle almost choked on her coffee, sputtering as she put down the cup and stared at the other woman. Before she could close her open mouth or form any words, Laura continued. "Back during the war, I worked here in Rome at the American Embassy. A man came in, supposedly looking for his lost brother. That man was Gabriel." Belle held up her hands to stop the woman, hardly believing what she was hearing.

"Lady, I don't know where you're coming from. You tell me you're my real mother, and then in the same breath you want me to believe that Gabriel is my father?" she shook her head, lost for words, and Laura used the opportunity to continue.

"Look at yourself, Belle. I'm Chosen, you know that. Have you ever taken the Blood?" Belle's silence was an answer in itself. "Yet here you are, looking in pretty good shape for a woman of sixty. You're right, we could be taken for sisters. You didn't need the Blood because you were already born with it," she explained.

"One of my parents had this blood-group, yes. Either my mother or my father," Belle started to interject.

"Yes, one of your parents. Your father, Gabriel," Laura went on, dismissing the nun's protests with a small wave of her hand. "Hear me out . . . ." she asked. "What a whirlwind romance that was," she chuckled, sadly. "We met, and then we parted. That about sums it up. There was an explosion, and he thought me dead. When I finally recovered, I thought he had abandoned me. I was on medication and then went crazy when I found out I was pregnant. Then, when I gave birth, after I came out from the anaesthetic, I was told you were stillborn. That's what Ryan told me, anyway," she paused, sipping at her coffee, allowing Belle to speak.

"You knew Ryan?" she asked.

"Knew him?" she chuckled sadly. "I was the one who killed him. My only regret is that I ran out of bullets!" she swore. "He stole you from me, Belle. Had me crying over an empty casket. There weren't enough tears in the world to wash away my pain." Belle was going to interrupt once more, but watching the woman's obvious emotion, she held her tongue. Could it be true? She looked again in the mirror, the skin-tone, the hair, a match for the photographs and memory of the man who had tried to kill her that night on the cliff-top.

"Ryan was my mentor," Belle explained in return. "He took me out of prison and brought me into the Church. Into the Sword of Solomon organization." She paused, hyperventilating a little. A sip of coffee was needed. Keep it calm, must remain composed. The tale was so far-fetched, yet it contained just enough of the truth to force her to accept the possibility, but then all good lies were concocted this way, just enough of the truth to accept the whole lie. "If what you say is true, my whole past is a myth," she realised.

"The Church lives on lies, Belle," Laura went on. "You've seen for yourself, just as I have, how the Sword of Solomon organization works. Most of the world doesn't know it exists, let alone what it does. Yes, a lot of it's actions are for the common good, but what you and I did over the years, we did at someone else's bidding. Someone we trusted. But I eventually found out that that trust was misplaced. Who's to say that our actions weren't to benefit someone else's personal agenda?"

Belle thought long and hard about that one. She knew the way Borgia worked. He did indeed have his own agenda, and doubtless some of the other council-members had theirs, too. If this were indeed the truth, there would be a reckoning!

"Let's just say I believe most of what you said. Why here and why now? I'm here because Gabriel is supposedly seeking me out, to kill me. Why are you here, and not him? From what I know of him, the odds wouldn't be likely to stop him. In fact I was counting on it," she admitted to herself.

"During that raid on the mansion, I killed one of Gabriel's best friends. He doesn't know about it, and I don't want him to find out," she explained. "I had to find you first, and explain the situation, to stop you mentioning it once he asks how we know each other."

"From what I remember, you didn't have much choice. You saved my life at the time," she remembered. "If you just explained the circumstances, he'd probably understand." Belle tried to reassure her. She could tell the woman was on edge. Then, strangely, she realised the secret she shared with Gabriel herself. Laura didn't know that Belle had met BOTH of them in the past. Neither wanted the other to find out. She could now see their reasoning.

"Belle, I've only just found him again, after so many wasted years. I don't want to lose him. It's too much of a risk. Have you ever loved someone so much, and thought you'd lost them? It hurts, believe me," Laura explained. Belle took another sip of coffee as she mulled over what the woman was saying to her.

"I need to think about this," Belle said, putting down her cooling cup of coffee. Laura's talk was bringing back her own painful memories of Jessica. "Be here tomorrow," she said, before suddenly getting up from the table, and discreetly re-fitting the throat mike, and switching it on. She left the coffee bar, not looking back, leaving the woman sitting there, alone and so forlorn, at the table. "Back on line," she announced softly to the watchers who she knew would be wondering what was going on inside.

"Any problems, Belle?" asked one of them.

"No, just one of the waiters who has a thing for Nuns. Can't argue with his taste," she passed it off, lightly. Walking along the street, she kept to her normal route, checking in with the various watchers. The woman's appearance and claims had unsettled her, and somehow she knew Gabriel wasn't going to show up today. She had seemed determined about contacting her before Gabriel could seek her out. The woman she had known only by the codename Chameleon, and whose name she had now found to be Laura.

The story had intrigued her enough to check it out, and check it out she would. She had access to Borgia's chambers, and that was where he kept his private computer. It would be an easy matter to download files, to go through later on her own machine, where she kept the latest decryption routines. Till then, best keep to the agreed routine. Just in case. Falcone would be expecting her shortly, and she was running slightly late. She picked up her pace.

*   *   *

In Borgia's chambers that evening, the sweet musk of sex filled the room, as the two naked bodies writhed together on the bed. "Yes . . . . yes . . . . Ohhhhhh . . . . Ohhhhhh . . . . Fuck me . . ." she moaned, clutching back at him as he rolled on top of her, his heavier body pressing her down. The mattress springs complained noisily beneath them.

"Hahhhh . . . . ahhhhhh . . . . like that . . . . you like that, don't you . . . ?" he grunted, rutting more savagely, pressing her facedown into the soft mattress. She moaned under him, turning her head so that her teeth sank into his arm savagely, drawing blood, as she enjoyed the sodomy. Borgia laughed, and merely continued to ride her mercilessly.

In the afterglow, the two damp bodies lay together, getting their breath back. At length Borgia got up and began to dress. "I must bring tonight to a close, my dear. Achille has called an emergency meeting of the council, to advise us of reports from his spies in the south. Gabriel was spotted entering on the ferry from Sicily. Arrogant bastard was dressed as a priest, but we have a description of the car he was driving."

"Good," she smiled, reaching for her underwear. "I have things to do, too," she admitted. "I have my own informants to talk to, and information to pass on," she smiled at Borgia, who leaned over and planted a kiss on her bare shoulder.

The two dressed together, and then left together. Borgia locked the door behind them.

*　　*　　*

Some ten minutes later, when Belle was sure that Borgia would be at the Council Meeting she had heard about earlier in the day, she entered the catacombs, and made her way along secret corridors and tunnels to the area where Borgia maintained his apartments. She used her own key to open the door, and went inside, closing and locking the door behind her.

Once inside, the smell of stale perfume hit her even before she put on the light. The faint smell of Jasmine was definitely not hers! She went into the bedroom, and her fears were then instantly confirmed. The rumpled sheets told the story of earlier passion. The bastard was two-timing her!

Her temper rising, she grabbed one of the pillows and threw it angrily at the wall, before managing to regain control. It was best if this visit remained a secret. Particularly if the tale the woman called Laura had told her turned out to be true.

Controlling her temper, she picked up the pillow and then replaced it on the bed. The study was where she would find his computer, and that was where she next went.

Sitting down, she booted up the machine, impatiently waiting for the machine to ready itself. She had watched him often enough to observe him punching in his password, the month reversed, and then the year. Complicated enough for most people not to be able to follow his nimble fingers, but then she had always been gifted with a very good memory. A gift she did not readily disclose, for it was an advantage she preferred to keep.

Once allowed access, Laura began trawling through the contents of his hard drive, searching for filenames, wildcards, links. She found her own name, that of Laura Donovan, Ryan and Gabriel. The files were indeed encrypted, but she was familiar with the type of encryption. A little time was all she needed.

She took one of the disks from his desk drawer, inserted it into the drive, and began to download files. It took less than two minutes. Switching the machine off, she vacated the apartment as easily as she had entered.

An hour later, she was back in her own apartment, at work on her own computer. Analysing the files, copying them, and then set to work decrypting them. She started work on her own file first, and once it was decrypted, she set the automatic program to work decrypting one of the others while she started to read of her own origins.

* * *

Later that night, after the Council Meeting was finally over, Borgia returned to his apartments. He had enjoyed hearing Ratti admit that his spies had lost Gabriel somewhere between Salerno and Rome. His old enemy was walking into his trap.

He chuckled to himself, as he went to his wine cupboard, and chose an acceptable vintage. He de-corked it, and left it to breathe on the sideboard, while he went into his study to check his e-mail.

He switched the machine on, entering his password automatically. Checking his e-mail, one of the files had two or three attachments, and he decided to download it to disk, to share one of them with one of the other members of the Council. He opened his desk, reaching for the pile of disks, when he paused.

It had been a green disk on top of the pile, the last time he had opened this desk. He was sure of it. Now the topmost disk was yellow. Always neat and tidy, Borgia was quite fastidious in his neatness. Someone had been into his desk, and if a disk was missing, that meant someone had been downloading files from his computer.

Quickly he went through his encrypted files, checking access dates, and he very soon found out the files which Belle had downloaded. All the files were connected, and the only possible connection was Belle. She also had her own key to these apartments. Somehow she had learned his password. She was quite resourceful, and, in his own way, Borgia was proud of her. But all things came to an end!

Picking up his phone, he dialed an oft-used number, and a woman's voice answered, sleepily. "It seems you were right, my dear. Our Belle has been misbehaving. Once she has served her purpose, you may kill her," he announced, simply. He could hear the sudden gasp of pleasure on the other end of the phone.

"My darling Alonso, you know how long I've waited to hear you say those words? The little bitch has had it coming for a long, long, time." He could almost imagine her smiling on the other end of the phone.

"I trust you'll let me watch?" he mused.

"I wouldn't have you miss it for the world," she chuckled as she put the phone down, and she turned to the sleeping figure of Bonetti lying next to her, gently rousing him from his deep slumber.

"Eve . . . . what is it? It's still night . . . ." he yawned.

"Easy, lover. I've just had a very interesting tip-off from an informant about your little terrorist," she smiled, gently raking her nails along the inside of his thigh, and she felt his reaction. "It seems she has returned to Rome for a special meeting."

"A meeting?" Bonetti was still half-asleep.

"Yes. Have you heard of the other terrorist known as Gabriel?" Bonetti suddenly became very awake. The name Gabriel was even older than Belladonna. Reputed to have been on a par with Carlos the Jackal. If the two of them were here in Rome for a meeting, something big was brewing. "I'll give you the details in the morning, darling," she promised. "But for now, roll over, it's my turn on top!" she grinned, and Bonetti obliged by turning over onto his belly.

*   *   *

Paulo Frattenzi scowled as he browsed through the dozens of photographs. It was a boring job, but one he had been chosen to perform, and he intended to perform it well. One or two of the Solomon agents were known, and if they could be identified from these photos, it would make their job that much easier. The woman's face masked in the headscarf pricked at his memory, though he couldn't quite place her. He put the photo to one side for a moment, whilst concentrating on the rest of the photos.

Later, he picked it up again, studying it hard. His eyesight was failing him of late in the evening light, though he was still too vain to consider wearing glasses. Then it dawned on him. Far from wondering what colour hair she had, it was her lack of hair that finally triggered his memory. The last time he had seen that face, she had had no hair at all, for he himself had just burnt it off. The woman who had killed the old Don. It had been her who had organized the raid in which his brother was killed.

The face in the photo was taken that day, yet she looked no older. He had heard rumours about these 'Chosen' of the Church, special envoys who somehow did not age. Which explained her importance to the Solomon organisation, why they went through with the raid on the estate to rescue her. Age had withered his own body, and he now walked only with the aid of a walking-stick, yet his wits were just as sharp as ever.

Ordinarily, having identified one of the Church's agents, they would watch her for contacts, but this was personal with Paulo. He would order her picked up on sight, at the first opportunity. He would question her at length, and enjoy it.

*   *   *

Two in the morning, and Belle poured herself a stiff measure of rum, the ice cracking loudly in the tumbler. She needed a stiff drink, for she had just finished reading the last file. True, it was all true.

Fantastic, but fucking true! There were too many details there for them all to be a fabrication, and from Borgia's own files too. Her cheeks were moist with still wet tears as she realised the lie she had lived with, all her long life.

She had lived all these years, believing herself to be the enemy of a man she must now call Father. Idly, she fingered her shoulder. The scar had long since healed. He had come so close to killing her.

She felt anger, but not hate. Hate between enemies was foolish. Respect certainly. Mutual admiration possibly, but not hate. Love? Inwardly she laughed. Oh, this was turning into a night to remember, she thought, and took a large swig of the heavy rum, shivering as it went down her throat. How can I love a man who tried to kill me?

Laura came to see her for her own private reasons. Belle gathered Gabriel had his own, and guessed correctly. She shared in both. She had not mentioned to Laura of her own earlier encounter with her supposed father. Not exactly the sort of family reunion you often hear about. She needed to sleep on it, but knew that sleep would be hard to come by after today. Parents she had never known she'd had, her lover revealed as a liar and a cheat.

She had thought the Cannucci's her natural parents, which made her treatment at their hands all the worse to bear. It had been the Church who had placed her with the Cannucci's. The Church was therefore to blame in her eyes. Her childhood innocence had been destroyed, and her life had changed quite irrevocably, some would say for worse. A reckoning indeed!

Chapter Sixteen

Sleep would not come easy for Belle, as she rolled about restlessly under the single silk sheet. When she did drop off, the nightmare came back to haunt her. She had not dreamt of the old man in years, and thought she had managed to put that part of her past behind her, yet now it was all coming back. Cannucci's grinning face as his weight held her down on the grass. The pain between her legs as her virginity was taken from her. The deep feelings of shame afterwards, the need to be consoled, and yet the woman she had called mother rejected her, unable to bring herself to meet her pained eyes. She had never felt so alone!

Continued sexual abuse followed, as the older man forced her into his bed, until the day Belle could stand no more. Looking forward to a life as nothing more than the old man's sexual plaything, Belle mixed the rat-poison in with the evening stew.

They were both still alive, writhing around in pain on the kitchen floor, when she took the carving knife and castrated the old man. He died screaming, and his screams were the most beautiful thing she had ever heard. The memory of her actions, and her own enjoyment in them, sometimes shocked her.

She propped herself up on a pillow, staring out at the dawning sky behind the cityscape. She had given up thought of trying to sleep any more that night. All that pain, the path her life had been forced down, had not just happened by chance. It had happened because the Church had taken a baby girl from her natural mother, and given her into the care of a pervert, to use and abuse, and eventually force into an act of desperation to keep her sanity.

The lies had continued after her recruitment was complete. The Church had forged itself a weapon, and one they had used willfully. Belle was reliving many years' worth of experience in her head as she lay there. How many lies had they told her? Even setting her against her own father. She smiled wryly as she remembered the awe with which she had viewed Gabriel's own plucking of her knife from the air, mere feet from Lucifer's throat. Her own skills with a knife had obviously been a gift from her father.

She bore him no grudge, for neither had been aware of the relationship at the time. If a reunion was forthcoming, it would be awkward to say the least. But there was a long way to go before such a reunion. The Church had wronged her, and the Church must pay. Vendetta was a way of life in Italy, and she had been raised as an Italian. On top of it all, her lover, Borgia, had used her as a plaything, two-timing her with one of the impressionably young novitiates no doubt.

She had not had much luck with her relationships, and this was the latest in a long line of failures. All things must end, she consoled herself.

$$* \quad * \quad *$$

Thirty miles outside the city, in another bedroom, someone else stirred restlessly in his sleep, disturbing his mistress who slept beside him. Paulo Frattenzi was reliving his time as one of Luigi Grimaldi's lieutenants on the old Don's estate. His mind drifted back to the day that the old man installed his new mistress in the villa.

Grimaldi had been called away to Sicily, and within days of his senior capo leaving, Morricone met the blonde at a strip club called Le Pomme D'or. Inspired by her act, he had himself introduced to her at the party after the club had officially closed, and asked her to join him at his table, later taking her back to his villa . . . In less than a week, he had moved her in, and she had started lording it about over the Don's men, acting above her station as they all thought.

She had been chosen by the Sword of Solomon to appeal to the Don's tastes, and Grimaldi's absence had obviously been arranged somehow. The timing was too coincidental. Grimaldi would never have allowed the woman to be moved into the mansion without checking her out more thoroughly.

She had been put in place to aid the renegade organization in robbing the Don of his art treasures, in a night of co-ordinated raids around Rome. She had insisted the old man had died of a heart-attack, but being found there standing over his dead body and signaling with a torch out of the bedroom window did not help her cause.

Her interrogation at his hands had been interrupted by the raid by the Solomon agents, revealing her claims about the other Mafia Don Ravanelli to be just lies, and the returning Grimaldi along with Paulo's brother Gianni had been killed in the battle which followed.

And now here she was, revealed as a Chosen, the hated ones of the Solomon organization, the ones who would not die, looking just as she had that fateful night. He had long since given up thoughts of revenge, yet now after all these years the opportunity suddenly presented itself. An opportunity too good to miss. Donatello's orders about the woman were not relayed to his immediate underlings. They would follow *his* orders in the field, and by the time Donatello found out about the unfortunate 'misunderstanding' it would be too late. The woman would be taken, and revenge would be his at last.

*   *   *

The morning could not pass quickly enough. Belle contented herself with briefing the watching Solomon team, and avoiding possible contact with Borgia. She was not quite ready to face him just yet. She needed to see, to talk to her mother.

'Mother', the sound of the word only brought back bad memories, yet mother she was. Her *real* mother.

All the files she had filched off Borgia's computer were quite thorough, and bore out Laura's tale exactly, giving even additional details that Laura didn't know. She would want to share in the revenge Belle was plotting.

*   *   *

Laura came late to the coffee bar. She had tried phoning Gabriel, to let him know she had made contact, but only Manuel was there to answer the phone. Relieved to finally hear from her, he did promise to relay the message.

Her presence in the street was relayed back by the alert Mafiosi, and Paulo's plan was put into action. He had told his men of the presence of one of the agents involved in the killing of his brother and Grimaldi. He wanted the woman taken.

The Solomon team operated as a mobile unit, spreading out before and after Belle by a good quarter of a mile, to give her optimum cover, and so they were not already in place to witness Laura and the net closing in rapidly around her.

As if sensing what was to come, ordinary pedestrians suddenly began picking up their pace, as they watched the slow build-up of Mafia muscle on the streets. Already in the coffee bar, this was not readily apparent to Laura, who was expecting her daughter to come in just as she had done the day before.

The first inkling she had that things were no longer going to plan was the appearance of the two heavies, moving slowly through the doorway. Behind them, outside, a black limousine pulled up on the opposite kerb, motor still running. She glimpsed other figures moving furtively in the distance.

Keeping calm, Laura sipped at her coffee. The two men moved towards the bar, seemingly ignoring her, and she hoped against hope this was just a coincidence, but at the same time changed her stance so that the slit in her skirt fell open as she leaned in towards the mirrored wall, and one hand slowly moved beneath to grip the tiny Beretta in the thigh holster.

Well trained, the two Mafiosi whirled on her as one, but Laura was expecting the attack, quickly turning over the table and kicking it into their shins as they came at her, screams ringing out around her from the other patrons, giving her the time to draw the automatic, and get in two quick and deadly shots before they could draw their own weapons. The tiny bark of the small gun would hopefully not carry out into the street, for there was only one way out, straight out, and she took it quickly, as the few customers and waiters behind her seemed frozen into immobility at the sudden deadly violence.

The gun held close to her side, hidden by her handbag, Laura exited the bar calmly, turning quickly away from the limousine, and walking at a brisk pace. The door to the bar opened behind her, and the screams spilled out onto the street. She started to run, and heard other feet behind her, pounding heavily on the pavement. Turning once, she fired off a shot from the hip, causing the pursuing man to throw himself down behind a trashcan to avoid the bullet.

Laura ran again. No return fire! What did that mean? It seemed more like Mafia than Solomon, and if she had been recognized, she doubted very much that they would show any restraint in their pursuit. Pushing her good fortune to the limits, she took off down one of the narrow alleys which ran off the main street, hoping to get to the road which ran parallel behind it, which was a busier shopping area where she hoped to lose herself. Her jacket was quickly removed, and thrown down behind a pile of refuse. The dress she had underneath was a different colour, and might help to lose her pursuers.

Before she could reach the end of the alley, the limousine pulled up, blocking the exit, and Laura cursed as she fired off a couple more shots at the driver as he tried to open his door. Back the way she had come, in the vain hope that all her pursuers had tried to head her off.

Just as she reached the end of the alleyway, Laura cried out as an outstretched leg tripped her as she burst out back onto the main street, and heavy bodies threw themselves on top of her as she cursed. The gun went off once more, uselessly in the air, as heavy hands wrested it from her, and punches rained down on her as she tried to fight back with legs, hands and feet.

It took four of them to subdue the wildcat, but eventually, Laura was beaten unconscious before an amazed crowd, way too frightened to intervene. Hurriedly, her limp body was carried to the waiting limousine, and dumped into the back seat. The four men got into the car with her, and others peeled off to go to their own transport. The car pulled away from the kerb hurriedly.

*   *   *

When the Solomon team showed up minutes later, it was to see the police swarming all over the place. Discreetly, they advised Belle of the disturbance, advising her not to approach any further. But when Belle ordered them to find out everything they could about what had happened, she ignored all their advice and came anyway, wanting to see things at first hand.

A Mafia operation, successful, though not without casualties. A woman had been kidnapped. Belle was livid, as she realised who that woman must be, and ordered the team to start questioning the bystanders. They needed a break while memories were still fresh.

When one of the team questioned her orders, Belle rounded on him savagely. "'This operation is under my direct control. You will follow my orders explicitly, and maintain radio silence from now on. The woman they have taken was a special covert operative of our organization. A backup arranged by me, in the event of anything unforeseen happening. She is a Chosen, and she knows things which could destroy us, and she must be rescued before they have time to work on her. You know what those animale are like!" she warned.

The Solomon agents did as she instructed, and began the laborious task of discreetly questioning the men and women, and trying not to attract the attention of the police while they did so.

*   *   *

In the back of the limousine, Laura was now conscious once more, aching in many places, but alive. Her eyes and mouth were taped over. Her wrists were taped up behind her back, and her ankles were likewise fastened. Sandwiched between two heavy-set men in the back of the car, she had no idea why she had been taken, or where. She was in no position to argue, and settled back in the seat, trying to regain her own strength in case an opportunity presented itself.

The men said nothing as the car sped along. No hint or clue as to what was happening to her. She had just shot and killed two of their number, yet here she was still alive. There was a purpose behind her abduction, but just what that purpose was, she had still to find out.

The traffic noise was diminishing as they drove along. Laura could feel the heat from the sun moving about on her body as the car turned and twisted, giving her a rough direction of their traveling. They were leaving the city.

The hands began to move over her body shortly after the traffic noise had indicated they had left the inner city. Laura stiffened, though helpless to resist, and tried to remain calm as meaty hands squeezed and fondled her breasts roughly.

The two men sandwiched her between them, and she could not squirm away as they enjoyed her helpless state. The two of them laughed crudely, as Laura forced herself not to cry out against the gag. It would only make breathing that much more difficult, and they wanted her to struggle. "Nice tits for a whore," one of them cackled, hefting first one and then the other.

The mauling continued in a detached fashion as the car continued on its way. The verbal taunts were typical and designed to make her frightened. It was something she had endured before, and she was mentally strong enough to remain in control of herself, blot out the fear. It was all part of the familiar softening-up procedure, meant to increase the anxiety, uncertainty and fear. Trouble was, it worked all too well. She forced her breathing to remain calm, switching off her mind. There was nothing she could do to stop it, just let it flow over her.

*   *   *

At length, the car turned off the road, and Laura heard gravel crunching under the tyres, evidence that they were off the main road, and probably at their destination. A few minutes later, the car stopped altogether, and she was hauled roughly out of the back of the car, a meaty hand smacking her buttocks, and making her protest in shock, muffled by the gag, to much frivolous laughter, and the four men frogmarched her across more gravel, before she felt paving stones under her feet once more.

The forced walk continued inside a large house, her heels echoing from the walls as she walked on parquet flooring. Three rooms at least, she was walked through, before finally being brought to a halt. Laura heard a muffled feminine chuckle, and a rasping voice ordered. "Take off the blindfold." Roughly, one of the men tore the tape from her eyes, and Laura recoiled as it almost took her eyebrows with it, making her eyes water uncontrollably.

A wizened old man stood in front of her, leaning on a cane. He was grinning as he studied her face. "Yes, it is her," he accused, as Laura tried to put a name to the aged face. Someone she knew? "Remember me, whore?" he asked, staring angrily into her face. "Such pretty hair," he smiled as he complimented, reaching out and gently caressing Laura's blonde locks, and then suddenly, Laura knew, the fear coming back instinctively as she sought to step back from him. It was Paulo, the bastard who'd used the lighter on her all those years ago. "Ahhhh, recognition in her eyes! Yes, good," he smiled thinly. "Perhaps you also remember my brother, Gianni? Gianni who was killed in that raid by your friends. My brother cannot be here to greet you himself, but I send you to see him shortly enough," he grinned. "In the meantime, Alexis here will make you at home, won't you my dear?" he beckoned his mistress forward, stepping back to let Laura get a good look at her.

Younger than Paulo now was, she looked in her mid fifties. She was dressed in a rubber basque, briefs and stockings. A black studded choker around her neck was her only other attire. Her smile was as merciless as Paulo's. "Welcome, my dear." Alexis smiled, cupping her chin lightly, and then running her hand up and down the front of Laura's body. "We're going to be great friends, I can tell," she chuckled as her hand slowly squeezed one full breast.

"You may have heard rumours about the Mafia, and their 'turkey-farms' . . ." chuckled Paulo. "How we make a memorable example of people who have crossed us. It's all true," he smiled cruelly. "Alas ill-health prevents me taking too active a role these days, but Alexis is more than adequate to the task, aren't you my dear?"

"Oh yes, Paulo," Alexis agreed, running her hand lightly up and down one of Laura's arms, like a butcher sizing up a joint of meat. "I do so enjoy my work!" she smiled.

"It will take a few hours to procure the services of our local doctor, but until then, Alexis will keep you amused, I'm sure. Take her away, and prepare her," Paulo ordered, and Alexis turned to lead the way. The helpless Laura was frogmarched after her.

*   *   *

Belle hovered in the background, pretending to give succour to some of the shocked bystanders, whilst her men questioned some of them about what they had seen. The police were also mingling about, doing the same thing, and sirens blared as ambulances approached the scene.

One of the detectives was staring at her, and she instantly averted her gaze, pretending interest in an old woman who was jabbering away incoherently. Casually, she moved away from the detective, working her way along the street away from him, pausing here and there, not making it obvious that she was leaving the scene. She spoke lightly into her throat mike. "The detective. What's he doing? I think he's onto me." She didn't risk a look back.

"He's following you. About ten yards behind. We'll cut him off," suggested one of her men.

"No, leave him. He's only one man. I'll take him out of the action. Concentrate on the job in hand. Get a trace on that car. I want results within the hour. She's a valuable agent, and we can't afford to lose her." Belle cursed her luck. Nothing was going right. She headed off down the street, turning quickly up the same alley that Laura herself had run earlier.

Keep moving away from the crowds, and if the detective kept on coming, no one would see what she would do to him. Keeping her pace even, she soon heard the sound of his footsteps echoing on the concrete behind her. "Sister, momento," he called out to her.

Belle stopped, and turned towards him, face bemused as she waited for him to close the distance between them. Bonetti approached her steadily, half-afraid he was making a fool of himself. Rome was full of nuns, yet there was something in the way she had handled herself back there on the street. Something he couldn't put a finger on.

His automatic was in a holster behind his waist, in easy reach should he need it. "Can I help you, officer?" Belle asked innocently, standing there calmly, hands hidden in her long sleeves, and one of them was already gripping the handle of the knife sheathed on her forearm.

Bonetti took out his notebook, and pencil. "Just a few questions, sister?"

"Sister Francesca," Belle answered falsely, any name would do. She too was aware just how many nuns were in Rome. Not impossible to check, but certainly difficult.

"I noticed you helping some of the shocked bystanders back there in the street. Did you see anything of the incident yourself?"

"Why no, officer. I came along just after it happened, alerted by the screams. I'm afraid I didn't see anything that would help you. I just did what I could to help the distressed. Did any of them tell you what had happened? I understand that two men were shot and killed. I will pray for them."

"Details are sketchy, sister, but we have a description of the car they used, and a license number. We are already running a trace," he admitted.

"Very efficient," Belle complimented. "Did you write the details down in that notebook?" she asked. Bonetti started to answer her, when he suddenly realized it was her who was now questioning him. Something about the tone of her voice made him look up, as Belle's hand came out from her long sleeve, a flashing edge of steel already reaching for his throat.

Belle lunged, the sharp steel extended and aimed for his jugular, and Bonetti flung himself back, putting up an arm to block the blow, crying out as the knife bit deep, and blood spattered wildly. Again, and once more, Belle attacked, all wrist and forearm in typical knifefighter style, as Bonetti rolled one of the trashcans at her to stall for time, as he tried to reach for his gun. Not giving him any time or room, Belle leaped over the rolling trashcan and Bonetti grabbed for her wrist, twisting as he rolled her over on the ground. More rubbish was strewn about as they fought on the ground, Bonetti slamming a knee up into Belle's crotch, which she only partially blocked with her thigh, and she head-butted the older man, stunning him momentarily.

Seizing the initiative, Belle used her free hand to snatch up a bottle out of the rubbish, and smashed it against the side of Bonetti's head, rendering him unconscious. Getting up from him, she sheathed the knife. He was out cold. No need to kill him, now. Looking around, she spotted the notebook, and quickly leafed through it, finding the license number.

Dusting herself off, she checked Bonetti's pockets, taking his identification. She activated her throat-mike. "Can you patch into Police Headquarters? I need you to pretend to be a police detective named Bonetti. They're running a trace on the car we want. I need that information fast. We have to get there before the police," she warned, and then passed on the license number and Bonetti's identification details from his wallet.

*   *   *

Falcone phoned Ratti's private number, when it became obvious that Belle was not going to turn up. "The girl is late," he explained. "I have tried to reach them on the frequency I have given, but there is no response. It is as though the entire surveillance team have ceased to exist," he explained, unable to give any theories. "Can Gabriel be that good?" he asked. A rasping chuckle was heard on the other end of the line.

Ratti was amused and puzzled at the same time. Falcone was right, even Gabriel wasn't that good. But it was amusing how Alonso's plans were falling apart. "Stay at your Church," he instructed. "I will make what enquiries I can at this end, and will advise you of a course of action within the hour. Something unexpected seems to have happened. Poor Alonso must be in a quandary indeed," he chuckled.

*   *   *

Belle and her team of Solomon agents made hurried preparations once the trace on the car had given them an address. The estate of Paulo Frattenzi, one of the lieutenants on the fringes of the Grimaldi Family. They were ill-equipped for a daytime raid on the estate, yet Belle did not want to wait until nightfall. Who knows what would happen to the woman she so desperately wanted to call 'mother' in that time?

She had heard the horror stories that the Mafia deliberately put out about their 'turkey-farms', where victims were kept and systematically tortured, with medical expertise on hand to keep them alive as they were deprived of their limbs one by one. Paulo Frattenzi had a reputation for brutality, and it was long rumoured his estate was one such 'turkey-farm'. This form of punishment was reserved for examples the Mafia wanted to make of certain of their enemies. It was a very powerful deterrent to anyone thinking of betraying their organization.

Utilising what assault weapons they could easily muster from safe-houses, and private stashes in the city, Belle lead a team of three cars north from the city, on the twenty mile drive to Frattenzi's estate. She was dreaming up an assault plan on the fly. No time for formal planning, it would all have to be sorted out by the time they got there.

She assessed her options. One of the cars could pass for a police vehicle, and they still had the detective's badge to bluff their way in through the main gates. It wasn't much of a plan, but she would have to make it work. Time was against her, here.

She knew roughly how these villas were laid out, with cctv cameras protecting the periphery, and dogs loosed after dark. A bold frontal assault was the best way, once they got past the front gates. One car approaching, and the other two staying out of sight, until access was assured. Then it would be fast and brutal, with no quarter asked or given. The Mafia were not known for their mercy, and the bad blood between their two organizations had existed since before the war.

*   *   *

Back in Rome, Bonetti recovered consciousness in the back of an ambulance, as an orderly attended to him, fastening up his sliced arm. It took him a few moments to get his bearings, and realize what had happened to him.

He forced himself to sit up, against the orderly's advice, and demanded access to the ambulance radio. Once he got it, he called for roadblocks on all the main routes out of the city. It hadn't been too long since the attack, and there was a faint chance he might catch her, but only a faint one. If she had any sense she would dump the nun's outfit at the first opportunity, unless she stayed within the city, and hid amongst the countless hundreds of sisters who walked the streets so freely. Bonetti cursed. How the hell could he get a search warrant for the Vatican?

He tried to understand the meeting. What was she doing there? Two Mafia hoods had been taken out. Had she done it herself? Why hang around, if she had? It didn't seem right for someone of her reputation. The two hoods were just nameless soldiers for one of the families. Taking them out like that would almost be beneath her, unless she had acted in self-defence. Maybe they had tried to enforce a hit on her. Dead men didn't talk unfortunately, and none of the eye-witnesses reported a nun at the crime scene. Another woman had been there. A blonde woman, who was seen being bundled into a car by more of the Mafiosi.

He reached for his notebook, realizing finally that it had been taken from him by the terrorist named Belladonna. What was her interest in the woman who had been abducted? There was an important link here that he needed to discover. A contact maybe. But a contact for what? There were too many of these unknowns, and unless he got real lucky real fast, she would slip through his fingers.

He used the radio again to call in to Headquarters, and checked up on the trace on the vehicle. He was then given the owner's name, recognizing Frattenzi. "Have someone pick me up from the hospital, and organize a search-warrant in a hurry. I want to get out there today, before they have time to hide any evidence," he ordered. It would not be the first time he had gone out to Frattenzi's estate with a search warrant, and on both previous occasions, there was nothing for them to find.

The turkey-farms used no special apparatus to carry out their heinous acts, and everything on the estate had another legitimate purpose to which it could be used, other than to commit torture. The Mafia were nothing if not ingenious.

*　　*　　*

Laura was taken into a generator-room, where numerous small machines were stored. A welding set and spare oxygen bottles was propped against one wall. A small chainsaw was on a bench, as were numerous other everyday tools you might expect to find in a workshop. The generator itself whirred away in the background, but otherwise the room seemed ordinary enough.

Two of the Mafiosi left Laura with Alexis and a third man, and they quickly set about partially dismantling some of the stored machinery, breaking up the components. Alexis was smiling at Laura while all this was going on. Pieces of wrought iron fabrications were broken up and then overturned, revealing a series of interlocks, which were used to then reassemble the different bits to form a new whole, one which she had heard terrible tales of. The Bed!

Less than four feet long, with slight protruberances at the corners, the device was simple enough. Easily dismantled as they had shown, it was no wonder the police had missed it in their earlier raids. A broad leather belt was taken from a locker, and a few industrial plastic ties, all easily available and just as easily explained. A body could be strapped to the Bed very easily, and once tied thus, movement would be impossible.

"Take your clothes off, girlie," Alexis ordered. "Time to put you to bed," she joked.

As the men untied her wrists to enable her to undress, Laura lunged for the other woman, determining to take her chance before the other two men got too close, but the third man was ready for her, and the butt of his gun slammed against the side of her head. She slumped helplessly to the floor, and Alexis ordered the men to strip her before strapping her onto the Bed.

The three of them did so with mixed feelings. The more flesh they uncovered, the more they thought of what a waste this was going to be, for they had seen Alexis at work before. When she was finished, Laura would be unrecognizable, and begging for death, if only Alexis would leave her tongue in her mouth. Even that was by no means guaranteed.

*   *   *

Belle used a pair of mini binoculars to peer down onto the estate. High metal gates, electronically locked. Cctv cameras looked down on the gates, and a pair of human guards was also on attendance to man the phone at the gate post. A long gravel drive lead through the trees which obscured the gates from the rest of the grounds. Good enough.

"You, Gino, with me. We'll use the detective's badge to get us close enough. The rest of you stay back up here till we put the gates out of action. Then get down there as fast as you can. We're not going to wait. If it moves, shoot it!" Barking out orders rapid-fire, Belle's authority was not questioned. The boldness of her plan was admired by some of them that knew her. Climbing into the car, she and the operative she had chosen to play detective put the car into gear, and drove off steadily down the road.

Belle adjusted her automatic, putting it behind her back. They drove up slowly to the tall metal gates. As they halted the car, the two guards came out of the small lean-to, and they approached the gates themselves. The cctv cameras swiveled in their direction. The window wound down, and Gino flashed Bonetti's badge momentarily. The two hoods didn't look very impressed. "Yeah? What can we do for you, officer?"

"I'd like to speak to Mr Frattenzi. There are a couple of questions I'd like to put to him," he answered brusquely, in what he thought of as an official manner.

"You got a warrant?" asked the other hood.

"No, asshole, but I do have an attitude, and if you make me go back and *get* a warrant just to ask a couple of routine questions, I'll take a very personal interest in making the rest of your life as miserable as is humanly possible. Now do I get to speak to Frattenzi or not?" he glowered.

The two men spoke in hushed tones to each other, and then one of them went into the guard-post to make a call. "Wait just a minute. I'll see if Mr Frattenzi will see you." Belle cautiously slid her hand behind her back, out of sight of the hoodlum, while they waited for the call to be made. A minute passed, in which time the phone call to the main house had been made, and a decision taken to let them into the grounds. He came back out, waving to his partner. "It's okay. They can go up to the house. Mr Frattenzi will give you half an hour of his time."

"Thank you so much," Gino grunted, sardonically, and waited impatiently for the electronic gates to unlock, and slowly begin to swing wide. They drove through in first gear, and then as the men began to close the gates behind them, stopped suddenly. Belle got out on the passenger side.

"Hey . . . . what're you . . . . " Belle shot him once, blood and brains flying out behind him to splatter the other guard, who reacted quickly enough to pull his own gun from inside his coat. Belle's partner double-tapped him, before he could fire, and he fell like a stone, red blood leaking out onto the gravel.

Immediately Belle turned her gun on the cctv cameras, and even with the silencer on the barrel, one shot was sufficient to put each out of action. Quickly, Gino went into the guard-post and reopened the gates. Then he put a bullet into the electronic mechanism, disabling it to make sure the gates stayed open. "Let's go!" cried Belle, who was already behind the wheel. Pausing to take a LAWS rocket launcher from out of the boot, the taller man got into the passenger seat.

"Ready to rock n roll, boss-lady," he grinned. Looking out the rear window, in the distance he could see the other two cars hurriedly making ground to catch them up, but they would be the vanguard of this assault. He was only sorry he wouldn't be able to use the rocket launcher immediately. Once the Chosen was found however, the Mafiosi would be fair game. The equipment they'd scraped together was hardly what they would have chosen for such a raid, but one had to make do with what was available. Gino liked explosions.

Reaching into the glove compartment, he took out a machine pistol. From under the seat, he brought out a compact Uzi submachine gun. Plenty of firepower should they need it. Paulo Frattenzi would have a dozen of more men on the estate, slightly outnumbering them, but they had the initiative and the element of surprise. Gravel sprayed out behind their wheels as Belle sped up the drive.

"When we get there, give me all the covering fire you can," Belle ordered. "Plenty of noise, and all from the one spot. I have to get into that house."

"No sweat, boss-lady. You want noise, Gino will give you noise!" he grinned. "Be a shame to bring this baby along and then not use her," he patted the LAWS.

"Just make sure you point it away from the house. Blow up one of their cars or something, okay Gino? Don't get carried away," she warned.

*   *   *

Within the house, one of the guards had, by now, noticed the inoperative cctv cameras. He tried to raise the gate-post by phone, and was not receiving any answer. Not expecting any trouble during the day, he asked one of the other men to go out to the gate and see what the problem was. Then he turned his attention to what he could see of

Alexis' new plaything on one of the other monitors. He liked to watch the sick bitch get her kicks.

*　　*　　*

In the generator room, Laura moaned as she came awake, the cold metal under her back told her she had been strapped onto the Bed, even before she tried moving her arms and her legs, which were now held securely by the industrial plastic ties. The broad leather belt was around her middle, and looped under the four jointed pieces of wrought iron. She was helpless, and naked, arms and legs spread out like a starfish, and now alone and standing looking down at her was the dominatrix.

"So pretty," complimented Alexis. "Such a shame I'm going to destroy that prettiness," she smiled cruelly, trying and succeeding in frightening Laura, who had heard the tales of what happened to the mafia's victims. "You know, they call these places turkey-farms because we process human beings, and turn them into turkeys," she explained. Alexis laughed, her voice echoing off the walls. "That's what you'll end up looking like when I get through with you," she promised, smiling thinly.

"Please, doing this to me won't bring his brother back." Laura tried to plead her case. The words slurred.

"Paulo just wants you dead, and he wants you to suffer in your dying. I can live with that!" she laughed hysterically. "I've gotten quite good at it, you know," she boasted, as she walked around her tethered prey. "The doctor is on hand to help control the bleeding, and ensure you don't die till we want you to. But then again, you're one of their Chosen aren't you? We might not even need him," she mused. "First we'll probably chop your arms off with the chainsaw, and leave you for a day or two. I'll take my time. The idea is for you to see yourself being slowly turned into nothing more than a piece of meat." Alexis chuckled. "All the time you'll be trussed up, totally helpless as we cut off various bits of your body. Nothing you can do except beg us to kill you. A lot of them beg," she delighted in telling Laura. "I don't listen, so don't waste your breath," she chuckled. "Then we'll come back and do your legs, maybe both together, maybe one at a time, depends on how loudly you scream I suppose." she cackled. "Then I think those big tits of yours will come off, and then I'll cut your tongue out. I

179

usually get bored by all the screaming by then," she promised. "I'll leave your eyeballs because I want you to see everything that happens to you, want you to see yourself being turned into a turkey!" she smiled sadistically. "We can keep you alive for a long, long time like that," she promised. "A living, paraplegic human turkey, and then finally we'll use a blowtorch to cook you nicely all over, all while you're still alive, and then feed you up to the dogs as their Sunday Dinner. They get a lot of roast turkey," she chuckled.

Alexis was getting quite seriously aroused as she enjoyed telling the helpless Laura of her impending fate, and the sight of her naked body so blatantly exposed as it was, she found quite appealing. Standing between Laura's splayed legs, she took the cigarette from her mouth, and mischievously flicked it to drop ash down onto Laura's pubic hair.

"Now what *will* I do to amuse myself till the doctor gets here?" she mused aloud, as Laura shivered helplessly. The large room was soundproofed against the screams which were always expected from the occupants, and so neither Alexis nor Laura heard the gunfire that started up at the front of the house.

* * *

Belle screeched to a brief halt as they approached the house, and she came out of the door already rolling towards the shrubbery which ran along the side of the mansion. Then Gino slid over behind the wheel, and revved the car up as he came into the main car park, firing through the window at the two men who were just coming out of the main doors. Both of them jerked like rag dolls as he stitched them up and down with the machine pistol.

Over the radio, he heard confirmation that the other two cars were entering the grounds, and he readied the LAWS, pulling back the tube, and the sight and trigger popped up. He got such a kick from using these things. He sighted on one of the cars on the far end, an antique Bugatti he noticed. Frattenzi liked his cars. A quick pull on the trigger, a jerk and a roar of flame, sent the missile on its way. KABOOOOOMMM! The car exploded, chassis flying about four feet into the air, before it came apart, showering metal everywhere, and black smoke rising in a thick billowing cloud.

"That should get their attention", Gino grinned. Shots were coming out of some of the ground-floor windows now, as Gino crouched down behind his car, returning fire. More shots soon followed as bodies came running, trying to pin him down behind the car. Where the hell were the other two cars?

Belle used the explosion and gunfire to distract the foot-soldiers inside the house, making her way quickly to the rear of the mansion, where she knew there would be doors in to the kitchen and lounge. Keeping low within the shrubbery, it took her less than a minute, during which time a war seemed to be breaking out at the front of the mansion, as Gino proved his worth.

Two hand grenades bought Gino the time it took for his reinforcements to arrive, as the two cars screeched up the drive, each pulling up at either ends of the small car park, spreading out covering fire. They now outnumbered the Mafiosi currently in the mansion, though they had the benefit of better cover. The firefight was furious.

Belle entered through the unlocked kitchen door, to find the chef hiding under the stout kitchen table. He looked up worriedly as Belle saw him. "Stay there, if you know what's good for you!" she warned, and then left the man, passing out into the main body of the hall, following the old wiring where it was tacked to the walls.

Fortunately, the wiring lead her to the rear of the mansion, away from the gunfire, and she soon found the control room for the security cameras. It was currently unmanned. A number of monitors showed the gunfight going on at the front of the house. It looked to be going well for Gino and his team. The Mafiosi could not keep heavy weapons here because of the chance of a raid from the police. The rocket launcher and machine pistols were proving quite effective.

Then Belle caught sight of one of the many other monitors, which showed Laura strapped onto the turkey-bed, and a strange looking woman in a rubber corset strutting around her, like a butcher deciding which piece of meat to take first. No time to lose.

There was a sketchy floor-plan of the building pinned up on the wall, with each camera number marked on it for maintenance and orientation purposes. Belle quickly noted the direction, and got moving. Out into the corridor, right, then left, towards the gunfire. Quietly now, for there were Mafia in the next room. Belle slipped quietly past, praying that Gino didn't decide to use one of the rocket-launchers in this end of the building.

Now left again, finger twitching and shooting the Mafia man as soon as he stepped outside the door. Two bullets sent him back into the room. Not knowing who else was in there, Belle quickly took one of the two grenades she carried with her and threw it into the room after him. Using the throat mike, she quickly alerted Gino. "They're onto me, Gino. Left side of the house. Pour it on, but remember I'm still inside."

The grenade exploded within the room, blowing out the door behind her as she scooted down the corridor. A tremendous fusillade of bullets was aimed at that side of the house, as Gino directed his team closer. Gunfire there was less fierce than from the other side of the house, as Belle's grenade had taken out another three of the Mafiosi. Gino was quick to realize what had happened and moved his men to take advantage, and breach the house. Knowing she could trust Gino, Belle concentrated her attentions on finding the room with Laura. Towards the rear of the left wing.

*   *   *

Within that room, Alexis taunted Laura. The industrial ties were almost cutting off circulation to her arms and legs, holding her motionless, and totally helpless. She was at the woman's mercy, and she could see none in her eyes. She boasted of doing this before to others. There was no one to help her, and her only chance was to beg for her life. "Please, I can get you money, a lot of money," she spoke hoarsely. Alexis laughed aloud.

"They all beg eventually," she scoffed at Laura's plight.

"Some would have pissed themselves by now, once they find themselves strapped in. You're doing well, but we'll see what your control is like when we start with the chainsaw," Alexis sneered. Laura was trying to hold it together, but it was very unnerving, the woman was right about that.

"A lot of money, maybe a million, if you let me make a phone-call." She could only call Gabriel, and she had no way of knowing whether he would be there to answer that call. Her stupid pride was going to get her killed. She shook her head, feeling herself starting to lose it. Her body began to shiver uncontrollably, and the dominatrix laughed to see her start to come undone.

"I'll let Paulo make that decision, though I think he'd prefer to cut you into little tiny pieces. He was very fond of his brother." Alexis came closer, and began to run her hand along Laura's leg.

"I didn't kill his brother," she pleaded.

"Whether you did, or whether you didn't, you're the one he blames, precious." Alexis leaned closer, cupping Laura's chin in her hand, and holding it up, as she leaned down and lightly kissed her on the lips. "Mmmm, sweet enough," Alexis chuckled. "You're mine to do with as I wish, until Paulo comes down. Let's play some games," she suggested, reaching down Laura's body and sliding her fingers through her pubic hair as Laura shuddered at the feel of her long fingers. Alexis chuckled, gripping the captive woman's pubic mound.

Her middle finger began to move slowly, mischievously, as she grinned down into Laura's face. Laura gasped, trying not to react as the dominatrix masturbated her, finger moving in slow circular movements that soon had her hips twitching in reflex. "Please . . ." she gasped. "Please, stop that . . ." she begged. Alexis grinned cruelly as she slid a long finger inside Laura's moistening vagina.

"Why should I stop? You obviously like it," she taunted the helpless Laura, and began working her finger slowly in and out as she chuckled to herself. "If you prefer, I could invite some of the men in here. I could just leave them the key and they could lock up when they'd finished with you," she chuckled at Laura's helplessness. "No, I think this is much better, just the two of us. Don't you ?" she smiled, before leaning to apply a hot wet mouth to one of Laura's aroused nipples, making the captive woman moan anew. "Come for me, Laura," she giggled, finger moving faster now. Laura gasped, biting her bottom lip as she tried to fight the unwanted rhythmic and pleasurable sensations. Alexis kept it up for what seemed like ages, enjoying having the helpless woman as her plaything, until finally Laura surrendered, crying out, and body spasming in her bonds as she was finally brought to an orgasm by the deviant woman's hot mouth and busy fingers.

Alexis smiled as she brought those fingers to her mouth and enjoyed the taste of Laura's moist juices. "Now it's my turn," she announced, straddling Laura's body, her own loins splayed above Laura's upturned face. "Play nice and the pain will be delayed," she advised, smiling cruelly. Then she squatted down, pulling the rubber gusset to one side, and those dark hairy loins smothered Laura's face.

Laura gasped as the clammy wet vagina pressed down onto her face, threshing her head to try and escape the obscene embrace, but one of Alexis' hands gripped her head, holding her there as she began to rock back and forth, moaning softly.

Laura fought against it until she could no longer breathe, and then realised she had no option but to do what the sick bitch wanted. Self-preservation was everything. Anything to keep alive a little bit longer. She put out her tongue, and Alexis gasped with pleasure as Laura was finally forced to perform cunnilingus on her tormentor. "Lick it!" Alexis ordered. "Make me come!" she moaned, surrendering herself to Laura's tongue.

*   *   *

Belle opened the door slowly, but the creaking hinges and now distant, yet audible, gunfire alerted the preoccupied Alexis, who straightened up suddenly and whirled around, grabbing a long screwdriver off the nearby workbench, quickly threatening the gasping Laura with it as Belle entered.

Belle had the gun trained on her chest. "Try it! I'd love an excuse," she spat at the woman, who kept her composure well. Alexis even smiled. "Drop the screwdriver, and untie her. Do it quickly," she ordered, not wanting to take any chances on Laura's safety.

Pouting momentarily, Alexis did as she was told, letting the screwdriver fall to the floor. She took a small sharp bladed knife from the table to slit through the industrial ties holding Laura's arms, and Laura cried out as the blood-flow was finally relieved. Using the slight distraction as Laura attempted to sit up, Alexis put the knife to her throat, crouching down behind her. Belle levelled the gun on her again. Alexis smiled more confidently. "Think you're good enough to shoot me before I slit this bitch's throat?" she grinned, confidently.

The gun roared a split-second later, in reply, sending blood and brains against the back wall of the workshop. "Yes!" Belle answered the corpse, then quickly rushing forward to help her mother, as Alexis' lifeless body slumped to the floor.

"God, I thought I was done for." Laura began to shake helplessly, as she allowed her daughter to cradle her in her arms.

"God may have heard you," she consoled her. She held Laura until she stopped shaking, and then used the knife to free her legs. Laura moaned as she tried to rub the circulation back into them. Her clothes were in a pile on the workbench, and she put them on painfully. "We must go. Out the back, the same way I came in." She helped Laura to walk. Activating the throat mike, Belle was in contact with her team once more. "Gino, we're coming out. Lay it on thick for the next couple of minutes, then start pulling out. Pick us up in the gardens at the rear."

They could hear the gunfire increase, and there was another explosion at the front of the house. Belle lead the way out the rear of the house, and Laura followed through the shrubbery, crouching down when the car came round the side of the house, guns blazing at unseen targets behind. Gino drove, with one of the other men in the car with him. Belle couldn't remember his name.

Laura was quickly bundled into the car, and they tore off back down the drive, with more gunfire and explosions coming from the front of the house. "We teach them a lesson today, eh Belle?" Gino grinned into the rear mirror. Belle looked out the rear window, pleased to see the other two cars begin their exit. Only sporadic gunfire followed them. "We lost Theresa," Gino apologised. "Marco took one in the arm, but we must have killed more than half a dozen of the swine," he announced. "I think I got Frattenzi, too. Old guy with a cane. I put a grenade into the room, and the cane was the only thing to come flying out," he laughed crazily.

"Do the other cars know what to do?" Belle asked, feeling Laura still shivering slightly against her.

"Usual routine," Gino confirmed. "Head east away from the city, and double back later. Hole up for the night and then we can touch base again in the morning."

"Good. Very good, Gino. Drop us off at my apartment. She looks in need of a hot bath and some fine cognac to warm her up again. Those bastards were going to chop her up." Gino swore. "Don't worry, I dealt with their chief butcher," she confirmed. "A little rest and she'll be fine." Gino nodded, and took the road left once he passed the large ornate gates.

The police would be heading this way rapidly. If they hadn't already known Belle's destination from her stealing the policeman's notebook, the mini-war that had just taken place would be soon reported. Black oily smoke hovered above the estate. Best get clear now while they had time. Roadblocks would be springing up all over the place, but planned to stop people leaving the city, not going back into it. Once they dumped the weapons, and dropped off the wounded man, there would be nothing obvious to link them to the afternoon's events.

Chapter Seventeen

Frattenzi's estate was like a war-zone by the time Bonetti and four squad-cars tore up the drive. One car stayed at the gate to check the two bodies, whilst the rest of them roared up to the main house, where three cars were still on fire, and dazed and wounded men were wandering about. Smoke still came from two of the internal rooms, though no visible flames were readily apparent. A few corpses were lain out on the small lawn running between the car-park and the mansion itself.

Bonetti recognized Frattenzi's body lying there, minus an arm. Dead at long last. No loss to the world. The shell-shocked foot-soldiers offered no resistance to the police, throwing down their weapons as they heard the sirens screaming up the drive. He took charge quickly, assigning men to search the house, and round up all the walking wounded.

He used the radio to order ambulances, and more forensic teams. This would be front-page news by morning, and he had best get the site secured before the Paparazzi and other news media arrived. He expected nothing much in the way of accurate information from the Mafiosi. Omerta was still much a way of life with these people, even though this seemed to be something other than internecine warfare.

The woman Belladonna was a known terrorist, with numerous assumed affiliations with the Red Brigade and other known subversive organizations. Could this be the start of some undeclared warfare between the Mafia and the Red Brigade? God knows they had never worked together before. Each group's aims were totally different. The Mafia worked to achieve their aims by corruption not outright anarchy and terrorist activities. Could one organization have somehow stepped on the others' toes by accident?

Answering a call from one of his men, Bonetti entered the mansion, stepping through the debris and still smouldering wreckage. He made his way towards the rear of the house, to the workshop, where he found the body of Alexis. Not much left of her head, but he had seen the woman on two separate raids on the mansion. The rubber clothing was enough to identify the sick bitch. She had a long police record in Vice. Nasty S&M games, and more, on the sex-club circuits, before Frattenzi took her under his wing. "Cover her up!" he ordered one of his men. "She wasn't that pretty when she alive, and she's a lot less pretty now."

The turkey-bed, he examined with interest. Noting and cursing at the ingenious construction. Unless they knew what to look for, it was no wonder his men had missed it previously. The industrial ties, cut up on the floor indicated that someone had been strapped into it recently. Was this the reason for the attack on the estate? Which individual was worth a raid of this magnitude to rescue? Who was this mystery woman? Where did she fit in to all this?

Bonetti's mind was working six to the dozen. Everything had started around the kidnap from the Viale Giulio Cesare. A blonde woman, so they said. He himself had had a run-in with Belladonna herself, whilst investigating. What was the unknown connection? It must be important for the raid to have been organized so quickly. The Mafia must have gotten mixed up in one of the terrorist's schemes somehow. He would need to question the Mafiosi thoroughly, and hope that their vow of silence did not extend to covering up for terrorists.

*　　*　　*

In Belle's apartment, Laura soaked in a hot tub of water. Some of the aromatic oils Belle poured into the water were refreshing and invigorating. She was now starting to loosen up, recovering from her ordeal. A glass of cognac by the side of the bath helped also. Belle came into the bathroom with fresh towels. "How are you?" she asked, genuinely concerned. It had hurt her to see the look in Laura's eyes when she had walked into the workshop. She had been on the verge of losing it altogether.

"I'm okay. Getting over it." Laura sat up in the bath, and reached for the cognac. "Not an experience I want to repeat," she forced a smile.

"You won't have to. I shot the bitch, remember?" Belle put the towels down by the side of the bath. "We can't stay here long, Laura. Once my people report the raid to the Cardinals, questions are going to be asked."

"Please, call me Mother." Laura reached out imploringly and took her arm. Belle stiffened momentarily, though allowed the grip.

"You don't know what painful associations that word has for me, Laura," she warned through pained eyes. "I'm not ready for that yet. 'Laura', it will have to be for now." Standing up, she smiled wanly, to reassure her, and left the room. Laura drained the large glass, and continued with her ablutions.

When she finally came out of the bathroom, wrapped in soft fleece towels, Belle indicated her wardrobe. "My stuff should fit you. Help yourself while I take a shower, and then we'd best leave."

"I have a hotel room," Laura suggested.

"Fine. That'll do for the moment. We need to work out what to do about Borgia," Belle said with a bitter finality.

"Let me contact your father." Laura suggested.

"My 'father' isn't here, and I've no intention of waiting. They'll be expecting me to go into hiding. Now is the best time to strike," she insisted.

"God, you're so like him, in temperament as well as your looks." Laura smiled, and reached out to stroke Belle's raven black hair.

"I'll take that as a compliment," Belle responded. "Use the phone if you wish, but with or without you, Borgia is going down!" she promised. "His time on this earth is done. I swear!" Turning, she went into the bathroom, and closed the door behind her.

"And the same bloody-mindedness!" Laura spoke to the closing door, managing a wry smile. Towelling herself dry, Laura inspected the contents of Belle's wardrobe. Everything had a designer label. The Church looked after her well, she thought. Once she was dressed, she tried calling Gabriel once more, but again only Manuel answered her. Gabriel had last been in touch a few days ago, to report he'd made contact with his allies in Sicily. That meant there was every chance he would be in Rome by now. "Manuel, I've found her. Tell Gabriel I've found our daughter. I'm with her now," she explained, and gave Manuel her hotel address. "Tell him to contact me there tomorrow. I've no idea where I'll be after then. Things could get a little hectic. Belle has a few loose ends she needs to clear up before we leave," she understated the situation, wanting Manuel to contact Gabriel but not to pass on her anxiety.

* * *

The news of the raid at the Frattenzi estate was relayed to Donatello Grimaldi later in the evening. Much information was sketchy, but enough that he was not relishing informing his friend Gabriel of events. One of his lieutenants dead, the estate wrecked and raided by first Solomon agents and then the police. Who knows what they would find there?

Gabriel took the news badly. He had never felt so helpless. He enjoyed his games of chess, yet normally the chess-pieces did as he wanted them to do. They did not take actions upon themselves, like this Frattenzi had done. "I am sorry, my friend. It seems as though Paulo had his own agenda," Donatello apologized.

"Well at least his agenda got him killed, and saved me the trouble." Gabriel was not in a good mood. "So now we've lost track of both women? Not good enough, Donatello! The city is going to be swarming with police now, to add to all the other complications," he shook his head, deep in thought.

"My men are out scouring the streets now," Donatello reassured him. "I have already doubled the reward I offered for information. We will come up with something, I promise you."

"If you don't, I'm going to have to take a more personal involvement," Gabriel promised. "I haven't been to Confession in too long a time."

* * *

Back at the precinct, teams of detectives were taking it in turn to question the captured Mafiosi, keeping them separated, and out of touch. Their lawyers could protest all night long, but they would not get to see them until Bonetti had answers. But the answers just wouldn't come. None of them knew who the blonde woman was, and knew nothing about her other than Frattenzi blamed her for the death of his brother, though that was thirty odd years ago, and that didn't make sense. They had no idea who had carried out the raid on the estate. It had all happened so suddenly.

He was on his sixth cup of coffee, going over his notes again, when Eve Maggio came into the squad-room, her face lit up in the most delightful smile. "Hi, lover," she greeted him with a light embrace as he got up from his desk.

"Eve, it's good to see you. I've had a shitty day," he held out his arm, and Eve saw the bandage on his forearm.

"Poor baby . . ." she fussed over him.

"I almost caught her! Almost!" he explained. "But the bitch got away from me, and then all hell broke loose at the Frattenzi estate." Eve's attention picked up as Bonetti related the day's events. The police version of events would make very interesting recounting to Alonso Borgia when next she saw him. So that was why the radio silence from the Solomon Team. Eve was putting two and two together as he told it all, the mysterious blonde woman, and the connection with Belladonna.

Laura was alive, she realised quickly. How delightful, she smiled to herself, wistfully, and Bonetti looked puzzled at her humour. "I have some good news for you," she related, to forestall his obvious curiosity. "One of my informants has come up with an address for this terrorist of yours," she quickly revealed, deflecting him for the moment. Laura and Belle were together finally. Eve was mulling things over in her mind, even as she gave Bonetti Belle's apartment address. The girl must have figured everything out from the files she had stolen off Alonso's computer. But Laura, alive? Well, if she was alive, then it followed Gabriel was nearby. Things were hotting up nicely.

Bonetti acted quickly with the information Eve gave him. Ordering a stake-out on the girl's apartment, he intended to supervise the operation himself. Reluctantly, he left Eve in the squad room, rushing out to catch a lift to the address she had given him. Eve remained at Bonetti's desk, going slowly over his case notes. If Bonetti was successful in capturing Belle, which she doubted, then one dark night in the cells, Belle and she would renew acquaintances. Otherwise, knowing the girl and her rashness, she had a good idea what her next move would be. Gabriel was the unknown here. Things would really get more interesting if he took a personal hand.

*　*　*

Bonetti's men took up their positions around the building. The landlord had confirmed that two women had in fact left the building less than an hour previously. The woman, answering to the name of Maria Caldone, had left with her new friend on foot, leaving her car in the lock-up garage under the building, which meant she was expected back.

He set his squad up to cover the building, commandeering three apartments in adjacent buildings, and taking up discreet positions on overlooking rooftops. When she showed up again, they would close in. It was going to be a long night.

* * *

Father Falcone held Confession in St Bartholeme's, still awaiting word from Achille Ratti on the events of yesterday. Waiting made him uncomfortable, particularly when he didn't know what he was waiting for. Ratti was ready to challenge Borgia for power within the Council, yet how he intended using Borgia's current operation against him he still didn't know.

He listened to a series of Confessions like an automaton, reiterating the blessings and condemnations by rota, as required of the individuals sitting in the adjacent booth. They related their sins, some petty, some not so petty. "Forgive me Father, for I have sinned," yet another voice spouted the same old words, yet these particular words seemed to have a new depth to them.

"Yes my son?" Falcone queried. "What is the nature of your confession ?" he asked.

"I have committed many sins, Father. I have murdered, for instance." The voice paused for effect. "At this moment I am seriously considering murdering a priest." Falcone froze as he heard the metallic sound of the gun in Gabriel's hand being cocked. "What can you say to change my mind, Father? Surely you wouldn't want me to commit such a grave sin?"

"My son, I don't know," Falcone hesitated. The figure viewed through the adjoining lattice screen was engulfed in dark shadows, and he only got the vaguest impression of the man. He didn't need to see the gun, the sound of the hammer cocking had been all the proof he needed. He felt rather vulnerable in the small Confessional. Just a thin wooden lattice-screen between him and the loaded gun.

"Oh yes, you do know, Father," Gabriel interrupted him. "So let's cut out the bullshit. I think you know who I am, and why I'm here." Falcone was no mug. He had guessed. "Belle wasn't just out enjoying the sunshine walking to and from this Church every day. She was being used as a 'stalking horse' to draw me out. Are you her controller?" Gabriel asked, keeping his voice low.

"No." Falcone answered truthfully.

"Something happened yesterday, Father. Something the Church didn't plan on. Tell me about it," he ordered. Falcone then told Gabriel as much as he knew, about the operation to keep Belle under watchful eye as they waited for Gabriel to make contact, and then the radio silence maintained by the team, after the Mafia interceded to kidnap a member of the public in the coffee bar where Belle normally made a brief pause on her walk.

"It was thought you might have something to do with that," Falcone accused.

"Sorry, not me, just some misguided former friends of mine. Fortunately for them, they're now dead. Anyone hurting either of those women will answer to me," Gabriel promised. Falcone began to see what had happened.

"This other woman, I take it she is known to you?" he asked, casually, voice not betraying his emotions at all. Almost willing Gabriel to deny what he so wanted to hear.

"You could say we all know each other, Father, but yes, I know her." Laura was alive! Thank God! Falcone tried to control his breathing. He had mourned for her once, when he had been told of her death in England. Now, to find out she was still alive, and back with Gabriel, brought him a mixture of sorrow and happiness he found hard to express.

"I do not wish harm to come to them either," he said at last, regaining control of himself. "Time is of the essence. If I give you her address, you will not have long to make use of it. Borgia still does not know any details of what transpired yesterday, but he will, before the day is out." Falcone explained, hurriedly. He gave Gabriel the address, and the name Belle was using.

"I'll have to take you on your word, Father. I hope for your sake it can be relied upon." There followed a few nervous moments of silence, and when Father Falcone came out of his cubicle to check, Gabriel had already gone.

*   *   *

Gabriel drove past the apartment building once in his car, taking a careful look up and down the street. Parking a few streets away, he hailed a cab, and drove through again, before getting out around the corner. "Thank you, my son," Father Patrick Ryan smiled benevolently as he paid the cab fare.

"Thank you, Father." The cabbie tipped his hat to the old priest, before driving away smoothly from the kerb. Turning, and feigning a slight limp, Gabriel started off back down the street in the direction of the apartment building. Despite the way most appearances could be disguised, you were always limited by your body's natural movement. Disguising the way you naturally walked was extremely hard for instance, and Gabriel had used a small stone in his shoe to help change his natural gait.

His eyes moved from side to side, under the brow of his hat, watching both sides of the street. Nothing obvious, but then he was dealing with professionals.

Going up to the apartment building, he entered the drab grey building, pausing briefly to nod to the concierge at the front desk. He took the elevator up. The concierge didn't pay him a second glance, which was not to say the Police weren't paying him quite a bit of attention. Numerous eyes had watched as Gabriel entered the building, but no one had really given much attention to the priest, just as no one gave much attention to the many nuns one saw every day on the streets.

Perhaps that was why Bonetti had suddenly come awake after a tiring night camped out on the adjacent rooftop. "Door's opening," one voice crackled over the shortwave radio.

Grasping the binoculars, Bonetti trained them on the apartment window. Not that one. Scanning along, he saw the priest standing inside Belle's apartment. He moved cautiously around the apartment, no trace of a limp anymore. Bonetti swore.

"I have the target. Repeat. I have the target . . . ." one of the marksmen called down.

"Negative . . . .Stand down." Bonetti keyed his own radio. "Repeat, do not take the shot. Let's keep things calm for now, eh?" Bonetti hurriedly reiterated. "Keep alert. Watch and wait for now," he ordered. Was this Gabriel? Descriptions of him were as sketchy as those they'd had for Belladonna. Only one way to make sure, he decided. "Attention all teams, I'm going in," he announced. "Take no action, unless he comes out without me. Repeat, take no action, unless he comes out on his own."

"You got big balls, Captain," one of the men on the roof muttered under his breath.

"Let's hope I don't get them shot off," Bonetti agreed. "If that *is* Gabriel, one man might be able to talk him out, without anybody getting killed. He needs to know just how many guns we've got pointing at him. If we kill him, we might never find out what the hell's going on around here," he warned his team. "Something smells about all this. I don't know what it is, but it's as though someone's stacking the deck here. We're just missing something, and I need to find out what that something is before more people get killed." Bonetti left hurriedly, taking the fire escape down to the street at the rear of the building, and then dashing across the road to the apartment building.

*   *   *

Inside the apartment, Gabriel moved slowly from room to room. The place was empty, he had been sure within the first few seconds. Faint traces of perfume remained, one of which he recognized. But where were the women now? There were no traces of anything untoward happening within the apartment. It was doubtful they would return under the circumstances.

So Laura had achieved her aim, and found her long-lost daughter. Only logical then that she would try and contact him. He would have to contact Manuel, and see if she had been in touch. Lingering, he wandered from room to room, through his daughter's rooms, trying to get a feel for the woman who lived here.

Admiring the décor, the plants, her choice of music, and alcohol, just seeking an insight into the woman he had only met once so briefly.

If Belle had told Laura the truth, what would she be thinking now? Would she say anything to Laura? Best not to think about it. There was nothing he could do about it now, so no good worrying. He would just have to play the hand Fate had dealt him when he met up with them.

He was perusing the books on exotic poisons, when there was a quiet knock at the door, which Gabriel had left locked behind him. He was at a momentary loss as to what to do, but then decided to answer the door. He did so to find Bonetti stood there.

Bonetti had chosen the direct approach, so as not to alert Gabriel, if it was indeed he. "Ah, I'm sorry, I thought this flat belonged to one Maria Caldone?" he questioned, the choice of speech enough to convince Gabriel he was police, even if he had no badge to produce. Best tread carefully.

"Indeed it is," Gabriel confirmed, for the middle-aged policeman obviously knew full well who lived here. "My niece. I let myself in," he explained, though he said nothing about the lockpick he'd used. "I, too, expected to find her here today."

"Father . . . .?"

"Ryan . . . . Patrick Ryan." Gabriel confirmed, as the portly policeman entered the flat. "And you are . . . .?"

"Captain Bonetti," he answered.

"Why are you looking for my niece, Captain?" he asked.

"She may be a possible witness to a crime that occurred yesterday. Just routine questions you understand, Father," Bonetti smiled, the weight of the gun pressed into the small of his back, as he walked warily around the man, not turning his back. Gabriel had already picked up on the man's alertness. His guise was obviously failing him. A tip-off perhaps, to get him out of the way. But then he was of no use to the Church locked up in prison. What then?

Bonetti was looking at him closely, his keen eyes seeing the cleverly applied make-up and recognizing it for what it was. Take off the moustache and the whitened hair, and what was left ran pretty close to the description they had of the man. Bonetti was sure this was Gabriel in front of him.

"We're both here looking for my 'niece'." Gabriel stated, emphasizing the word. "Let's clarify a few things," he smiled. As Bonetti watched, Gabriel opened his jacket slightly, revealing the shoulder holster and gun under his left arm. His head turned slightly on one side as he regarded Bonetti. "I will assume yours is behind your back? Standard police position?" he smiled. "Leave it there."

"And if I don't?" Bonetti asked, not wanting to sound intimidated.

"You'd never clear leather," Gabriel advised. "Don't get me wrong, Captain. I don't want to hurt you, but I will if I have to."

"Likewise," Bonetti agreed, refusing to be stared down. "I'd stay clear of the window if I were you. I have marksmen all around the building," Bonetti revealed. Gabriel mused, and then tapped lightly on his own chest. Bonetti heard the hard rap, recognizing the sound of knuckles on Kevlar.

"I used to be in the Boy Scouts. Always prepared," Gabriel joked, but moved away from the window nevertheless. A shot would not penetrate the vest, but might break a rib quite easily. "All this for me? But how did you know I'd be here?" he then asked, hoping to get some answers.

"Not for you, but for the woman you came here to meet. Belladonna," Bonetti answered. "It was a surprise to see you walk in here so calmly," he admitted. "What are you two terrorists planning?" he asked. Gabriel shook his head, amusedly.

"I'm no terrorist," he insisted. "and Belle, whilst admittedly a bit of a problem-child, is no true terrorist either," Gabriel started to explain.

"Not from where I'm standing. Both your records go back years. You were involved in scores of terrorist attacks across Europe," Bonetti added.

"I admit, some of the things I did in Spain could possibly be misconstrued, maybe a bit in Argentina too, but generally the rest is disinformation by certain parties, to blacken my name, blaming me for their own misdeeds," Gabriel tried to explain, but the police officer's mind already seemed made up.

"Bullshit!" Bonetti announced.

"Hard to disprove, I know," Gabriel conceded.

"Give me the gun, as a sign of good faith, and we walk out of here nice and calmly. No one needs to get hurt. We can talk this through at the station."

"Captain, I can't do that. I spoke the truth when I said we were related, and we're not terrorists. I need to find her, and when I do, you'll hear nothing from either of us ever again. We'll go away. Simply vanish," he assured him. Bonetti shook his head.

"I can't do that. You'll never get out of here alive if you try anything."

"Watch me," said Gabriel, grim-faced. As the two men faced off against each other, the doorbell rang suddenly. Both men froze momentarily, and then Gabriel walked slowly over to the door and opened it. A second priest stood there, and he had a gun leveled at Gabriel's stomach.

*   *   *

Outside from one of their vantage points, the police could only watch helplessly as a second priest entered the apartment building. It was too much of a coincidence, but there was no way they could warn Bonetti, as he'd left his radio behind on the roof.

*   *   *

Gabriel backed off slowly, as Father Falcone walked into the room. Bonetti couldn't believe what was going on. "Is there nothing sacred to you people? Posing as priests and nuns?" he was disgusted.

"Actually, he isn't posing, Captain. He really is one," Gabriel smiled wistfully. Falcone moved the gun slowly back and forth, keeping both of them covered. He kept his distance.

"Forgive the gun. I heard voices, and wasn't sure what was going on. I'll put it away in a moment," Falcone offered. "Nice trick," he complimented Gabriel, eyeing his clerical attire. "A wolf in sheep's clothing indeed." Going over to the bureau, he picked up the telephone, and made a call. Once he heard the party pick up at the other end, he handed the phone to Gabriel. He took it and brought it to his ear, and a rasping leathery voice spoke to him.

"Mister Gabriel," a leathery voice spoke. "Forgive this introduction, but of necessity, we cannot meet face to face. My name is Achille Ratti." Now *this* was *really* unexpected, Gabriel thought, as he listened to the voice of one of the most infamous members of the Council of Vampires.

Bonetti only heard one end of the conversation, and so had no idea what was going on. Falcone was already clued in to what the conversation was about, and remained calm, yet watchful. He still had the gun out, though not obviously threatening either of them. "Make some coffee," Falcone suggested to Bonetti, indicating the kitchen. "We'll still be here when you get back," he smiled thinly. Bonetti went into the kitchen, giving the OKAY signal at the window in case his men were getting worried. He was not in control of the situation, true, but things were developing, and his instinct told him to let them develop. He filled and then switched on the kettle, looking around in the cupboards for cups, milk etc. When he came back into the room, both Falcone and Gabriel were seated. No gun was evident any more. Bonetti put down the tray with the coffee, and they all helped themselves, adding milk and sugar to suit their individual tastes. It was Gabriel who spoke first.

"Captain, there is indeed a lot of terrorist activity taking place in Europe. Most of it is organized from right here in Rome itself. We won't go into details." He caught the warning glance from Falcone, and decided to play along for now. "The good Father and myself now seem to be working towards the same end, in trying to put a stop to this, by taking out the man we think is responsible," he explained.

"You mean kill him, as opposed to arrest him, don't you? Who is this man?" Bonetti asked, sipping his own coffee as calmly as he might under the circumstances.

"His name is Alonso Borgia," Falcone explained. Bonetti's eyes widened, recognising the name.

"The same Alonso Borgia who runs the big nightclub?" Bonetti asked.

"The same," Falcone confirmed. "This man has subverted a beneficial organization for his own aims. He has done much harm over the years."

"Give me the right information, and I'll have him arrested. With enough evidence, I don't care how powerful he is, he'll go to jail." Falcone scoffed, and Gabriel smiled amusedly.

"You have no idea who we're talking about, Bonetti. You won't find evidence against this man. It doesn't exist. You just couldn't get near him legally," Gabriel explained. "He is the one who has falsified evidence against me over the years. He is responsible for Belle's activities, too. He gave the orders."

"It is all true, I'm afraid," Falcone confirmed. "It is in everyone's interests if this man were to just disappear." He waved a hand in the air to emphasise his point. Bonetti looked from one man to the other. "We can get you computer records to verify the man's guilt, but not until he is out of the way," he explained.

"You, a priest, are prepared to discuss murder? What is this world coming to?" Bonetti asked incredulously. Falcone smiled grimly.

"Murder is such an earthly concept, don't you think?" he replied. "God gives life, and he also takes it away. Borgia is one such life. If you knew his real identity, you would already believe him dead. I will say a prayer for him, but only after he is gone from this earth. Which may prove to be more difficult than you think." Falcone caught Gabriel's eye. Did he know?

"So what really happened yesterday? Any of you two bosom buddies care to tell me?" he asked, putting down his cup.

"A friend of mine was trying to contact Belle," Gabriel explained. "Someone in the Mafia recognized her, and decided to kidnap her. Belle followed, and we think she managed to rescue her from their clutches." That really was as much as Gabriel knew at this moment in time.

"Why? No one goes against the Mafia like that without a reason." Bonetti stated.

"The woman kidnapped was Belle's mother." Bonetti's eyes widened. A lot of things were suddenly much clearer. Vendetta he could understand.

"But the scale of the operation, the death and destruction? One woman caused all that ?" he asked in disbelief.

"She had help, but from people who would no longer consider themselves her allies, once the identity of her mother is made known," Falcone offered. "She had to lie to them to get their help. These are the people responsible for much of the death and destruction, Captain. The girl is but a minor player. Borgia is the main force behind all this. It is he that gives the orders. It is him we must remove."

Bonetti sat there, letting all this talk of conspiracy and subversive organizations just wash over him. None of it was straightforward, but if he could make it all go away, the less paperwork there was for him to deal with the better. "Tell me more," he suggested.

Chapter Eighteen

As Gabriel, Falcone and Bonetti were all sat around the table discussing Borgia's downfall, Laura and Belle were just about finishing their breakfast in Laura's hotel room. Neither had slept that well, despite the comfiness of the twin beds. Laura placed an overseas call to Gabriel's estate, and spoke briefly to Manuel, only to find Gabriel had still not checked in with him. Belle had blood on her mind, and it didn't look like she was going to be able to talk her into changing her plans.

The strong coffee tasted good, though she knew it wasn't doing her blood pressure any good. Still, she'd managed to kick her addiction to cigarettes after so long. Only using one 'crutch' was an improvement surely? "Why tonight? Why can't you wait?" Laura asked Belle.

"Because I know where he'll be tonight, out parading in the limelight he so adores," she insisted. "After yesterday, word will go out. I won't be allowed into the catacombs. They'll take me before I get anywhere near him."

"The Church has wronged us both over the years," Laura agreed.

"Wronged? Wronged ? You killed Ryan for God's sake! Just for a lie. Didn't it feel good? My reasons for killing Borgia are a lot stronger!" Belle insisted.

"Tell me. Let the anger out," she tried to empathise with her daughter. Belle sat there, coffee growing cold in the cup as she held it cradled, staring into her lap. She was almost shaking, the cup starting to rattle lightly against the saucer until she put it down.

"Ryan and his friends let you believe I was stillborn. That crime was bad enough in itself, but what they did to me was even worse," she started to explain, her voice faltering a little here and there. "They fostered me with a farmer and his wife, the Cannucci's, the man and woman I believed to be my real parents until the other day. I killed them both!" she admitted, staring wildly into Laura's eyes. "I murdered my own 'parents', and it was the happiest day of my life . . ." and then it all came flooding out.

Laura could only sit there and listen as Belle recounted the story of her abused childhood, one horrific detail after the other, before sobbing and falling into Laura's arms as she cradled her heaving chest against her.

"Oh Belle . . . . Belle . . . . " she started to cry too, the tears running freely down her face as she sought to comfort her daughter. No child should have to suffer what Belle had gone through. God only knows the emotional and mental problems she had had to deal with after she had killed the Cannucci's, believing them to be her real mother and father.

As her own rage had needed to quench itself with the death of Ryan, so Belle's needed to be assuaged with the death of the man she believed responsible for her own troubles. Alonso Borgia. Mother and daughter together if need be. No one was going to harm her daughter as long as Laura had a say in the matter. She hadn't found her, found Gabriel, after all this time, to stand idly by. Dysfunctional family they might be, but family nevertheless. Bound by blood!

*   *   *

By lunchtime, Belle had outlined all her plans to Laura. Tonight was the re-opening of Borgia's nightclub after a long renovation. Borgia would be there in person to bask in the glory of his hedonistic clientele. Belle already had tickets to the affair. Mingling with the partygoers would get them inside, and close enough for her to make her attempt at Borgia. When Laura asked her how she intended to smuggle weapons into the place, past all the undoubted security, she simply smiled, and took out a bottle of nail varnish from her handbag, shaking it lightly from side to side, although what was in the bottle, as Laura found out, was not quite nail varnish.

"One scratch from me, and he'll be dead within minutes. I just wish it was more lingering and much more painful. But at least he'll know who was responsible before he dies," she promised.

*　　*　　*

From Belle's apartment, Gabriel phoned his estate in Buenos Aires, and spoke to his manservant Manuel. He swore inwardly when he learnt of Laura's attempts to contact him, and made a mental note of the hotel, and the name that she was registered under. He phoned the hotel, asking to be put through to a Ms Louise Tackett, but got no response other than a curt apology from the concierge, who could only reiterate that Ms Tackett was not presently in her room. Seeing his annoyance, Bonetti forestalled his imminent departure by reminding them of the police marksmen around the building.

"If I go along with this crazy scheme, I want cast-iron evidence that I can use to clear up the mess when we're done," he insisted.

"You'll have it," Falcone assured him. "Once we obtain access to Borgia's files, I will copy everything you need and send you the disks. Or you can pick them up yourself from my Church of St Bartholeme," Falcone offered.

"You mean you really are a priest?" Bonetti scoffed.

"You wish me to say Mass? I only speak it in Latin, I'm afraid," Falcone smiled.

"How the Church has changed." Bonetti gave a wistful smile.

"Not as much as you think, my friend," Falcone smiled back.

"Very well. I'll go out first. Give me ten minutes before you follow, and that should give me enough time to allay my team's reservations. Then the two of you can come out. I go with you. I'm not leaving you out of my sight," he warned.

"Things could get dangerous." Gabriel warned.

"If you two double-cross me, things could still get damn dangerous. You don't know Commissioner Falco." Bonetti left the two men in the apartment, taking the lift down to reception, and then went out onto the street, where one of his men rushed over to meet him.

"Captain, we were worried. What happened up there? Is it our man?" Bonetti shook his hand, trying to appear not in the least concerned.

"No, it's been a mistake. The woman is involved in some charity work as part of her cover, and arranged a meeting with the two priests, which she has apparently forgotten. Fairly understandable under the current circumstances, I'll take them downtown myself, and ask them a few more questions. Have a car brought around for me," he instructed. "Maintain your surveillance on the apartment, and ring me at the station if anything transpires," he ordered, before going back into the building.

Gabriel and Falcone came back out of the building shortly with Bonetti, and the three of them drove off in the police car, which Gabriel persuaded Bonetti to leave, in favour of his own, which was parked a few streets away. Then Gabriel drove the three of them to Laura's hotel, as Bonetti gave directions. Once there, Bonetti's official manner persuaded the concierge to let them into the hotel room. "What happened to your badge?" asked Falcone.

"Don't ask . . . ." Bonetti answered brusquely. The three men began a systematic search of the apartments. It was Gabriel who found the notebook, though it was Falcone who explained the diagrams that Belle had drawn out on the pages.

"It's Borgia's nightclub," he explained. "It must be where they are going. She must be going after him herself. God knows, she has justification. It's reopening tonight, and is sold out. We won't be able to get any tickets at this late stage."

"Then I guess we'll have to gate-crash," smiled Gabriel grimly. "I need to use the phone. I think my friends will be of more use in this than yours," he spoke to Falcone.

"I need to use the phone, too," announced Bonetti. "If that's Borgia's club, I may be able to get hold of some better plans." Gabriel then called Donatello, informing him of what had happened, and what they thought was going to happen tonight. He discussed options over the phone, telling Donatello what he needed. If Gabriel was going up against Borgia, he would need help. Falcone seemed to hint that he knew Borgia's little secret, and Gabriel needed to talk to him about that. But it was best that Bonetti be kept in the dark. The less the policeman knew the better.

"Would you leave the two of us for a few minutes?" Gabriel asked Bonetti, after he had completed his phonecall. Bonetti looked puzzled at the request. "We're not planning on running out on you. I just need to discuss something that you don't need to know. Something you can honestly deny if it ever came up in the future," Gabriel explained.

After debating with himself for a few moments, Bonetti shrugged, and headed for the bathroom. "This is getting to be a habit," Bonetti complained. "I could do with a dump, anyway." He closed the door behind him. Falcone seemed to be waiting for the question, and so Gabriel asked it.

"How much do you know about Borgia's origins?" This time Falcone shrugged.

"He came to the council the same way most of the others came, as I understand it. But while all of the other council members suffer from ailing health, Borgia remains fresh and relatively youthful looking. Blood-stocks are depleted, and their efficacy shortens with each ingestion as you know. For all our scientific endeavours, we cannot recreate it. The Council is now fading, yet Borgia remains in fine health. Ratti first mentioned it to me many years ago, and suggested I do well to read up on some of the more esoteric books in the Papal libraries," he explained.

"He *is* a vampire, Falcone. Make no mistake about that," Gabriel confirmed. "Forget what all those books of yours tell you, all the fairy tales you've read, the folklore and old wife's tales. This is a real live vampire, and you'd better know what we're going up against," he warned. Falcone nodded, and leaned forward to listen. Gabriel sounded like he knew what he was talking about. "As you have seen, Borgia does not shun the daylight. None of the old 'tried & trusted' methods will kill this vampire. Forget your holy water, your garlic. Shooting him will only disable and possibly slow him down. A stake through the heart might do it, but beheading is the only sure way I know of killing him. Even then, I'd make sure to burn the body. He's tremendously strong, and extremely fast. I've gone up against him once before, and almost lost. I was real lucky," Gabriel admitted. "Tonight, in a crowded nightclub, we don't stand much chance of pulling that off, so we go in purely to rescue the women. They have no idea what they're up against, and their ignorance could cost them their lives. If I had a choice, I'd stay well clear of Borgia. He doesn't frighten me, but I know it's a fight where the odds would be in his favour. As it is, I don't have a choice, but I'm not going in all gung-ho and trying to do the impossible. I'll take him down alright, but not when the odds are in his favour."

"I can get you into the catacombs," Falcone admitted. "With Ratti's help, that is possible. Are those the sort of odds you would like?" Gabriel nodded.

"Close quarters, and with the right preparation, yes even on home ground I could take him out. We might need access to Belle's flat again. There are a few things there I could use. But let's concentrate on tonight." The flushing of the toilet warned them of Bonetti's imminent return. "Borgia's computer. It's totally isolated from the external telephone networks. How are we going to hack it?" Gabriel asked.

"It has an infrared port, which I can use to transfer data to a small portable computer, with an in-built gold-card modem." Falcone explained. "If you give me a suitable e-mail address, I can hook it up to a mobile phone and forward those files to you, as well as to Ratti. I won't need access to an outside network. Full co-operation was promised, and that you shall have, for the moment. You may pass on whatever information you think the policeman needs. I will trust you to be discreet. It is in no one's interests that the affairs of the Council are public knowledge."

"Agreed, then," Gabriel confirmed, as Bonetti came back out of the bathroom.

*   *   *

The advert in the newspaper ran to a full page, proclaiming Borgia's nightclub as the best in Rome. The illustration showed hints of the interior, where it was claimed live action gladiatorial combats would be staged nightly. Not phoney hi-tech combats as broadcast by television companies around the world, but real traditional combat, as had taken place in the ancient heyday of the original Colosseum, which had been used as a model for the new nightclub's interior.

Though smaller in size, the interior decorators had done Borgia proud, with a sunken arena 50 yards in diameter, around which, at a higher level, the tables and boxes of the guests would be able to look down and witness the combats. Away from the arena area, the gambling tables and bars would occupy the rest of the guests who had no stomach for bloodshed, for Borgia had let it be known unofficially that the combats he staged would not be faked, and would be to the death. It was his intention of paying criminals to fight it out amid the sawdust of the mock arena, or perhaps a drugged member of the public against some of his professional athletes. Either way, blood was always popular with the masses. They would watch, and cheer like the cattle they were, a recreation of the mob of ancient Rome.

Borgia could hardly wait to inaugurate his new club. But matters pertaining to Belle and Gabriel preyed heavily on his mind. The Solomon Team had finally broken radio silence this morning to report in of yesterday's events, of how Belle had sidetracked the team on some personal mission against one of the Grimaldi lieutenants.

Bearing in mind the stolen files from his computer, it took little guesswork to fathom the identity of the mysterious Chosen who had been rescued from Frattenzi's villa. But behind all this, where was the man called Gabriel? It was he that was supposed to take the bait, not the mother. Where were they now? His own teams had reported the stakeout at Belle's apartment. Had she been reunited with both parents, and were they now all laughing at another of his glorious failures? Oh, how Ratti would love that to come to pass.

All he could do was order his own teams to deploy around Grimaldi's villa, for he was Gabriel's most logical contact point. Phone lines were being monitored, not that he expected Gabriel to make much use of the telephones. He knew what to expect as regards security of conversations in today's technological age. If he was hasty enough, or desperate enough, they might get lucky. It was a big IF. He was not in the best of moods to receive Eve's phone call. Sensing his mood, she got to the point. "She's going to try for you tonight, Alonso," she warned.

"How do you know this?" he asked.

"I know *her*, remember? She stole your files and found out about all the lies you've told her over the years. You kept her real parents from her, and gave her to a pervert to play with. Naughty boy! Looking at it from her point of view, I'd kill you myself," Eve chuckled. "Believe me Alonso, she's coming. I don't know whether the rest of her family will show up, but Belle will be there tonight," she warned. "She'll be aware of the alert we'll send out whenever one of our agents goes missing or rogue, and know tonight is the best chance she's going to have to get at you. Knowing that, we can arrange for a nice little reception committee for her."

"What do you suggest, my dear?" Borgia liked the way Eve's mind worked. It was almost as depraved as his own. He chuckled as she outlined her plan. "Very well, my dear, but remember, we can't afford to kill her until we have Gabriel. I'll see to security myself," he promised.

*   *   *

The partygoers and revelers began arriving early, and Borgia's security staff checked everyone's tickets, searched all handbags, and gave one or two a random body search. Once this was done, they were allowed into the refurbished nightclub, marveling at the extravagant and decadent fittings and expensive furnishings. Gold and purple drapes and wall-hangings, lavishly decorated the walls. Opulence was everywhere, or so it seemed. The waiters and waitresses were all dressed in ancient roman slave-costumes, and carried wine around the room in gourds instead of bottles. It all added to the atmosphere. Was this what ancient Rome was like? None of the revelers knew. Even Borgia didn't know, but his knowledge was better than most. It was the atmosphere that counted. Wine flowed freely. Drugs were more expensive, but readily available.

Everyone was of a rush to get the best tables in the many encircling tiers which overlooked the arena, and they were soon filled. Latecomers had to content themselves with the gaming rooms in the rear. The sunken area was covered in sawdust and rose petals, and was otherwise bare. At opposite sides, iron gates covered dark openings, where the combatants would enter the arena. It was rumoured that Borgia had a permanent medical facility under the arena, where injuries could be treated, and surgeons and doctors on permanent standby for these combat evenings. The crowd were keen to see blood being spilt in the arena, to christen it as it were.

Borgia was dressed not as Caesar, as some might have thought, for he did not deem it appropriate, and might appear as too ostentatious, but as a roman senator, as were some of his senior security staff, who had advised him against the rash plan of Eve's. They had the descriptions of the two women they were expected, and a rough description of the man. They had orders to let the women through, unless the man was with them.

Truth to tell, Borgia did not think Gabriel was likely to try entering the club through the front doors. He gave him more credit than that. Security all around the club had been tightened. The events of these last few days had convinced Borgia that Gabriel was not among the players yet. Either he had been using the woman Laura to contact Belle, fearing to approach Rome, or something had gone wrong with his friends in the Mafia. He agreed with Eve, who thought the women were currently acting alone, which made their capture all the more important if they were to bargain with Gabriel. Stalking-Horse tactics were now out of the question after Belle had learned the truth.

Two birds in the hand would suffice to draw Gabriel out. If his Mafia friends were double-crossing him, it would mean his resources would be limited. With both his daughter and her mother in his power, Gabriel would have to come against him himself. If need be, he would send Gabriel a piece of his family at a time until he showed himself. Belle especially needed to learn a lesson in both loyalty and humility. He would enjoy watching Eve teach that lesson.

Tonight's guests were in for a surprise. He had already told the men who were scheduled to appear, that they would not be required. He had another spectacle to offer up to the jaded revelers. He chuckled when the cell-phone rang, and he answered it to be told that Belle and Laura had been spotted queuing up outside the club. "Very good, you know the drill. Allow them in, but keep the cameras trained on them all the time. Everything is so far going to plan."

*   *   *

The two women shivered slightly as they shuffled along with the rest of the queue toward the ornate entrance. Evening wear was meant for internal use, and the cool evening breeze was raising goose-bumps on their arms and legs. They were dressed as typical revelers, white one-shouldered gowns, in typical roman style, of longer length than the slave costumes the waitresses were wearing.

As they got to the doors, their handbags were searched, and then they were allowed in. Mingling, they ooohhed and they ahhhhed at the impressive décor with the rest of the rabble, though constantly looking about them for Borgia's security people and Borgia himself.

They took a table on one of the higher tiers, four rows above Borgia himself, where he sat in the equivalent modern reproduction of a royal-box, every inch a Caesar, whilst not dressing as one. He was lord of this manor, and everyone there knew it. Belle recognized politicians amongst the crowd, some with their wives, others with their mistresses. All of them greeted Alonso affectionately. His power was growing by the day, as he courted all the important people in Rome. Some were swayed by friendship, others by blackmail, but swayed they all were.

Cctv cameras were trained on the two women all the time since they had entered the building, and another discreet call on his cell-phone advised Borgia of their position respective to him. He had two security men sitting with him, though no weapons had been found on them when they had been searched at the door. He wondered how Belle intended to do it. Her unarmed combat skills were excellent, but then so were his. Using the cell-phone, he called Eve. "They are both here, as you predicted. Sat a couple rows above me, to my left. My security is in place, and I'm eager for the show to begin," he chuckled.

Laura and Belle acted as any of the other revelers, agitated and seemingly eager for the evening's entertainments, drinking their wine from complimentary goblets of gold-painted pewter. "Just as I thought it would be," Belle reassured her mother, who fidgeted next to her, as her trained eye spotted Borgia's security people mingling with the crowds, more alert than the rest of the masses, and thus easily spotted if you knew what you were looking for. "Two men close to Borgia. Once the fight starts in the arena, there'll be a lot more mingling as people will try and get a better view. We'll just drift closer to his box, and while you take one guard, I'll take the other. One scratch is all it will take. It'll look like a heart-attack for Borgia, and until the two guards regain consciousness, no one will be aware of our involvement. Then we set the fire alarms off, and get the hell out in the confusion," Belle explained.

*   *   *

Outside, from an adjacent rooftop, Gabriel watched the queuing crowds being admitted to Borgia's nightclub. On the roof of the club was a swimming pool and small bar area, currently unused. Too small for public use, and probably intended either for personal use or private parties by Borgia. Bonetti's influence had enabled them to obtain copies of the publicly lodged building plans, blueprints which showed the layout of the place, and even brief details of the security measures that had been installed. Gabriel had no way of knowing if there were others.

The fire escape could not be accessed from the ground, and all doors leading to the fire escape from inside the building were alarmed. Doubtless the door from the roof to the internal stairs would be alarmed as well. The huge skylight window which looked down onto the mini-arena, currently revealing a plethora of ever-changing coloured lights, was the way Gabriel intended entering the place. Not exactly discreet, but that wasn't his intention.

Shock-tactics to stun the opposition into motionless, and give him valuable seconds to make his entrance, and do what he could to find and rescue the women, who were there somewhere inside. Falcone and he would handle that side of things. Bonetti would secure the main front doors for their exit, and it would be in a hurry, he had no doubt.

Donatello had cars on standby at every adjacent street around the club. One car would take them away from here, and the others would do what they could to foil any pursuit. Falcone checked the hang-gliders, as black as the all-over suits the two of them wore. Samurai swords strapped to their backs added to the impression of ninjas, an idea suggested by Gabriel in case they managed a shot at Borgia, and fortunately Donatello had managed to source a couple of such sharp-edged weapons in the time required. Gabriel himself checked the ropes, harnesses and rappelling gear.

Each man carried an Uzi strapped to his chest, and an automatic in a shoulder holster. Gabriel favoured a Beretta, whilst Falcone went for the more powerful Glock, both small and neat, but deadly in the right hands. They had sufficient firepower if called upon to use it, but Gabriel hoped to avoid a bloodbath, relying on the magnesium flares and stun grenades he also carried.

* * *

Back inside the club, the revelers were getting impatient, and so was Belle. On their second goblet of wine, which was noticeably watered down, she was sitting on the edge of her seat, impatient for her chance to approach Borgia's table. At last, something was happening.

Borgia stood up, and turned to wave to the audience around him. "Ladies and Gentlemen, doubtless you have heard of the type of entertainment Borgia's will become famous for, a glorification of our ancient and proud heritage as Romans. Sadly tonight's intended performance, has unexpectedly had to be rearranged." There were gasps and some moans from the crowd of disappointment before he continued. "However, I have now arranged something a little special for you, as a taster of things to come here at Borgia's." Music blared from hidden speakers, and instruments long since thought obsolete sounded out suitably impressive fanfares, as one of the iron gates in the arena was swinging slowly open, and all heads turned to watch as a single figure stepped out into the lighted area.

The spotlights revealed the sawdust of the arena was covered in rosepetals, and a cold shudder went through Laura's body. It looked like the floor was covered in blood.

Walking to the centre of the arena, the lone figure acknowledged the cheers of the crowd. Dressed in sandals and metal grieves, a short leather skirt, leather and metal breast-plate, and a metal helmet, with perforated face mask, carrying a short sword. The gladiator stood there, in full view of the cheering audience, accepting their acclaim, raising the short sword in salute to Borgia, as one by one the gasps went up. There were real breasts behind the breast-plate, for the gladiator was female!

"Signore e signori, may I present EVE!" Borgia announced. The revelers looked on in amazement at the armoured woman who stood amid the sawdust. Female gladiators were not unknown in ancient times, but they were rare. This certainly looked to be a special treat Borgia was laying on for the opening night, but she was standing down there alone. Where was her opponent ?

*   *   *

The gladiatress simply stood there, motionless, short sword now held down by her side in her right hand, accepting the crowd's loud acclaim. Then, slowly and very deliberately, she raised her head, looking up at one particular table.

She held the stare as everyone in the place gradually followed the direction of her gaze. Laura was puzzled, for everyone in the club was now looking their way. Theirs was the table the female gladiator was so obviously looking at. She said nothing, maintaining her silence, just continued to look up at their table, and all around the whispers and the gossiping started increasing in volume. Laura looked across to Borgia, who met her stare and smiled knowingly.

She looked across to Belle, and found her to be visibly shaking, trying to control herself as she glared down at the woman in the arena. Only the eyes and her lower chin were visible under the helmet, but those eyes met Belle's, and she knew instantly who they belonged to!

"Belle, we've been made. It's a trap!" Laura warned, trying to get her daughter's attention. Belle's view was fixed on the masked gladiatress, skin tight and whitening, and she hardly felt her mother's hand on her shoulder.

"I know," Belle said under her breath, trying to remain calm. She glowered down at the silent figure in the arena. The hair was the same vivid shade of red, though worn much longer. Why she had thought her dead, knowing what she did of the increased longevity of some of the Church's agents, she didn't know. She had thought their paths would have crossed much sooner if that had been the case. "If you get the chance, take Borgia out. Otherwise get out and save yourself. You can't help me in this." Belle hissed under her breath, and then stood up.

Gasps went up all around as she stood up, acknowledging the female gladiator's stare. Amid the hubbub and whispering, the gladiatress finally spoke. "Coming down to play, little girl?" she taunted.

*   *   *

Belle was still visibly shaking, trying to get her anger under control. She was failing, and failing fast. Emotions were too strong for rationale. She had waited too long for this. Give in to your rage, part of her was saying, while the more rational part was warning her to maintain control. The rage was winning, and her inner voice knew it. Jessica's ghost was calling out to her. Alright then, use the anger!

"You *want* me, bitch?" she screamed, a touch of hysteria in her voice as she fought to retain some control, and standing to acknowledge and confirm the curiosity of the crowd. Looking briefly down at the dress she was wearing, she tore it from her body with one swift movement, and the crowd gasped as she stripped herself right down to her panties. The dress was too long and cumbersome to permit the quickness of movement she would need. The shoes quickly followed. Belle had no thoughts as to her near nudity, she was focusing on one thing and one thing only. The woman waiting to be killed in the arena below. Today would be the day Jessica's ghost would finally be laid to rest. "You *want* me? Then here I come!" she cursed, and jumped up onto the table amid gasps and screams, and started a furious run, jumping from table to table as she approached the lower tiers, scattering drinks and people alike in her wake as they tried frantically to get out of her way.

Reaching the balcony, she leapt out and away, executing a perfect double somersault, before landing at a crouch, about ten yards from the waiting female gladiator. The revellers applauded the acrobatic feat, crowding around the balcony like the mob of old, all scenting the blood and animosity already heavy in the air. Laura looked down horrified, not understanding anything of what was going on.

She had never seen such a look of pure, unadulterated hate on her daughter's face, even when she had been talking about the Cannucci's. Belle remained crouched, balanced on the balls of her feet, unarmed, yet ready and waiting for the other woman to make her move, snarling defiance.

"Cute moves, little girl. Someone taught you well," the slightly muffled voice chuckled, and then the helmet was slowly lifted, and Eve/Angelica smiled cruelly across the width of the arena floor at Belle. "Have you missed me, Sweetness?" she sneered. "This is just like old times."

Chapter Nineteen

G abriel and Falcone heard the roar go up from the club opposite as they were making their final preparations, Falcone adding blacking to his face. He wanted no one there to identify them, or reveal his open assault on a Council Member. Gabriel too, made use of the blacking. Apart from their eyes, they were almost invisible in the blackness. The hang-gliders were light and sturdy. Borgia's roof was some three stories below, and more than four hundred yards away. An easy flight, but a difficult landing as the roof was unlit, and with only the light from the illuminated rooftop pool to orientate themselves.

The night-vision goggles were on their heads, but not in use yet. Bonetti had arranged for all power to the building to be cut on a prearranged signal, which Gabriel would give by using a cell-phone to call one of Bonetti's many acquaintances in the Municipale.

"Time to go," announced Gabriel, checking his watch. He and Falcone took up their hang gliders, and clipped both their harnesses onto the frames. Gabriel went first, a short run up to the parapet of the roof, and launched himself into the night. Falcone watched as he dropped below the edge of the roof momentarily, before rising into view once more, and then angling his silent flight towards the lower rooftop.

Gabriel exalted in the feel of the night winds lifting his mono-wing. He knew the winds as no other, and was quick to adjust to the small nuances as the gusts changed direction, being channeled through the artificial canyons formed by the modern day buildings.

The lower roof came up fast, and Gabriel knocked over two chairs as he landed, before coming to a stop, and unclipping himself from the glider frame. He gave a thumbs-up to Falcone, and then began clearing the area of chairs to permit Falcone a smoother landing than the one he had had himself. As it was, Gabriel needed to use a helping hand to avoid Falcone toppling into the swimming pool as he landed. Once both men had stored the gliders out of the way, they went to peer down through the large skylight into the club below.

*　　*　　*

Angelica regarded Belle coldly, noting the musculature on her athletic body with a tinge of sadness. Such a pity she had never enjoyed it. "Never let it be said that I didn't offer you a fair fight," she smiled cruelly, and began unbuckling her chest plate.

The crowd applauded Angelica/Eve as she removed her armour to match Belle's own current state, though beneath she wore a small short shift instead of going bare-breasted. She kept on the sandals and grieves, whilst Belle remained barefoot, still crouched and expecting an attack, wary of the short sword the woman was carrying.

As Angelica acknowledged the crowds' cheers, saluting them with her short sword, Borgia approached the edge of the balcony. "My dear . . . ." he called to Belle, who glared up at him. "I think you might need this," he smiled down at her, and threw a short sword into the air. All eyes followed it as it landed point first amid the sawdust and rose petals. Angelica stepped back away from it, graciously allowing Belle to move forward to collect it, smiling a knowing smile as she did so, warily.

Hardly had Belle's hand closed on the hilt of the short sword, when Angelica lunged forward with lightning speed, and the crowd roared as it got to its feet, surging forward. The two swords met with a loud CLANG, as Belle managed to parry the other woman's blow with difficulty.

Grunting, and with a wild expression on her face, Angelica took the fight to Belle. Again and again she cut and slashed at her. Again and again, Belle met the blows, the force of which ran down her forearm painfully, as she was forced back. Above them the crowd roared loudly, crushed against the balcony to get the best view. This wasn't a staged combat, it was the real thing. It was like the ancient mob of old, they could smell the blood about to be spilt. Those two women down there were really trying to kill each other.

The short swords were heavy, and sharper than those used by ancient combatants. Belle was unaccustomed to using one, whereas Angelica obviously was not, showing a great degree of skill in the way she was handling hers. Laura looked down horrified, as her newfound daughter was in the fight of her life, when a hand clamped down hard on her shoulder.

Laura looked up, to find the two security men stood behind her. "Mr Borgia requests the pleasure of your company at his table," one of them said, smiling grimly down at her. Hardly a request under the circumstances, but it served her purpose, and Laura stood up and allowed them to escort her to Borgia's side, where he had cleared a space for her at his table.

"My dear Laura, so nice to meet you at last," he said enthusiastically, as she accepted the seat next to him. "I dare say you're a bit confused as to what's going on down there?" he chuckled. "The two of them are old friends," he explained. "With more than a bit of bad blood between them. I'm afraid," he added. "Oh, nice move!" he applauded, as Belle forced her way out away from the wall of the arena.

No matter how hard Belle tried, Angelica brought the fight to her, keeping in the centre of the arena, dictating the conflict, taunting her in a voice just loud enough for her alone to hear. "Did you ever see the body, Belle? Did you ever see what I did to her?" Belle tried to ignore her words, for she knew they were designed to make her angry and reckless, but Jessica had been her first love, and she found she was fighting with tears in her eyes.

"When they bury you, Angelica, I'm going to visit your grave once a year, just so I can piss on it!" she cursed, parrying yet another fierce blow, and launching one of her own, but then Angelica stepped nimbly to one side, putting out a foot to trip Belle and make her stumble.

The crowd roared, seeing Belle fall, and Angelica lunged forward, the short sword arcing down for the kill, but Belle's longer leg shot out, catching Angelica below the knee. The bare foot slid off the metal grieve on her shin, enabling Angelica to avoid the full force of the blow, but she too fell, turning her fall into a roll away from Belle, as the two women separated once more, and both regained their feet, circling once more.

Laura was finding it hard not to clench her fists, and she was careful when holding one hand up to her mouth as a lock of Belle's hair was severed as she narrowly avoided a blow by the other woman. "I did tell Eve *not* to kill her, just teach her a lesson, if that's any consolation," Borgia smiled cruelly.

"Belle might surprise you yet. I've seen her in action, and she's pretty good." Borgia merely smiled amusedly.

"Not much chance of that," he explained. "The fight was over as soon as she picked up the sword," he explained almost casually. "The leather handle has been soaked in a soporific, absorbed through the skin, it will make her more tired the more she fights." Borgia grinned. "One of Belle's own concoctions, I believe. Eve is just playing with her for the audience." Laura felt a shock go through her. A trap indeed.

Whirling suddenly, before any of the two security men had an inkling of what she intended, Laura raked her nails down Borgia's bare arm, and he cried out in shock as bloody furrows opened up on his arm. "Die you bastard!" she cursed, standing suddenly as the two security men grabbed for her. But Borgia held up his other arm, and they let her go. Borgia sat there, staring brazenly up at her, and then back at his arm, as the flesh around the wounds noticeably began to darken.

It was fast-acting, whatever it was, Laura thought. Pleased she had followed Belle's move to paint her own nails with the same poison. "So that was how she intended to do it. I should have guessed." Borgia forced a smile, though she could see he was in pain. Breathing hard, and face flushed, and he watched calmly as the flesh on his arm coloured, dark then light, dark then light, throbbing painfully. "It hurts, if that's consolation," he admitted, though remaining remarkably calm under the circumstances. Laura could only sit and watch, the ring of steel on steel from the arena below now secondary in her mind. Slowly, the reddening flesh lightened in colour, and slowly the flow of blood from the red furrows began to congeal. "A nice move on her part, but such a shame it was designed to work on mere humans," and his mouth opened in a wide grin, extended white canines now pronounced and exposed in public for the first time as he revealed his true nature to her.

Horrified, Laura was frozen into immobility for a few moments, until she forced herself into action. Standing up, she overturned the table towards Borgia, and before he could start to recover, leapt over the balcony herself to join the two engaged combatants in the arena, both of them whirling around to see the new arrival land ungraciously in the sawdust.

"The sword! You're being drugged! Drop the sword!" she warned Belle frantically, and threw a handful of sawdust into Angelica's face as she aimed a blow in her direction, rolling to one side frantically as the heavy blade chopped the air inches from her.

Cursing, Angelica rubbed her eyes as Belle closed her down. Drugged it might be, but Belle had no choice but to use it. She had to end this quickly. A flurry of blows rained down upon the partially blinded Angelica as Belle fought to press her own advantage, but Laura was right, she could feel a slight lethargy creeping into her body. Her blows were weakening. But Laura was weaponless, and if Angelica had the chance, Belle knew she would butcher her without a second's remorse, just for spite! Like Jessica all over again.

As if knowing this, Laura knew that she had to help her daughter, and she flung herself in a forward roll as Angelica turned her back to deal with Belle's assault. Angelica cried out as Laura crashed into her legs and she toppled over backwards.

Seizing her opportunity, Belle dropped her own sword and flung herself at Angelica, the three women grappling and rolling around in the sawdust as the watching crowd roared. Angelica screaming in frustrated rage as the two women fought to force the sword from her hand. Both the two women were skilled combatants, and punches, chops and elbow-strikes slammed into Angelica's body.

Resilient she certainly was, but in such close quarters against two such foes, she was losing the physical battle. It was only when she finally bared her own fangs and sank them savagely into Laura's neck that the sudden shock and extreme viciousness of her own attack brought her some respite.

Laura went suddenly immobile at the surprise of seeing a second set of fangs, and then came the pain and pleasure of the bite itself. Belle was just plainly horrified, and sat back on the sawdust, as the 'thing' in front of her tore open her mother's throat, red blood quickly staining the white robe she wore. She gawped helplessly as Angelica let her mother's body drop semi-conscious to the sawdust of the arena floor.

The face that turned towards her, open maw crimson with her mother's blood, was like nothing she had ever seen on this earth before. Fangs so white and long and sharp. Then the old Angelica was back all of a sudden, as she closed her mouth, hiding her true appearance from the watching masses who were unsure what they had just witnessed. "Now it's your turn, little girl!" she hissed, picking up the short sword once more while Belle remained motionless and shocked on the ground before her. "Borgia wants you alive," she spat out. "But guess what?" she grinned evilly. "I don't!" and the sword rose and fell in a savage blur. Weaponless, all Belle could do was to put a hand up to ward it off.

*   *   *

Up on the roof, Gabriel and Falcone had watched, horrified at the combat taking place in the arena directly below them, and unsure as to how to intervene without causing possible harm to Belle or Laura. The sight of Laura falling to the arena floor, covered in blood, galvanized both men into action.

The magnesium flare dropped down from the skylight, Falcone priming it with a two second fuse, and it went off about 30 feet above the arena floor, as Angelica raised her sword. Everyone screamed as they were blinded by the terrific sudden glare. By the time the flare had dropped to the sawdust, and gone out, everyone that had been looking down into the arena area had been blinded.

"Now!" Gabriel said into the cell-phone, as he readied his night-vision goggles. Falcone was already clipping his own harness onto the skylight frame. Seconds later, the building was plunged into darkness as all power was cut off by Bonetti's friend at the Power Station. "Go!" he gave the command, and he and Falcone dropped down into the darkness.

Abseiling down, they dropped like silent ghosts into the blackness, listening to the screams from the stunned crowd, some of whom where recovering from the initial optic overload only to find the place still in darkness, and totally disoriented as Gabriel had planned. Everyone was milling around in a panic, and no one was attempting to stop their descent.

Peering down into the arena, he saw the female gladiatress run off out through the open barred doorway, and he managed to fire two quick shots after her, but unsure as to whether he had hit her or not. Belle and Laura lay prone on the ground. He began scanning the milling crowd as he dropped, but he could see no sign of Borgia.

Falcone alighted first, unclipping himself from the rope, and running to where Laura lay, her throat a bloody mess. "Laura . . . ." his voice was pained, and Gabriel almost picked up on it, as he quickly unclipped himself and ran to where his daughter lay, quickly checking her pulse to assure himself she still lived, and quickly breaking out some bandages from a small pack strapped to his thigh, to form a makeshift tourniquet to try and stop the bleeding.

Falcone quickly broke out a field-dressing of his own from the small pack clipped to his belt, and applied it to Laura's raw throat to stem the bleeding. He took her up in his arms, and then turned to find Gabriel had already slung Belle over his own shoulder. He was speaking hurriedly into the cell-phone. "We're coming out. Neutralise the doormen!" he spoke to Bonetti.

*   *   *

Outside the building, upon hearing the message, Bonetti strolled casually around the corner and along the opposite side of the street. The two heavies were frantically talking on a mobile cell-phone, trying to make sense of all the screaming coming from inside the building, but as yet none of the panicking revelers had so far made it downstairs in the darkness.

When he came level with the entrance to the club, he pulled out the riot-gun from under his raincoat, and aimed the gas-grenade directly into the front lobby, where it hit the wall behind the two heavies and went off, spraying tear-gas in all directions. Dropping the riot gun, he pulled his automatic and dropped behind a parked car to offer covering fire if it was required. The two heavies were doubled over, coughing and eyes streaming as they fought to catch their breaths.

Gabriel and Falcone fought their way out with the two women, Gabriel shooting two of Borgia's men as they tried to stop them coming out from the underground facility and upto the upper levels. The main doors burst open, with Gabriel giving more instructions into the cell-phone, and a car came hurtling around the corner, screeching to a halt in front of the club. Falcone put one of the women inside the rear of the car, and then stepped aside as Gabriel got in with the second. Falcone took the passenger seat, as the Mafia driver pulled away. Bonetti made himself scarce, as there was no immediate signs of pursuit from Borgia's men.

Inside the car, Gabriel was phoning Donatello, asking for directions. "We need urgent medical help, Donatello. A clinic or private surgery. One of the women has a throat wound, and the other has lost a hand," he revealed sadly.

*　　*　　*

The night was a long one. The drive to the private hospital seemingly endless, with the field-dressings on the two women's horrific injuries dripping blood. Finally, trained medical staff took the two unconscious women into their care, and it was all Gabriel and Falcone could do to wait helplessly as hands more skilled than their own took care of the women. This private clinic was one used by Donatello and his family, and was as secure as anything they could find. Donatello ordered round the clock surveillance for the place whenever it was in use, and he beefed it up by pulling people away from his own estate.

*　　*　　*

Back at Borgia's club, now that the panic was over, and the clientele removed from the building, the power was working again, and Borgia fumed in his private office. Gabriel, for it could have been no other, had engineered the raid on his establishment, and both women were now gone, hostages no more. The severed hand which Eve/Angelica dropped messily onto his desk did little to appease him. "You have the nerve to call that a bargaining tool?" he scoffed.

"Pack it in ice, and it's still possible to reattach it," Eve explained. "It's all we have, so make use of it," she suggested.

"The Council will not be satisfied with that!" Borgia brooded. "Ratti may succeed in ousting me over this latest debacle. Unless I can turn things around." Eve said nothing, and sat down across from him, careful not to lean on her bandaged shoulder where one of Gabriel's bullets had clipped her as she had fled. Borgia called the medical team in the underground facility as Eve had suggested. "I have a body part for cryogenic storage. Send someone up to collect it," he instructed.

"What are you going to do?" she asked. Borgia scowled across the desk at her.

"Nothing I can do for the moment but wait. I had word earlier that Donatello Grimaldi had began pulling men away from his own estate. Doubtless he seeks to aid Gabriel and the women. I told our own people to follow and see where they went. When I get word on that, we'll know where Gabriel is holed up. Then it will be time to hunt!" Borgia grinned. "Let him think himself secure for the moment. He will not expect me to take the fight to him. Phone Grimaldi. Tell him what we have, and that we offer it in exchange for Gabriel. If he wants his daughter to regain the use of that hand, he will at least think about it. While he does, it will distract him enough for him to let down his guard. Then I'll take him!"

*   *   *

Eve did indeed make the call to Grimaldi, who was surprised that anyone in the Solomon organisation had access to his private line, and he sat there quietly fuming as the woman gave him details of the night's events, and what was on offer. She gave him a number for Gabriel to call, accepting the offer, and then she hung up.

Donatello reached into his desk, and pulled out his automatic, sliding back the chamber and ensuring there was a full clip. "Giuseppe, round up what's left of the men. We're going to pay a call on Mr Borgia's club. It's time these Solomon bastards learn that the Grimaldi's may not be the biggest of the Families, but no one fucks with me or my friends!"

*   *   *

While Grimaldi was busy organizing his troops, Borgia's expected phone-call came through, advising him of the private clinic which was now patrolled by a dozen armed mafia foot-soldiers. "You stay here, and if he calls, make the offer, and arrange an exchange for tomorrow. His daughter gets her hand back, and we get him for our scientists to play with. Make it sound a genuine offer," he warned. "While he broods on that, he may lower his guard. He won't leave the women, and as long as we know where they are, we know where he is going to be."

"There was someone else with him when the lights went out." Eve revealed. "Lucifer?" she posed the question.

"They have worked together in the past, true. But one by one, or both together, tonight, I'll have them!" he promised.

*   *   *

At the clinic Gabriel and Falcone impatiently awaited news from the doctors who were attending to both of the two women. At length one of the doctors came out to see them, and they were relieved to see that he had a slight smile on his face as he greeted them. "Good evening. I am Doctor Malinari, and I have some good news for you," he began, and both men felt instantly relieved. "The young lady with the throat wound has been successfully operated on. There was no damage to the vocal chords, and although there might be some noticeable scarring, we expect a full recovery. Strange blood-group the young lady had. We couldn't get a match for it, and so had to use plasma, which seemed to be acceptable"

Falcone nodded simply, greatly relieved that Laura would recover. "And the other woman, doctor?" Gabriel asked. The doctor frowned, and then shook his head in a puzzled manner.

"The loss of the hand was a relatively clean cut, but again, the blood loss was stabilized with plasma, when we couldn't get a match. It seems both women have some obscure blood-group. I couldn't very well make a donor of one for the other's sake. They've both lost too much," he explained.

"I share that blood-group, doctor," Gabriel was quick to explain. "We're family. If you need more, just ask," he offered. Malinari nodded, and then continued.

"Both wounds had already started to heal themselves by the time the women were brought in here," Malinari announced. "It was very strange. Gentlemen, I have seen nothing like this in all my years. Is there something you should be telling me about these women?" He looked from Gabriel to Falcone, neither of whom said anything. "Very well. Both women are currently sedated for the night. They will need their rest, but should be conscious by mid-morning, and well enough to receive visitors. I will ask my staff to make up some beds for you in two of the unoccupied rooms. Signor Grimaldi's men are patrolling the grounds. Everything is secure," he reassured them, and then turned and walked off along the corridor, before turning to the right and disappearing from sight.

"Thank God they both will live." Falcone crossed himself. Gabriel couldn't quite join him in his belief, though he did indeed feel relieved. The two women had no idea what they were going up against, and he blamed himself for not being more honest with Laura about his reluctance to allow her to seek Belle out on her own. Now Belle was minus a hand. Would she hate him for that, too? Just as he hated himself?

From Laura's throat injury, it was obvious they had a second vampire to worry about, the female that they had been fighting with in the arena. What part did she play in all this? Despite his reading on the subject, Borgia himself had been only the second vampire he had come into contact with, so his experience at such things was very limited. If his assumptions were correct, the vampiric parasite was carried in the host's blood, and as long as Laura had not ingested any of her attacker's blood, then she would not be affected by the assault. Other opinions differed, the more widespread his reading had become. Another opinion was that as long as the bloodletting was not fatal, then the victim would recover. Or was it such that the mere bite itself could inject some of the vampiric parasite into the victim? In which case, Laura would need to be watched for outward signs of any such change. If that happened, Gabriel did not know what he would do.

Falcone sat beside him, saying nothing, and head bent in silent prayer. Gabriel looked out of the window into the night skies. Feint clouds drifted across the half-moon. It was going to be a longer night than he had thought.

Chapter Twenty

Borgia drove himself across the city in his private limousine. The address he had been given was for that of a private clinic to the south of the city. It took him nearly forty minutes to get there, and he drove past the walled grounds unhurriedly, taking note of the positions chosen by Grimaldi's men. One such was on each corner of the walls, and he expected others to be patrolling the grounds internally. Somewhere inside the three storied building that he could see over the wall, was his enemy Gabriel, and the two women.

He would need caution and stealth to slip inside without alerting Gabriel, but once the prize was his, a simple phone-call would bring a squad of Solomon agents to take care of the Mafiosi, and deliver Gabriel to the Council. The women, he would claim as spoils of war. Neither would survive this night. If Lucifer was indeed inside the building too, then his was a third life he intended to take, for his bloodstream was known to be tainted, and of no use to their scientists. It would taste sweet enough, though.

Borgia cruised the adjacent streets, looking for a suitable place to park, and eventually deciding upon a tree-lined avenue two streets to the south of the villa. Walking on foot, Borgia seemed to be part of the night, gliding rather than walking, as he approached the fifteen foot high walls. He watched the clouds across the moon, timing his movements for when the night was at its darkest, hiding in the shrubbery of a neighbouring house, as he positioned himself midway between two of the Mafiosi, and bided his time. Borgia was a patient man, but he needed this over by morning.

At length, after perhaps ten minutes had gone by, the two Mafiosi's heads were turned away from each other, and the darkness had descended upon the street. Borgia moved, like a shadow stretching across toward the walls, and then rising almost without stopping, to pause momentarily on top of the wall, before disappearing over it. One of the Mafiosi's heads turned, catching the merest glimpse of a shadow, but by the time he had turned, Borgia had vanished from view, and he shook his head, thinking his eyes had played tricks upon him.

Inside the grounds, Borgia crouched in darkness on the other side of the wall, using the cover of a small tree to survey the distance to the villa. The main entrance was on the opposite side of the villa, but a back door remained to the kitchen areas. Looking up, Borgia noted the windows, and which of them were open. The old stone with which the building was constructed was loosely jointed, and would be easily climbed by one such as he, plenty of toe and handholds. One merely needed the physical strength, of which he had plenty in abundance.

The garden and lawns were black and grey in the faint moonlight, and the shadows cast dark pools, which Borgia used to mask his approach. He had already spotted the next three of Grimaldi's men, two of which were stood smoking together by the rear door, and the third was dutifully patrolling along the edge of the garden. He would be the first to die. Borgia waited in silence and shadows.

*   *   *

Inside the building, Gabriel and Falcone were shown to their rooms, just along the corridor from where the two women were resting. Gabriel stowed his gear under the bed, and got on it to lie down and get some rest. He knew sleep would now be impossible. In his own room, Father Falcone did much the same, though kneeling in prayer before getting on his own bed. He was already working out details of tomorrow's raid on the Vatican's catacombs. How to get Gabriel in and out again afterwards, with no one the wiser.

Falcone dwelled on his loyalty to Ratti, his love for Laura, and the forced friendship with the man who had taken her away from him. Could he let that happen? Gabriel was there in the next room, an easy target should he decide to give in to such evil thoughts. But could he kill Borgia on his own?

Ratti's plan had been to discredit Borgia, earning Gabriel's gratitude for his aid in recovering his daughter, and oust Borgia from the Council. But Ratti had never been a field operative. You did not leave such an enemy alive. Killing him had been Gabriel's suggestion, and one which Falcone had gone along with readily, for it was surely no sin to kill such as he. Borgia was an abomination, as was the woman who had torn out Laura's throat.

Gabriel had accepted Ratti's offer of aid, and the promise of no further persecution by the Church, in return for the sworn guarantee of a yearly delivery of a pint of Gabriel's own blood to the Council. Such a delivery would be sufficient to keep the Council members and their most trusted agents alive, but would be insufficient to stockpile. A compromise which Gabriel had accepted. It was Ratti's intent to restore the Council to its original aims of furthering the good works of the Church, instead of following some maniac's personal agenda. If the Church left him alone, then he was prepared to leave them alone.

*　　*　　*

The second attack on Borgia's club was more unexpected than the first, for the Mafia had never moved openly against the Sword of Solomon before. Gunfire at the main entrance was the first indication Eve received of anything untoward, and then the Mafia foot-soldiers, led by Donatello Grimaldi himself, had gained access to the building.

Using the cctv cameras via the remote console in Borgia's office, Eve saw the strength of the infiltration. Almost a dozen men, against a handful of Solomon agents, and ordinary security personnel. The place was not designed to withstand a siege of this magnitude, and although she barked out defensive strategies to her men, Eve knew this was a battle already lost. Time to cut her losses.

Whilst the fighting was going on, Eve slipped out one of the fire doors. Alarms were already going off, so one more was hardly noticeable.

Downstairs, splitting up his men, Donatello ordered four of his men down to the underground chambers, housing the medical facility, while he himself lead a clear-out operation up to the higher floors. He wanted to teach Borgia a lesson he would not soon forget, and they took no prisoners. Everyone they met was assumed to be a Solomon agent, and dealt with accordingly. From time of entry, it took less than ten minutes to kill all of Borgia's men. Three of Grimaldi's own people were also dead, and two wounded.

When he received word from the rest of his team that the severed hand had been found in a small cryogenic container, he ordered the club burnt to the ground. He left the place without a backward glance, as dark smoke began spiralling up to the darker heavens. The cryogenic unit was there on the seat next to him, as his driver drove the limousine south. The doctors at the private medical facility were amongst the best in Italy. With luck, they would be able to re-attach the hand. Fortunately it had been preserved well, on a bed of crushed ice. The battery in the base of the unit was still reading 80%, so the temperature would be maintained for quite a while yet. He had heard of a few cases where full mobility had been restored. He hoped for the girl's sake that this would be true in this case also.

*　　*　　*

In the grounds of the private clinic, Borgia smiled as he lowered the body of the first guard silently to the ground. He had taken the man from behind, breaking his neck in less than a second, before he knew what was happening, then he edged his way to the side of the building, away from the kitchen doorway where the other two men were still smoking. He was waiting for them to move and separate. If he left them, they would soon discover the absence of the third guard.

Minutes passed, and they eventually stubbed out their cigarettes. They moved apart in opposite directions, one of them towards the position that Borgia had chosen, and he took him quickly, rising up out of the shrubbery like a ghost, his skin all white in the pale moonlight. The guard almost had time to mouth a scream, but then Borgia's large hand clamped over his face, and his fangs clamped down on the man's throat.

The third guard was taken even more simply. Wearing the jacket of the second man, who was of similar build, Borgia merely walked straight up to him. Keeping to the shadows, the man never spotted anything wrong until it was too late, and then Borgia finally stood alone in the garden. Ignoring the kitchen door, for he didn't know how many men were inside the building, Borgia began to scale the outer wall, fingers and toes finding easy purchase in the broad gaps between the stones, and his strength sufficient as to enable him to climb easily.

*   *   *

Falcone stirred restlessly, for sleep wouldn't come. He got out of bed, and swilled his face in the small washbasin, washing off most of the blacking, which was difficult with it being grease-based. Opening his bedroom door, he went out into the corridor, and along to Laura's room.

He opened the door quietly, to see her lying there asleep. Her throat was bandaged, and there was a plasma drip attached to her arm. Other sensors were attached to a nearby monitoring machine, which would keep the main desk informed as to any changes in her condition. He checked the chart fixed to the end of the bed. He had done enough missionary work to be familiar with such things. Her condition was stabilized, and rest was perhaps the best thing she needed right now.

Could he really let her go back to him? Their affair had been brief and fiery, and Laura had ended it all too soon. She had made a mistake, she'd said, and left it like that. No appeal. It was simply over. She was a strong woman, perhaps too strong in certain ways. He admired that quality in her, but found it hard to let her go. His faith was of little help in matters of the heart.

Seeing her like this, lying there so helpless, brought back so many sad memories. Nothing he could do but pray for her, and so he sat down on the chair beside the bed, and bowed his head in silent prayer.

*   *   *

Borgia paused at the first floor window, sniffing the air from within. Someone was in there, but the smell was old, and mixed with medication. Not a smell he recognized. He entered silently and quickly, eyes making out the slim emaciated figure in the bed, an old man, fast asleep in a drugged slumber. He was no threat, and so Borgia left him to his dreams, quietly opening the door to the corridor, and peering out. At this hour, he did not expect many people to be up and about.

He stepped out into the corridor, moving quietly along as he checked each closed door to see the patients' names, scrawled on a white card, and slotted into a small nameplate on each door. Passing the stairwell, Borgia heard traces of a hushed conversation from the floor below, and passed by quickly. He soon satisfied himself that his prey was not on this floor. That left only one other, and he cautiously went up the final flight of stairs to where he knew Gabriel would be waiting for him.

Peering over the last few stairs, Borgia noted the empty corridor and dim lighting. Everyone here too was retired for the night. Good. He moved up to the top of the stairs, breathing slowly and deeply, trying to scent out his prey. The strong smell of antiseptic and medications were interfering with his own keen sense of smell, and Borgia could not isolate his prey. Frustrated, he moved off, intent on a room by room search.

The first such room he tried contained a young boy, and Borgia stood there, intent on the watching the youngster's chest slowly rise and fall, the thick vein in the side of his neck pulsed slowly, and Borgia found himself imagining the sweetness of the boy's blood. Controlling his urges, he closed the door, and went on to the next, opening it slowly. This room was empty, although the bed looked as though it had been slept in. Borgia closed the door, and moved on.

*　　*　　*

Gabriel lay awake on his own bed. He had heard Falcone moving about earlier, though he had not disturbed him. Now he could hear other doors faintly being opened and closed. It was a bit late for a doctor to be doing his rounds and checking up on his patients. Puzzled, he lay there, wondering what it was that was plucking at his mind.

Suddenly it struck him. For all the doors being opened and closed, he could not hear the sound of any footsteps out there in the corridor. Someone was going from room to room, and being as quiet as they could. He rolled out of bed, silently, listening for more sounds. As soon as he opened the door to his own room, whoever it was would see him, and so he preferred to just wait, and listen for the moment.

*　　*　　*

Falcone was nodding off in the chair as the handle turned slowly on the door. It slowly opened, and Borgia peered in, smiling as he saw and recognized Laura lying there in the bed. He stood there in the doorway for a moment, as he decided whether to take her life now or later, when a sudden movement from behind the partially opened door alerted him, and then he stepped into the room to see a startled Falcone fearfully fumbling for his gun.

"Falcone! You would *dare* go against me?" Borgia was furious at the discovery of Falcone's deception, and batted the gun helplessly out of his hand before he could bring it to bear on him. The chair went over as Falcone tried to avoid those massive hands, his knee coming up into Borgia's balls, but the only effect it had was a small grunt, as Borgia's weight forced him back against the wall. Falcone's eyes bulged as the massive hands fastened around his neck, squeezing mercilessly. "I'm going to rip your throat out, Falcone." Borgia's face broadened in an evil smile. Then it broadened even further, as Borgia's canines began to extrude slowly as Falcone watched, horrified, as the life was being slowly choked out of him.

*   *   *

"Why don't you pick on someone your own size?" came a voice from behind, and Borgia turned to see Gabriel framed in the doorway. The Beretta in Gabriel's hand roared six times in rapid succession, sending six hollow-point bullets thudding home in Borgia's huge frame. He could hardly miss, but as he had rightly guessed, despite the internal damage they caused to his body, they only served to enrage him, and Borgia roared in pain as he flung Falcone helplessly against the wall. "Come and get me, Fatso." Gabriel taunted, as he stepped away from the door, and began running down the corridor, eager to get Borgia away from Laura's bedside.

Downstairs he could hear sounds of alert, as the gunfire had served its purpose, and Donatello's men would be seeking to assist him. Behind him, he could hear Borgia snarling like a wild animal as he pursued Gabriel once more. The stairwell to the roof beckoned, and Gabriel used it, scant seconds ahead of his pursuer. He needed more space to move if he was to stand a chance against Borgia.

Borgia ran after him, finding the narrow stairwell difficult to navigate, and slowing him down, but he got to the roof to find Gabriel waiting for him. "Another rooftop. Just like old times," he grinned. "And this time there is no swimming pool." He reminded Gabriel. "It is a relatively small height. Jump and I'll jump with you," he warned. "Face me honourably if you dare," he taunted. Gabriel stood his ground, knees slightly bent, and one hand holding a knife low, against his leg, where Borgia could not see it. "I'm going to crunch those hollow bones of yours, and grind them till you beg me to stop," Borgia promised, looking forward to humbling his nemesis. "Then I'm going to take a great delight in killing those two lovely women of yours." Then he stepped forward towards Gabriel, who chose that moment to throw the knife in a neat underhand arc. Borgia barely had time to register the glint of steel in the moonlight before the knife buried itself deep in his jugular. "Akkhhhhhhhh!" he cried out, blood bubbling from his throat as he clutched at the blade to drag it free.

"This time I'm ready for you, Borgia," Gabriel announced, and pulled from his pocket what looked like a small bulbous rubber douche-bag, which he quickly un-corked, and then lunged forward, squeezing the rubber bladder, to empty the contents full in Borgia's face, and stepping quickly back as the acid did it's work.

Borgia screamed into the night sky as the corrosive fluid burned at his flesh, and most importantly his eyeballs, blinding him. He flailed around in agony, helplessly trying to catch hold of Gabriel, who kept out of Borgia's longer reach.

Calmly, Gabriel unclipped the magnesium flare from his belt. Operating the fuse with his thumb, he then flung himself at Borgia, and as the smouldering head went back in a roar of pain, he forced the flare down into Borgia's mouth, the magnesium igniting a half-second later, lighting up his entire skull from the inside.

Borgia's body shook, but no sounds escaped his mouth, for the magnesium was burning so hotly that his tongue had simply vanished, almost instantly. His face was a jack o' lantern come to life, horribly contorted as he writhed in agony the rooftop. "Die, you bastard!" Gabriel cursed as he stood there watching him.

* * *

Donatello's men met Gabriel as he came back down from the roof, minutes later. "Don't go up there!" he warned, and then went back to his bedroom. Moments later he came out again with the samurai sword, and then he went back up to the roof. The Mafia cringed away when they saw what he carried on his return, burned and blackened though it was, it was still just recognisable as the remains of a human skull. Gabriel carried it downstairs, and into the cellar where he knew there would be a medical incinerator in the basement. Opening the door, Gabriel threw it inside, and then closed it. He paused to turn up the thermostat all the way up to the red.

Going back upstairs, he found Falcone being attended to by the medical staff, who were busy strapping up his shoulder. Other than that, he seemed to be unharmed. He looked in on Laura, and then on Belle, who were both still unconscious. Borgia was finally dead, but his legacy lived on.

He heard a car pulling up outside, and looked out of the window to see Donatello angrily shouting at his men, and Gabriel went down to greet him. Donatello was giving the cryogenic unit to Malinari as he arrived. "Gabriel, my friend, they tell me the bastard is dead at last!" he grinned.

"Let us hope so, Donatello. Let us hope so," he agreed.

*   *   *

The next afternoon, the two women were now conscious, though notably subdued by their ordeals. Gabriel found Falcone in Laura's room when he went up, and the low conversation ceased as soon as he entered the room. Both of them looked guiltily at him, as though he was intruding, and so he left the room briefly.

Falcone came out a few moments later, and he paused in the corridor to speak briefly to Gabriel. "I go now to complete my end of this bargain. I will send you Borgia's files, and you may give selected information to the policeman. We part today as allies. Do not count on it in the future," he warned. Looking back once at Laura, he spoke again. "I suggest that you take better care of her than you have done so far." He turned on his heels and walked off down the corridor before Gabriel could think of a response. Instead, he went into Laura's bedroom.

She smiled at him as he went to her side, and held out her hand, which he took and squeezed. "I should have listened. You were right. I'm sorry," she spoke softly, her voice still pained.

"I'm sorry too." Gabriel admitted. "I should have been more honest with you," he regretted. "Did they tell you what happened to Belle?" Laura nodded.

"They took me in to see her earlier," she admitted. "She's in shock still, and she needs love more than anything, Gabriel. The love she never had as a child. She's dealing with it, but it's not easy. Doctor Malinari says there is every chance they'll be able to reattach the hand. With the right drugs, and those special regenerative powers, I think she'll be fine." Gabriel didn't share her enthusiasm.

"I don't think it's going to be that easy."

"What do you mean?" she asked.

"Haven't you ever wondered why my wings never grew back?" he asked, with a saddened expression, and Laura's chin dropped at the sudden realisation of that simple truth. "The Church has experimented on my kind over the years, once their blood became poisoned and they were no longer of any use to them. I captured copies of their files years ago in Madrid," he added. "Those regenerative powers have already started working to mend the amputated limb as best they can. The bones are knitting, and the flesh is healing over. Once any part of the body is completely severed from the host, any attempt to reattach it is doomed to failure. Her body will reject the hand, despite the drugs they use. Even with all this technology and skill, there isn't a surgeon in the world who can reattach her hand." He let his words sink in, as Laura grasped fully what he was saying to her.

"You mean she's going to remain crippled like that for the rest of her life?" Laura looked horrified.

"I don't know," he admitted, shaking his head slightly. "I need to think on it." Laura didn't understand and pressed him further.

"What do you mean, 'think on it'? You just said there wasn't a surgeon in the world that could help her." She looked exasperated.

"I do know someone," he admitted. "But getting his help will not be easy. He's not exactly *of* this world, and we're not exactly friends." Laura's chin dropped once more.

*   *   *

Later, Gabriel went in to see his daughter. He simply did not know what sort of a welcome he would get, and his slow footsteps were heavy as he entered the room. Belle looked up briefly from the bed, where she cradled the bandaged stump of her right wrist on her stomach. She said nothing as Gabriel stood there, staring down guiltily. He came around the bed to sit on it, and took her left hand in his own.

"Don't blame yourself." She forced a pained smile. "Shit happens." Her voice was trembling, and she said nothing for a few moments, as Gabriel just looked at her, lost for words.

"I was so looking forward to you teaching me that knife-catching trick," she blurted out suddenly, and then she broke down altogether, sitting up in bed and hugging him as she cried her eyes out, chest heaving against him, and there was nothing Gabriel could do but hug her back, and cry along with her.

Epilogue

After cleaning up at Borgia's club all day, Bonetti was beat. He was pleased to find Eve waiting for him at his flat. She had let herself in with the spare key, and was busy cooking him a meal in the kitchenette. As he did every night, he switched on his computer and checked his e-mail, his interest picking up when he saw the size of the file being downloaded. *Big* file! "How long till the meal's ready, honey?" he called to Eve in the kitchen.

"About twenty minutes," she answered back.

"I think I'll take a quick bath. It's been a long day," he announced, and went into the bathroom. He ran the bath as he was undressing, and had a quick shave.

In the living room, Eve came out of the kitchen, and noticed the flashing flag which announced the e-mail had downloaded. She sat down at the keyboard and began to read the files that Gabriel had forwarded.

Bonetti was enjoying a nice long soak in the hot water, when the bathroom door opened. "I thought you might like to listen to some music while you enjoyed your bath," Eve smiled, as she brought in the portable radio, and plugged it into the shaver socket. Switching it on, she made to place it on the toilet seat next to the tub, when her fingers let go, and the live radio dropped into the bathwater. "Ooops!" she smiled wistfully, as Bonetti's body contorted and threshed in the water. Death by electrocution was not a nice way to go.

Leaving him there to enjoy his death, Eve went back into the room, and redirected the e-mail to her own e-mail address, and then set about systematically erasing files from Bonetti's pc. Deciding not to waste the food, she then ate her half of the meal, before scraping the rest down the waste disposal, and then doing the washing-up.

Taking care that no one saw her leave, she locked the apartment door behind her. Her position with the Police Department had been useful to Borgia, but now Borgia was obviously gone and it was time to move on. Shit happens!

THE END